Stay a Little Longer

DOROTHY GARLOCK

Stay a Little Longer

**Doubleday Large Print
Home Library Edition**

GRAND CENTRAL
PUBLISHING

NEW YORK   BOSTON

Grand Central Publishing
Hachette Book Group
237 Park Avenue
New York, NY 10017

Printed in the United States of America

Grand Central Publishing is a division of Hachette
Book Group, Inc.
The Grand Central Publishing name and logo is a
trademark of Hachette Book Group, Inc.

ISBN 978-1-61664-283-9

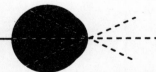

**This Large Print Book carries the
Seal of Approval of N.A.V.H.**

This book is lovingly dedicated to
Kelly and Jason Brubaker
and Baby Bru

A Long Time Gone

All the flags were waving
All the band's music blared.
I took her in my arms
And said how much I cared.

I promised her that I'd return
(Though not like this . . .)
When I took her in my arms
For a good-bye kiss.

There are no flags a-waving
After eight long years.
There is no music playing,
No sound of long-dried tears.

I've come for just a glimpse
Of the girl I left behind.
But she must never see me
To that I am resigned.

For I was lost a world away.
I'm not the man she wed.
The face she loved no longer mine,
The man she knew—is dead.

—F.S.I.

Stay a
Little Longer

Chapter One

Carlson, Minnesota—October 1926

RACHEL WATKINS wiped the sweat from her brow with the back of her hand while absently moving a strand of her coal-black hair from her green-flecked brown eyes. Though the early October day carried the crisp chill of autumn, the inside of Will and Clara Wicker's small home blazed as if it were the hottest day of July; water boiled in a cast-iron pot on top of the wood-burning stove and candles flickered in every corner, their meager light sending faint shadows dancing across the walls.

"Oh, Rachel . . . it hurts . . ."

Clara Wicker lay on her back in the bed,

one thin-boned hand spread across her enormous pregnant belly. All of the color had drained from her thin face except for the dark purple circles under her eyes and her bitten, red lips. Her blonde hair, slick with sweat, was drawn back from her face. Beads of moisture stood out on her forehead. Her eyes were closed tightly and her breathing was shallow. Not particularly pretty, Clara's face was now a mask of agony.

"It's to be expected," Rachel comforted her.

"Ohhh!" Clara answered, her cry almost a moan.

"It'll be over soon."

Gently, Rachel wiped the sweat from Clara's pain-chiseled face. Looking around her, she took inventory of all that she would need to bring the young woman's first child into the world; the extra sheets that had been prepared for the birthing, a nightdress, towels, clean rags, and a dented bucket for water. Everything was as ready as it could be.

"You sure you know what you're doin' . . . 'bout birthin' and all?" Will Wicker asked from where he meekly stood at the head of his wife's bed, his voice little louder than a whisper. He nervously shifted his weight from one foot to the next, his small, dark eyes flickering back and forth from Clara to Rachel, never lingering for long. His filthy fingers, the fingernails caked with dirt, twitched uneasily as he rubbed one thin hand over the stubble of his bony jaw. His clothes hung loosely on his small frame, just as sweaty and soiled as the body they covered.

How did Clara allow this man to lie between her legs?

"I do," Rachel answered simply.

"Wouldn't it be better if your mother was here?" Will followed.

"I've already told you that she couldn't make it."

"But don't you think . . . that . . ." he stammered. "You know . . . given that . . ."

"There isn't time for this." Rachel took a deep breath, trying to settle her growing dislike for the man. From the moment she'd been summoned to the Wickers' ramshackle house at the far outskirts of town, she'd hoped that Will would simply accept that she was every bit as capable as Eliza Watkins of bringing a newborn child into the world. Instead, he'd eyed her warily from the moment she'd set foot in his home, as if she had come to harm instead of help. So far, he had contented himself with a few derogatory comments. She hoped that was the way it would remain.

"I'll need you to bring me the water when it's time," she told him.

"Don't worry 'bout me none," he answered. "Ain't no—"

Before Will could say another word, Clara moaned in pain as blood-tinged water gushed from between her legs and formed a puddle around her feet on the mattress.

Sensing Clara's panic, Rachel did her best to settle the pregnant woman. "Don't worry about the water," she said calmly. "We've got plenty of rags and oilskins to keep things dry. This happens to every woman when giving birth to her child." Covering Clara with another clean sheet, she grabbed a pair of rags and tucked them between the woman's legs to catch the remaining fluid.

"I'm . . . I'm sorry . . ." Clara struggled to say.

"There's nothing for you to be sorry about," Rachel said with a soft smile.

At a sudden rustling behind her, Rachel turned to find that Will had moved from the head of the bed and quickly shuffled over to the ramshackle home's lone window, as far away from his wife as he could get without going outside. The look on his face was one of utter revulsion and horror. Clearly, the sight of Clara's body preparing to give birth, readying itself to finish what had begun when Will had planted his seed inside her nine months earlier, had completely unsettled him.

"That there . . . that there . . ." he stuttered, "ain't . . . ain't right!"

"Will . . . Will . . . don't . . ." Clara struggled to say through the vicious waves of pain that washed over her, one shaking hand stretched toward her husband, desperately urging him to return to her side.

"I can't, Clara," he answered with a shake of his head. "I just can't."

A small cry escaped Clara's lips and the hand that she had offered to her husband was withdrawn, instead clenching into a tight fist that she pounded heavily on the mattress. Her head swung from side to side as she rode out a spasm that hurt so much her eyes, though still open, couldn't seem to focus on either of the faces around her.

"Help her!" Will shouted at Rachel.

"I'm doing all that I can," she answered as calmly as she could.

"Maybe Doc Clark is back," the man kept on. "Maybe he can do this!"

Clarence Clark was Carlson's new doctor, having recently arrived from the state college. For many years, the town simply made do without a full-time physician, relying instead on the folk knowledge that had been brought from the Old World, mostly a mixture of Norwegian and German home remedies. Though Dr. Clark was a young man in his early thirties, he had proven to be an excellent caregiver and was well respected. If not for an emergency in his wife's family that had taken him from town, he would have been where Rachel now sat.

"We don't need Dr. Clark's help," Rachel said, her eyes never leaving Clara.

"Then we should get your mother," he insisted. "She'll know what to do!"

"She can't help us," Rachel answered curtly.

"But she'd know—"

"We don't need her!"

Though Rachel had remained calm through Will Wicker's suggestion that she needed Clarence Clark's help, she bristled at the insinuation her mother was more capable than she. Before the doctor's arrival, Eliza Watkins had been the midwife for the birth of nearly every child in Carlson. Her opinion had been sought for every sort of illness or condition, even those outside of childbirth. But then Mason Tucker had gone off to war . . .

And everything had changed!

Nowadays, Eliza Watkins almost never left her room in the house she owned with her brother, Otis. She contented herself with fretting incessantly about those unfortunate enough to get too close, working herself into fits of worry. She agonized over the slightest sign of a cold, the hidden danger of a flight of stairs, or the tiniest of cuts. To combat these imaginary threats, she hid herself away. Even now, in Dr. Clark's absence, she couldn't bring herself to help. Instead, the burden once again fell to Rachel.

As a child, Rachel had never been her mother's favorite; that honor had always belonged to her older sister, Alice. Where

Alice had been fawned over, eagerly encouraged to follow her dreams, Rachel had forever been second fiddle. When she'd been told what to do, there was no other expectation than for her to agree. Thankfully for the Wickers, she'd watched her mother deliver babies so many times that there was little that could surprise her. They were in safe hands. In the end, it seemed that everyone now depended upon her.

Her mother, her uncle Otis . . . and especially Charlotte.

"Look at me, Clara," Rachel encouraged.

Hesitantly, the pregnant woman's eyes fluttered open and stared into Rachel's face, not seeing her, but using her voice as a point on which to focus her mind while her muscles knotted and pulled. Her voice cracking, she answered, "It . . . it hurts, Will . . . Rachel . . ."

"It won't be long, Clara," Rachel soothed.

"Is she supposed to be hurtin' like this?" Will asked from the far corner, his voice finally returning after Rachel's rebuke. He looked at them over his shoulder, as if he couldn't bear to bring his full attention toward the bloody, unsettling sight. "It don't seem right."

"Take one of these rags," Rachel told him, holding a swatch of cloth out for him, "and dip it into the water bucket, then use it to wipe the sweat from her brow."

"I—I can't," he said with a shake of his head.

"Stop asking questions and complaining about things you know nothing about. Clara and I need you to do this one simple thing," Rachel commanded, the fire in her heart momentarily bubbling to the surface. "We need to make her as comfortable as we can. Whining about how this looks isn't going to do her any good."

"I'm not whining," Will countered, succeeding only in reinforcing Rachel's accusation. Still, his resolve to stay away from his wife's side wavered. Slowly he made his way to where Rachel knelt, snatched the rag from her hand, and clumsily dunked it into the bucket. Making his way to the bed, he began absently to wipe it across Clara's blazing forehead.

"Just try to keep her cool," Rachel furthered.

"I'm here, Clara," Will softly reassured his wife.

"Oh, Will!" she exclaimed before another

pain came and went as rivulets of water ran down her red cheeks.

"It won't be long now, Clara," Rachel said confidently. From her experience at her mother's side, she could see that the Wickers' new child would soon make his or her entry into the world. "If you need to holler right out and loud, don't you hold yourself back. Even if they hear you over in Cloverfield, you just rear back and shout. Take hold of the sheets and push when I tell you to. That's a good girl . . ."

Clara's body shook as agonizing contractions washed over her, leaving her with little control of her mind or her body. Her shouts rose in intensity, filling every space of the small home. Still, she did as Rachel told her, pushing her small body to expel its burden.

"Clara! It's coming!" Rachel shouted from the end of the bed. "I can see the top of its head!"

The pregnant woman's eyes opened wide. "Will!" she screamed.

"I'm here, darlin'," Will answered, his eyes searching his wife's face, his unease nearly completely forgotten. "You just keep pushin' . . . let it come. Don't hold yourself back from the hurtin'."

"Listen to him!" Rachel added.

Just as her mother had taught her many years before, Rachel let a sense of calmness wash over her; this was a time that required both a steady heart and hand. Everything about the birth of Clara Wicker's baby seemed normal, but any delivery could go wrong in an instant. Still, she knew that she would do anything in her power to make sure nothing happened to either mother or child. Placing the palm of her hand on the hardened mound of Clara's abdomen, she waited for another contraction.

"Ohhh . . . oh, it hurts!" Clara bellowed as heavy pain assailed her.

"Push, Clara! Push!" Rachel urged.

Clara did what she was told and her child arrived. The head came free and then, a mere blink of the eyes later, the shoulders. Rachel waited for the final push, then gathered the baby to her. She reached for the linen string, tied two heavy knots on the umbilical cord, and cut between the knots to sever the cord. The baby was covered in birth blood. She grabbed a towel and cleaned the child frantically, pressed by the realization that something was wrong; the tiny chest was not moving, the eyes were sealed shut.

"Rachel . . . I don't . . . I don't hear anything," Clara gasped.

"Is . . . is somethin' wrong?" Will added.

Refusing to become distracted, Rachel gave no answer, her mind racing over her mother's many lessons before alighting on the answer. Quickly, she hurried to the dented bucket of well water and plunged the newborn infant into the cold water up to its neck. She poked her finger into the child's mouth when it gasped. "Breathe!" she whispered fervently. "Breathe!"

"What's happenin'?" Will insisted, stepping away from his wife's side.

"Stay back!" Rachel barked. She knew that there were people who depended on her to do the right thing, to take care of what was precious to them and keep it safe. Her entire adulthood had been spent doing just that. She wouldn't fail now.

Suddenly the tiny chest heaved, and the little mouth opened and drew air into the lungs. The resulting scream was both fierce and tiny, but it sounded like the sweetest of church music to Rachel's ears.

"It's . . . it's not dead or nothin'?" Will asked cautiously.

"No, by God!" Rachel laughed. "Listen to that scream!"

Crossing the room, Rachel placed the tiny bundle of flesh on a towel. She rubbed the baby briskly, moved its tiny arms and legs, then turned it over and rubbed its back until all of its skin had turned a healthy pink. He was both full and fit.

"You've got a beautiful baby boy," she told the new parents.

"I've . . . I've got me a son?" Will asked.

Rachel nodded.

"Did you hear that, Clara?" he exclaimed, turning back to where his wife lay, utterly exhausted despite her beaming smile. "We got us a son! She said we done got us a son!"

"A son," Clara echoed.

Rachel continued to work the baby's tiny arms and legs, smiling happily when the little muscles responded. Little hands flayed the air, fingers fully outstretched. A cry of protest came from his mouth, and he opened large, beautiful blue eyes. Just as her mother had always told her, she knew that what she had witnessed was a living miracle.

Every child was just that . . . a miracle!

"Look at what we got there!" Will shouted from beside Rachel. Staring at his new-born son, his face lit up with a brightness she'd never seen before. "Just gander at them bright eyes! There ain't a better-lookin' boy that ever did come into this here world!"

"Let . . . let me see him," Clara said.

Rachel held a blanket to the fire and warmed it. Wrapping the baby, she cuddled him against her and carried him to his waiting mother. Kneeling beside Clara, she placed the baby in her arms. Clara gazed upon her new son with as much amazement as love.

"Has . . . has he got everything?" she asked anxiously. Her fingertips lightly stroked the fuzz of dark hair.

"Yep! He's got the right number! I counted!" Will exclaimed proudly as his eyes bounced from his wife to his son. "Ten fingers and ten toes to go along with 'em! Now all he needs hisself is to get a name."

"I thought . . . we'd already decided," Clara said. "You'd picked a name."

"I did," Will nodded. "If it's all right with you."

"It is."

"Then his name is Walter." Will beamed brightly. "After my father."

Having never given birth to a child of her own, Rachel always marveled at how quickly women could recover from the ordeal of birth. After experiencing a pain the likes of which couldn't be adequately described, their recovery was nothing short of remarkable. She found herself amazed that Clara could so much as raise her head to look at her child. The color had begun to come back into her face and her eyes seemed a bit livelier. She looked exhausted, worn out, but the pain had disappeared.

What she was witnessing was the beginning of a new life, not just for Walter Wicker but his parents as well. From this day forward, they would go on together, their lives entwined; father, mother, and son. This was a time of happiness and joy, of hopes and dreams, expectations and even fears. Nothing would ever be the same again.

Just like nothing was ever the same for me!

Rachel turned away from the Wickers as the shadow of a frown crossed her face. Try as she might, she couldn't stop herself from thinking of what had happened eight years ago that very day. Memories of the day assaulted her from all sides. The entire time she had been inside the Wickers' home, she had been fighting a constant battle against her remembrances, though it was clear that the parallels were too close to avoid.

She knew all too well that the birth of a child was not always an occasion for joyous celebration. Sometimes, the beginning of one life can signal the end of another. When such a thing happens, it's up to the survivors to pick up the pieces, and that was what she'd been doing for the last eight years. Picking up the pieces.

Chapter Two

RACHEL LEFT THE WICKERS with the promise she would return the next day to check on the baby. From the tiny house on the outskirts of Carlson, she headed home without any hurry, content to enjoy the beautiful day. High above, the mid-October sun shone down with pleasant warmth, enough to hold off the persistent fall chill carried on the breeze. Lazy wisps of clouds skirted the far edge of the horizon. All around her, the trees showed signs of the changing of the seasons: elms, oaks, and maples exploded in spectacular colors; brilliant reds, deep purples, and even burnt oranges.

The day is too beautiful for the trip I have to make, she mused.

Carlson sat to the northeast of the capital city of Minnesota, St. Paul, and its sister city of Minneapolis. Primarily a farming community, it was home to less than a thousand inhabitants. The tall, leafy cornstalks that had stretched skyward in the stiflingly humid heat of July had been almost completely harvested, families spending night and day reaping the fruits of their many labors. Farming was so essential to the town's well-being that school was suspended during the busiest days of the harvest.

Like thousands of other towns in Minnesota, Carlson was situated on a lake. As she made her way toward Main Street, Rachel caught glimpses of Lake Carlson through the spaces between homes. Open where it butted up against the town, the far side of the lake was lined with majestic evergreen trees that sheltered wild game. Mallard ducks lowered themselves to the lake's glassy surface, their flight ending as they slid gently into the deep blue water. An abundance of catfish and walleye swam beneath the surface.

The sound of saws cutting through wood and nails being hammered came to Rachel's ears as she neared her family's boardinghouse. Carlson was clearly a town on the rise. New buildings seemed to spring up as readily as the corn that was the town's lifeblood. Passing Hamilton's Grocery, Abraham McLintock's barber shop, and Miller Livery reminded Rachel that while the rest of the community was enjoying prosperous times, her own life seemed stuck in the quagmire of decline.

Stopping in front of the post office window, Rachel took a good look at herself in the glass reflection. Coal-black hair, one of the features she was happy to have inherited from her mother, fell just below her narrow shoulders. Greenish-brown eyes looked back at her over high cheekbones, a petite button of a nose, and full lips. Her clothes certainly weren't the latest fashion sent north from Chicago, but her blue blouse and skirt fit her narrow waist and full bosom flatteringly. There was no shortage of bachelors in Carlson who entertained thoughts of taking her as a wife; but with all of her responsibilities, romance was the furthest thing from her mind.

"Afternoon, Rachel," a voice called from behind her.

Struggling mightily to find a smile to fix upon her face, Rachel turned to find Sophus Peterson leading a team of horses down the street, his wagon nearly overflowing with a load of enormous orange pumpkins being brought to market. One of her many suitors, he tipped his straw hat and gave her a wink before he walked past her.

"Not if it took a hundred years," she muttered under her breath and continued on her way.

The boardinghouse she called home sat just off Main Street and across from Carlson's train depot. Rachel stood in the road and stared up at the building her grandfather had built with his own two hands shortly after his arrival from Pennsylvania. He'd originally come to Carlson in the hope of tapping maple syrup from the thousands of trees in the area, but had ended up having about as much luck as if he'd tried to squeeze blood from turnips. He'd died fifteen years earlier with little more to show for his many labors than what he had when he first arrived; he left only the house as a legacy to his two children. Rachel's mother, Eliza, had decided to turn it into a boarding-house when times began to get tough. Drifters and seasonal workers rented the four available rooms a week at a time, and the Watkinses had somehow managed to eke out a living.

The building had required but not received improvement in the years since her grandfather's passing. The exterior was in dire need of a new slathering of paint; what little remained from the last coat was chipped and weather-beaten, with several warped planks pulling free from the frame. One of the windows on the upper floor was cracked, a recent occurrence that would have to be fixed before winter. Even the sign that read BOARDERS WELCOME wasn't immune to decline; one of the bolts that secured the sign had come free, leaving half of the word WELCOME to hang listlessly in the breeze.

With every passing year, the number of boarders seemed to dwindle; on most days the family felt lucky to have a single room occupied. The only glimmer of hope had appeared years earlier when Rachel's sister, Alice, married Mason Tucker, whose father was at once the proprietor of the town bank and the wealthiest man in Carlson. Mason had promised to help care for his new bride's family, but then he had gone off to war and . . .

"Damn it all," Rachel swore.

A fluttering at one of the upper windows attracted her attention and she looked up just in time to see her mother's porcelain-white arm quickly withdraw from the sunlight. Rachel sighed. Most days, her mother did little more than sit at her window and watch the world go by without her, worrying all the while. Today appeared to be no different. Waiting for word of the Wickers, she was by now quite impatient. Rachel was certain to get a tongue-lashing when she went inside.

The laughter of a young girl and the playful barking of a dog suddenly rose from the rear of the house; Charlotte and Jasper seemed to have escaped Eliza's panicked oversight long enough to make their way outside. Rachel hoped that Charlotte was being careful; if she were to come back indoors with a bloody scrape or bruise, Eliza wouldn't let her outdoors again for a month! Rachel regretted that she would soon have to pull the girl away from her fun.

What a life for a small girl!

The inside of the boardinghouse was only slightly better than the outside; dusty banisters lined the once majestic hardwood staircase that rose from the door toward the rooms on the second floor. Chipped tables and chairs filled the small dining area tucked off to the left of the entrance and next to the kitchen. Though she often tried to polish the rich woodwork her grandfather had built throughout the house, Rachel could clearly see the many blemishes and warps. While it must have been something to behold when it was first built, the place now looked shabby.

Otis Simmons, Rachel's uncle and her mother's older brother, came from behind the dining room's cast-iron stove humming a tune between gulps from a bottle of whiskey. Drops of the amber liquid ran down his stubbly chin and heavy jowls.

"Don't you think it's a little too early to be drinking?" Rachel asked.

The sudden sound of his niece's voice startled Otis so badly that he stumbled, nearly dropping his bottle. Sheepishly, he stared at Rachel like a child caught with his hand in the cookie jar. Though in his mid-fifties, Otis *was* childlike, even comical. He insisted upon combing his few gray hairs across his otherwise bald head. His dingy clothes strained mightily against their seams and buttons on his enormous body, and he had a cockeyed smile that lit up no matter how much he'd had to drink. For an instant, he tried to hide his bottle behind his ample waist and pretend the liquor didn't exist, but then he just smiled mischievously.

"I don't know if I'd be willin' to call this a drink," he offered defensively.

"If it's not a drink, then what is it?" Rachel asked, willing to play along with her uncle's shenanigans for the moment.

"This here ain't nothin' but a nip," Otis explained. "In my book, that sure ain't the same thing as a drink."

"What's the difference?"

"Oh, my darlin'," Rachel's uncle exclaimed with a heavy slap at his knee, "drinkin' is somethin' you do sittin' down at a bar while pourin' yourself a big glassful, whereas nippin' ain't nothin' more than takin' a few sips here and there. Drinkin' you do with your friends down at the tavern or, if you're a particularly lonely sort, yourself. Nippin' is somethin' that can be done 'bout any time of day. Hell, I ain't above nippin' first thing in the mornin'!"

"That's all too apparent," Rachel pointed out with a disapproving look.

"I'm livin' proof that there ain't nothin' wrong with it! Why, most fellas my age couldn't hold half the liquor I can put down in a day. I'm a modern medical miracle if I do say so!"

"I don't know if that's a claim I'd be too proud of."

"That's 'cause you ain't a drinker or a nipper." Otis guffawed. "If'n you were, you'd think I was mighty amazin'!"

Rachel walked over to the check-in counter and frowned as she counted the number of keys still hanging from the pegs; it looked as if they still had no new boarders. "No matter what it is you think you're doing," she said, "it isn't appropriate behavior when you're supposed to be behind the counter waiting for new guests to come in."

"Takin' a tug now and again from this

here bottle's about the only way this fella is gonna get any entertainment." He shrugged. "Gets more than a bit dull waitin' for people that ain't never gonna come. You can't blame me for needin' a little pick-me-up!"

"Maybe if you'd go out and fix that sign, we'd get new guests."

"Ain't I already fixed that thing?"

"No, you haven't," Rachel retorted, her temper rising to where she could barely contain it.

"Then I'll do it today!" Otis exclaimed as if it were the most brilliant idea he had ever heard.

"You said the same thing last week," Rachel complained.

"But this time I done mean it!" he bellowed as he raced back toward the tiny closet from where he had come, his ample midsection jiggling with every thunderous step. Rachel could only sigh; even if Otis hadn't hurried away to get as far from her complaints as he could, his good intentions would surely evaporate just as soon as he realized he was still clutching a bottle of whiskey. While her uncle was as sweet a man as could be, he was as useful to the house as a three-legged plowing horse to a farmer.

In the end, she knew that if she wanted the sign rehung, she'd have to do it herself.

Rachel's mother's room on the upper floor of the house faced the street and train depot beyond, her two windows affording her a view of Carlson's newest arrivals and departures. The interior was dark and gloomy; heavy lace curtains allowed little sunlight to penetrate, and the oil lamps were lit only in the darkest hours of night.

Eliza Watkins's favorite place to hold court over her tiny fortress was a small table next to one of the tall windows, its surface littered with used teacups and saucers. There was also a vase containing a single rose, long since dead and drooping, most of its petals fallen. Two chairs sat waiting for another guest to join her, but it had been many years since a social call was paid upon the co-owner of the house.

Rachel was hardly inside the door when her mother set upon her, breathlessly asking questions. "Is the child all right?" Eliza said in a rush. "Was the birth okay?"

After all the years her mother had sequestered herself in her room, Rachel was still momentarily surprised by Eliza's show of compassion. Though it would have taken a team of wild horses to pull the older woman from her exile, such resolve didn't mean that she worried only for those around her. Only hours earlier, Rachel had pleaded with her mother to accompany her, begging her to come and do what she was skilled at: bringing a new baby into the world. But the horrible memories of what had happened eight years earlier proved too strong to budge her, and so Rachel had gone, as many times before, alone.

"It was a healthy baby boy," she answered with a smile.

"He had all of his fingers?" Eliza prodded, starving for the tiniest of details. "All of his toes? There weren't any complications? Did you remember to tie off the birthing cord the way that I taught you, because if you don't there can be complications!"

"Everything was fine," Rachel assured her. She decided against telling her mother about newborn Walter Wicker's short struggle for breath; there was no point in needlessly worrying her further.

"Oh, thank God!"

Eliza Watkins had been a beautiful young woman, and that beauty hadn't deserted her as she aged. Her silky hair, already bone white, was pulled back fashionably and piled atop her head. Piercing green eyes had once held many a man in rapt attention. Her features were delicate, almost fragile, but though she was small of frame, it was clear that she wasn't a woman averse to work; her hands, in particular, were still strong. She showed her age only in the many wrinkles that lined her cheeks, underscored her eyes, and furrowed her brow.

"Why did you go out without a coat, or at the very least a shawl?" she asked her daughter. "You could have caught your death of cold! You know how quickly the weather can change this time of year!"

"It's a beautiful day, Mother." Rachel sighed. "You should know, you've done nothing but watch it from your window."

"Why must you always ignore my advice? Alice never defied me!"

Rachel had long ago accepted that she would never be the apple of her mother's eye; that was an honor reserved for Alice, even though she had died eight years earlier. The constant comparisons could still rankle, but she'd long since learned how to swallow her upset.

"You don't need to worry so," she remonstrated.

"It's a mother's right to worry about her children," Eliza argued, wringing her hands compulsively; there had been times over the last several years when she had chafed them so badly that they had bled. "The way you traipse out the door without a second thought, all willy-nilly and carefree, why it's nothing short of a miracle you haven't ended up just like your poor sister!"

"Mother . . ." Rachel said, her voice trailing to a whisper.

As difficult as Alice's death had made life for Rachel, she sometimes forgot how heavy a toll it had taken on their mother. Eight years ago that very October day, Eliza Watkins had done everything she could to save the life of her oldest child, while struggling to bring her first grandchild into the world. It didn't matter that Alice hadn't wanted to be saved, that she'd wanted nothing more than the cold embrace of death. Eliza carried the burden of

Alice's death as her failure and nothing less, a failure that had cost them all dearly and from which they had never recovered.

Before Rachel could say anything else, could offer some small condolence, her mother turned back toward the window and dabbed at her eyes with a handkerchief. "I'm sure you noticed that Charlotte's already escaped outdoors," she said. "She's just like you were at that age . . . she won't listen to a thing! If you turn your back for a second, she'll be gone."

"I heard her and Jasper playing around back."

"That mangy dog of hers might be as sweet as honey," Eliza explained, "but I worry about all of the ways he could hurt her, even by accident. Besides, just imagine all of the fleas he could be carrying!"

"Jasper's a good companion for her," Rachel said.

"Regardless, she was out the door only seconds after you left!"

"I don't know just why she was in such a hurry to escape," Rachel answered. "While I'm sure the nice day was part of it, better odds are that she ran out as much to avoid me and where I'm going to take her."

"Does she know what today is?"

Rachel nodded. "It is her birthday, after all."

"And that's why she needs to go to the cemetery," Eliza said, turning back toward Rachel and again wringing her hands.

"Don't you worry that you're punishing Charlotte by insisting that I drag her out there year after year?" Rachel asked. "It can't possibly be good for such a young child to be confronted with the fact that she's without a mother."

"I don't ask that you take her there to remind her of what she doesn't have," Eliza argued, "but to remind her of where she comes from. You never so much as mention Alice's name in front of her."

"That's because I don't want to upset her!"

"She needs to know who her family is!"

"She has a family here with us."

"Just because Alice is dead doesn't mean that she's not Charlotte's mother."

Rachel's protesting tongue fell silent and they returned to the awkward silence between them. In the eight years since Alice died while giving birth to her daughter, this was an argument they often revisited. While they both had a profound interest in Charlotte's well-being, they differed on how to provide it. Rachel knew that this year would be no different from the last or the year before that; she would take Charlotte out to visit Alice's tombstone alone, regardless of the fact that it was her mother's desire.

"Are you sure you won't come with us?" she asked with little hope.

"No, no, no," Eliza answered without any hesitation. "I just . . . I just can't . . ."

When Rachel closed the door to her mother's room behind her, she could already hear the first of the older woman's sobs.

Chapter Three

RACHEL WALKED SLOWLY down the long, oak-lined street toward Carlson's cemetery with a heart as heavy as it was determined. The burnt-orange October sun brightened the cloudless afternoon sky, pleasantly warming the earth, while a listless breeze lazily shifted the tufts of dirt kicked up by her feet. Somewhere in the distance, a farmer purposefully burned the remnants of his fields, already beginning the necessary preparations for the next season, and the rich scent wafted over the town. But as beautiful as the fall day was proving to be,

Rachel found that she could not tear her attention from her niece.

Charlotte trudged along behind Rachel, silent save for the occasional huff of complaint, her head hanging down toward the ground. Bouncy blonde braids danced over her shoulders, brilliant blue eyes looked out from under long lashes, and her cheeks were nearly as red as her lips. In her favorite blue dress, adorned with bright red buttons, she was certainly a beauty. Even at just eight years old, Charlotte was the image of her mother, except for the penetrating look that Rachel clearly recognized as having come from her father. Unfortunately, on this day her mood was as ugly as that of a chick that just missed getting a fat junebug.

"It's not as if this visit is punishing you," Rachel offered.

The child remained silent.

"Look," Rachel pointed out, "even Jasper is enjoying himself."

Charlotte's constant companion, a shaggy dog, ran ahead of them, darting from one side of the road to the other, his eagerly sniffing nose never leaving the ground for very long. Mouth open, his pink tongue hanging from one side, he truly seemed to be having the time of his life. Part Labrador retriever and part collie, Jasper had a black coat that was randomly splotched with patches of white, down to the tip of his long, bushy tail. Though Eliza often complained that he could be a danger to Charlotte, Rachel saw him as a gallant protector. Every bit as good-natured as he was good-sized, he rarely left Charlotte's side, even when he followed her to school; more than once, Charlotte had sneaked him inside, much to her teacher's consternation.

"He ain't either," Charlotte said stubbornly.

For the briefest of moments, Rachel found herself startled by the sound of Charlotte's voice; ever since she had been forced to stop her playing behind the boardinghouse, the little girl had remained mute, choosing to sulk instead of talk. "Yes he is," Rachel countered. "He's bouncing around and enjoying himself."

"I ain't no dog," Charlotte mumbled.

"Don't say 'ain't,' Charlotte."

Jasper seemed to recognize that he was the subject of conversation and turned

his head back to them for a moment before resuming his wayward sniffing.

Charlotte had always been quick to throw
temper tantrums and to argue, far more
prone to give a frown than a smile; she
was as hard to predict as she was to control. Even as an infant, the sound of her
wailing could be heard over the thunderous noise of trains in the depot across the
street. Eliza constantly complained of her
sinful disobedience, of her refusal to do as
she was told. Rachel often tried to practice Otis's advice, an admonition to be patient with the girl, but there were days . . .

What kind of mother have I been?

"I didn't want to come here. I want to
play jacks," Charlotte complained.

"You can play jacks when you get home."

"It'll be dark when we get home!"

"No it won't, Charlotte, I—"

"I don't care what you say." Charlotte,
lagging behind, stuck her tongue out at
her aunt.

"We're going to visit your mother," Rachel
replied calmly. "We—"

"I don't have a mother!"

Rachel cringed at the harshness of the
words. Deep down, she knew that this was

part of the reason Eliza refused to join them on their annual visit to view Alice's grave marker. To hear the spiteful words of her daughter's child was a harsh reminder of all that they had lost. Hiding in her room was easier than facing the truth.

Rachel knew that she didn't have such a luxury; she accepted her responsibility to keep Alice's memory alive in Charlotte's heart. Although Eliza had doted upon and loved Alice so unconditionally, jealousy had never entered Rachel's heart. Quite the contrary, she had idolized Alice. Four years younger, Rachel had dreamed that she would grow to be just like her sister; that she would be the one to receive broad smiles as soon as she entered any room; that she would have a beautiful wedding attended by every man and woman in Carlson; that she would meet a man as handsome and charming as Mason Tucker . . .

Frowning at the thought of her sister's husband, Rachel sighed deeply; it still seemed far too soon to reconcile her feelings for Mason. While she'd hoped that the passage of time would erase her memories of the man, it instead seemed to strengthen them, regardless of the anger she still felt toward him.

"Hurry up so we can go home," Charlotte demanded, breaking into her aunt's unwanted thoughts.

"Be patient, we'll go in a few minutes."

"All right!" she squealed with delight, so satisfied that her burden would soon be lifted that she began to run ahead, with Jasper playfully bounding along at her side.

"Charlotte!" Rachel called, but her niece wasn't listening.

Not for the first time since that fateful day eight years earlier, Rachel wondered if she had somehow failed her sister. Heartbroken by Alice's death, she had taken the burden of raising the newborn infant willingly, feeling that it was what her sister would have wanted; but even with her mother and Uncle Otis's help, she'd felt overwhelmed from the start. Raising a child had proven far harder than she could imagine. Certainly, she'd done her best, but she wondered if that was enough. She couldn't help but believe that Alice would have done far better.

If only she'd had the will to live . . .

Carlson's cemetery lay just to the south of town, atop a low hill dotted with a pair of majestic trees that stood silent watch over the somber gray tombstones. A black wrought-iron fence encircled the sacred grounds, its gate hanging open on squeaking hinges. Flowers were scattered across the graves, the remainders of previous visits from other mourners. From inside the fence, one could see most of town, along with a spectacular view of the far side of Lake Carlson and the pine trees beyond. But Rachel rarely took the time to marvel at the vista; the thought of her sister lying asleep forever in the black earth was too overwhelming.

"Oh, Alice, I'm doing the best I can with your daughter." She sighed before pushing open the gate.

On the day Mason Tucker left Carlson to head off to war, Rachel had stood next to her sister on the train depot platform. The weather had been beautiful, unseasonably warm with only a scattering of clouds to mar the sky. The red, white, and blue of the American flag had been draped everywhere.

Although tears streamed down both her and her sister's cheeks, pride had filled their hearts at the sight of the town's men marching off to fight for their country. In the middle of the first row of marchers, Mason had stood out; his new uniform was crisply pressed and impressive as it spread across his broad shoulders, and the brilliant brass buttons shone in the spring sun. It was as if he had stepped right out of one of the many recruiting posters plastered around town. With his military cap perched atop his head, he had turned back to them and smiled so warmly at Alice that Rachel knew no one could doubt their love for each other.

"Don't worry," she'd consoled Alice. "He'll come home safe and sound."

Alice had tried to put on a brave face to her ever-growing loneliness and worry. To be separated from her new husband so quickly was a difficult burden to bear. Every day she wrote Mason, telling him all about her daily life but not including anything she thought might worry him; then, little more than a month after the train carried Mason from her, she found out that she was pregnant.

"We are a newly married couple," she'd said, beaming, the day she told Rachel. "It's to be expected!"

Just a few days later, it seemed as if every person in Carlson knew the good news. But even as she accepted all of the warm congratulations, Alice remained uncertain as to whether she should write and tell Mason.

"Why in heaven's name would you keep it from him?" Rachel had asked.

"Because he doesn't need anything else to worry about," Alice replied with as much conviction as she could muster. "If anything were to happen to him because he was distracted, I don't know if I would be able to live with myself!"

"Don't you think that if he knew there was about to be another Tucker in the world he'd be even more careful?"

"Well . . . but . . ." Alice had stammered.

In the end, Rachel's argument had won out. On the day that Alice finally decided to tell Mason about their unborn child, she sat in the parlor, hands shaking, and wrote a long letter. When she finished, she let no one, not even her sister, read it. Her eyes were filled with tears when she had handed it to the post-man.

And then she had waited . . . and waited . . . and waited . . .

Weeks passed without a letter in return. She was just about to write another identical letter, to assume that the first communication had somehow been lost within the war's confusion, when Mason's father, Sherman, had appeared at her door in the company of a military man she didn't recognize. Both of the men wore somber expressions.

"What's the matter?" Alice blurted. "What has happened?"

Sherman Tucker had done all of the talking; the military man had done little more than stare silently at his feet. Private Mason Tucker was officially missing, presumed dead. He had last been seen by another soldier entering a small ravine along the front in a French valley she had never heard of. Seconds later, a shell had detonated beside him, sending the very earth skyward. When the smoke cleared, all that was found was the shattered wreckage of his rifle and a few blood-soaked tatters of his uniform.

"But . . . but . . . his   body . . . his . . ." Alice managed to choke out.

"My dear, sweetest Alice," Sherman answered, pulling her to him as she dissolved into tears. Rachel, while not in the room, had heard every heartbreaking word through a partially open door.

During the difficult days that followed, all the citizens of Carlson came to pay their respects to Alice. On the morning of the funeral, a miserable March drizzle fell. With the entire town swathed in black, an empty casket was buried in the cemetery.

Alice's despondency grew by the day. As the weeks slowly passed into months, what little hope she held that Mason's reported death had been a mistake finally faded. Without that slim chance to buoy her, the greatness of her loss began to overwhelm her.

Though Rachel spent most of her days at Alice's side, it became obvious that her sister was retreating from her own life. She rarely spoke, ate barely enough to nourish a mouse, and even began to refuse to go outside. Even as her unborn child grew in her belly, the loss of her husband, her one

true love, proved greater than the hope of
the life yet to come.

"What are we going to do when the baby
comes?" Eliza had fretted.

"Don't she know what she's doin' to that
little one?" Otis added.

Rachel had no answers.

Then, just short of nine months to the
very day that Mason left Carlson to do his
duty for his country, Alice went into labor.
Having helped deliver countless dozens of
children, Eliza felt confident that she could
bring her own daughter through the birth
safely. All of the necessary preparations
had been made, all of the pots of water
and sheets and rags gathered, even the
cradle that had once held Mason as a child
was brought to the room; but nothing could
have adequately prepared them for what
was about to happen.

From the very beginning, the birth proved
difficult. Shortly after Alice's water had
broken, she began to bleed excessively.
To make matters much worse, Eliza soon
discovered this would be a breech birth,
that the baby was coming out backward;
instead of the crown of the baby's head,

one tiny foot appeared. The last time the midwife had seen such a thing, the child had been stillborn, strangled by the umbilical cord. With all of her experience and hope she could muster, Eliza set about rescuing her unborn grandchild.

"No one's dying here," she promised.

Through it all, Alice hardly uttered a sound. Once in a while, air hissed through her clenched teeth. Occasionally she grunted. She never shouted. Her skin was clammy to the touch, deathly cold. Even as Rachel urged her to continue pushing, to follow her mother's advice, it seemed as if her sister were somewhere else.

When Eliza finally managed to bring Alice's newborn child into the world, the baby was silent and blue. As her mother rushed to save the infant, Alice continued to pour out her life's blood onto the bedsheet. Rachel stayed at her sister's side, tears streaming down her cheeks as she watched Alice willingly slide into the darkness, never fighting what was to come. Alice had stopped living the moment Mason's father and the military man had given her the news of her husband's death. This was the end she desired.

Even as the baby wailed its first cry, a weak, plaintive noise that sounded like a kitten's mewl, it was too late. Alice never even looked upon her daughter before she died. They named the child Charlotte, a name Alice had, in better days, once remarked that she liked.

On that day, Rachel lost her sister and became a mother to her sister's baby.

Rachel stared solemnly at the gray stone of her sister's grave marker as a whistling wind raced between the rows of headstones. Uncomfortably cold, she rubbed her arms for warmth; she was unsure if her chill was because of the temperature of the wind or where she stood. At the edge of the cemetery, Charlotte ran after Jasper, chasing the happily panting dog around the base of a tall spire tombstone.

The words carved into the stone were a cold reminder of what she had lost:

ALICE TUCKER

1895–1918

BELOVED MOTHER, WIFE, SISTER,

AND DAUGHTER

SHE LIVES WITH THE ANGELS

Even when Charlotte was an infant, she had cried incessantly when she was brought to the cemetery. On the most beautiful of days, no amount of rocking or cooing ever managed to quiet her. Now she had become both uncaring and defiant. Rachel could hardly imagine what difficulties lay ahead in the years to come.

"Charlotte," she called to the little girl. "Come over here."

Though Rachel was certain that she had been heard, the child gave no indication. She continued to chase Jasper around the cemetery.

Rachel sighed. "Charlotte," she said, louder this time. "Come here!"

This time, Charlotte actually came to a stop, turning her head and fixing a hard stare upon her aunt. "But I'm playing!" she complained, her lip puckered and insolent.

"We came up here so that you could have a few moments with your mother," Rachel replied with as much patience as she could manage, "and that is exactly what we are going to do. Now please just come here."

Reluctantly, Charlotte tramped over to

where her mother eternally slept. Her arms folded across her small chest, she pouted unpleasantly. She stamped her foot angrily, and, her frustrations overflowing, kicked a couple of loose stones, sending them ricocheting off her mother's tombstone.

"Stop that!" Rachel ordered.

"She don't care if I kick her old stone," Charlotte cried. "She's already dead!"

"You're being naughty, Charlotte," Rachel said, hearing Eliza's many warnings echoing in her head. "All I'm asking for is five minutes of your time. I think you owe your mother that much."

Charlotte stood in silence, occasionally wiping her nose with the sleeve of her blouse.

"Isn't there anything you want to tell her?" Rachel prodded.

"No."

"Don't you want to tell her about school or your friends? What about Jasper and all of the things you do with him? That would be just fine! Your mother always loved dogs."

"I don't want to talk to her about anything!"

Charlotte cried, her fists balled tightly at her sides, an angry red flush spreading across her face. "Why do I have to spend my birthday here talking to a dead person? I hate it here! I hate it!"

"Charlotte, I—" Rachel began, but her niece had already dashed away from her and was making her way toward the cemetery entrance. Without pausing, she pushed open the squeaky gate and kept on running, never looking back, Jasper, as always, right behind her.

Rachel sighed heavily. "I'm sorry, Alice . . . I tried . . ."

Slowly, her attention turned from her sister's grave marker to the one lying beside it—Mason's. Cut from the same stone, the carving was simple:

MASON TUCKER

1893–1918

HE GAVE HIS LIFE FOR HIS COUNTRY

Unlike her sister's grave, Rachel knew that Mason's was empty, a symbol lacking in substance. Looking at his name sent a spasm of agitation racing down her spine.

In the eight years that had passed since Mason left Carlson on the train, Rachel had discovered hatred for him in her heart. She knew that it was not rational, that it was not fair, but she couldn't help but be mad at him. If he hadn't left for the war, if he'd only managed to keep his word to Alice and stayed safe, none of the horrible things would have happened: her sister wouldn't have given up on her life, Mason would have returned to the future that awaited him in his father's business, and Charlotte would have grown up in a loving home with two parents who would have treasured her.

And my own life would have been so different . . .

Mason's death had changed all of their lives . . . but none more than hers. The burden of raising Charlotte had largely fallen on her; Eliza had found demons that prevented her from being much use to anyone, and Otis had only slid deeper into his bottle. Mason's family had promised to help, but . . . that was yet another matter. The fact remained that nothing in her life was as it was supposed to be . . . nothing.

Yet she found that the worst burden to bear was that she was failing Charlotte. Failing miserably.

Though he was already dead, Rachel hated Mason Tucker more with every passing day.

Chapter Four

MASON TUCKER WOKE with a sudden start, his eyes immediately trying to adjust to the darkness of the train car. The boxcar creaked and groaned mightily as it swayed, clickety-clacking across the iron rails, but he could have sworn that he had heard a footfall. Little light came through a crack in the car's door from a full moon shining in the fall night beyond, and he hoped it would be enough. He knew that his life was in danger.

They mean to kill me!

When he had climbed into the boxcar just south of Milwaukee, there were two men already inside; a beastly ox whose raggedy shirt was nearly bursting at the seams and whose jowls were streaked with grime, and his companion, a wisp of a man with a porkpie hat perched atop carrot-orange hair. No words had been spoken between the three of them, no offer to share what food they might have had, but simply a nod of each of their heads, the traditional greeting of fellow travelers.

But there had been something in their demeanor that spoke of trouble.

Mason lay on his blanket, the cloth sack that contained all of his belongings clutched to his midsection. Slowly, he raised himself from the floor and strained for another tell-tale sound . . . There it was . . . another creak.

Two figures passed the illuminated door before once again being swallowed by the darkness; one large silhouette leading a smaller one. For the briefest of instants, something glinted in the larger man's hand, twinkling as if it were a star in the night sky. Mason knew instantly that it was a knife.

"Is he sleepin', Horace?" a reedy voice asked; it must have been the smaller man.

"Shut yer hole, Del!" a deep baritone hissed. "Are you wantin' to wake him?"

"Naw!" Del whispered back, ignoring Horace's advice.

"Goddammit! I said hush!"

Mason tensed, readying himself for the fight that was about to come. The life that he had chosen to lead, the life of a hobo, was certainly not without dangers: roust-abouts for the train companies wielded wooden clubs with reckless abandon, the police never gave a damn about what cir-cumstances drove a man to live in such a way, and getting off in the wrong commu-nity could be hazardous. But mostly there was the trouble caused by other riders.

More than once, Mason had been forced to defend himself. Most of the time, the at-tacks were the last acts of desperate men, feeble older men incapable of providing for themselves any longer, starving or sick. But occasionally it was something much more dangerous.

This was one of those times.

There was no doubt as to why the men were after him; they wanted to pilfer his belongings. His cloth sack didn't contain much: a couple of mealy apples, a change of clean, well-worn clothes, a broken pocket watch, and, concealed in a couple of socks, a handful of coins. But it was plenty to a couple of desperate men, more than enough to kill for. Little did they know that his true treasure wasn't kept in the sack but next to his heart; someone would have to pry it from his cold, dead fingers to get it.

Another creak of a floorboard . . . the attack would come soon.

"Do him! Do him quick!" Del barked.

Mason sprang to his feet. The suddenness of his movement momentarily surprised the attackers. In the time since he was awakened, his eyes had sufficiently adjusted to the darkness so that he could see both of them clearly. Taking measure of the knife in the larger man's hand, he wrapped his blanket around one fist and forearm.

"That ain't gonna be enough to help you." Horace grinned wickedly.

"Think not?" Mason grunted, biding for a bit more time.

"We'll see," Del snarled.

Far more quickly than would be expected of a man his size, Horace lunged forward and swiped at Mason with his knife, clearly a well-practiced move meant to disembowel his victim, but he found that his prey was nimbler than he'd thought. Mason sidestepped and threw a punch that snapped the man's head back and bloodied his nose.

"You son of a bitch!" Horace spat angrily.

Mason could see that his blow, while hard, had done no real damage other than to make the man angrier.

"Get 'im, Horace!" Del cheered, moving along the edge of the fight.

Bellowing like a bull, Horace charged Mason in an attempt to use his larger size to his advantage. This time, he was more successful. As Mason once again attempted to move out of the way, the big brute managed to snag him with one meaty hand, pulling him in as if he were a roped calf. Mason landed an elbow to the back of his attacker's head, a blow that would drop most, but the huge man barely wobbled.

Horace's humongous hands clutched fistfuls of Mason's coat and he found himself lifted up off the floor of the boxcar. He was about to kick out with one of his dangling feet, to drive a knee into the man's gut, when he was hurled through the air as easily as a doll thrown by a child. He slammed into the unforgiving side of the car and crashed hard to the floor, the air driven almost completely from his lungs.

Without pausing, Horace came at him with the knife. Somehow, Mason managed to get one end of his blanket free from his arm and looped it around the hand clutching the knife. A struggle of sheer strength ensued, as each man strained against the other. With his feet having regained sure purchase on the well-worn floorboards, Mason managed to take a quick step behind the other man's shoulder and then slammed one foot into the back of Horace's knee, driving him down toward the floor of the boxcar.

Maybe . . . maybe I can . . .

Just as Mason was about to throw a vicious blow to Horace's chin, his other opponent darted in and jabbed his ribcage, stunning him. Even as pain shot wickedly across his body, Mason was grateful that the little bastard didn't have a knife of his own; otherwise he would have been a goner. Still, it was enough to take away his advantage; Horace pivoted and pulled Mason down to the floor, where they began to wrestle.

"You ain't gettin' away," Horace panted, his face inches away.

"You'll not get my plunder."

"Oh, ain't this fun!" Del hooted from the side.

The two men rolled first one way and then the other, all the while the knife remaining clutched in one of Horace's hands, constantly threatening to find its intended mark. Sweat stood on Mason's brow, the muscles of his arms nearly shaking with the strain, but finally he found an advantageous position. With a heave, he pushed up from the floor and Horace fell away from him, his weight carrying him to the open door.

"Oh, my sweet Lord, no!" he screamed.

As Horace scrambled for any handhold he could find, his face was a mask of raw panic. Forgotten, the knife fell from his hand and clattered onto the stones that raced across the ground below. He clawed at the edge of the boxcar until somehow his fingers managed to grip its rough edge.

"We wasn't gonna hurt ya," he protested in desperation. "Honest, we wasn't!"

"He ain't lyin', mister," Del added.

"Yeah, and it snows in July." Mason walked over and smashed the heel of his booted foot down onto the man's clinging fingers. With a yelp of pain, Horace fell back from the train and was lost to the night.

Turning swiftly on his heel, Mason found Del wide-eyed behind him, his face a mixture of fear and disbelief at what had happened to his companion. Shaking hands rose to his small chest in a plea for mercy.

"Now . . . now wait just a second . . ." he begged.

"Not so tough now that you don't have your friend to protect you," Mason snarled, his anger growing with every step he took toward the man.

"You don't . . . don't gotta do nothin' to me, mister . . . I weren't gonna . . ."

Before Del could utter any more words of protest, Mason grabbed him by the front of his wretched coat and slammed him hard into the side of the boxcar; the man collided with such force that his rheumy eyes seemed to rattle in his sunken head.

Up close, his mouth and body reeked of rot and decay, roiling Mason's stomach.

"No doubt this is something you've done before," Mason accused.

"It ain't," Del said with a severe shake of his head. "Honest! We was just a bit hungry is all!"

Mason knew that he was lying; it was hard for him to imagine that a man Horace's size maintained his girth from the meager scraps he found traveling the rails. It was far more likely that the two simply preyed on the weaker men and women who were unlucky enough to encounter them. If they had been successful that night, there would have just been another body somewhere down the long road . . .

"Don't hurt me none, mister," Del continued to plead. "I won't—"

"Preying on folks who are down and out isn't right," Mason shot back angrily, cutting the man off. "It isn't honorable. You don't deserve any less than what your friend got."

"No, mister! Don't—"

With one swift motion, Mason hurled Del out into the night to share the same fate as Horace. The man's plaintive screams filled his ears for only an instant before being lost to the whistling winds.

Back in the corner nearest the open door, Mason bent down and snatched up the rucksack that the two men had brought with them onto the boxcar. For an instant, he considered doing to them what they had intended to do to him; to take their things as his own. Just like anyone unfortunate enough to find himself on the rails, there were things that he needed. But then his conscience got the better of him and he instead tossed the sack out of the train. Who knew . . . with a little luck, someone else would find it at first light.

"I'm getting fed up with this life," he muttered to himself.

Mason stood for a long while, looking out of the train at the landscape that flashed by. Under the full moon and brilliant blanket of stars, it was beautiful; freshly harvested fields disappearing in a blink, turning into thick groves of elm trees or the shimmering surface of a placid lake. For a brief moment, a pair of loons could be seen gliding through the night air.

Wisconsin in the fall gave Mason

pause; the seasons were too much like those back in Minnesota, back in Carlson, back in his hometown. Though more than eight years had passed since he had last laid eyes upon it, memories of the town sprang to his mind as clearly as the very stars above him. Rather than getting weaker with time, his recollections gained strength with each elapsing year. If he were to close his eyes, he could still see the bright flowers that lined Lake Carlson, William Hamilton's grocery, the look on his father's face as he sat behind his desk and patted his ample stomach, but especially . . .

"Alice," he whispered into the night. "Do you love me still?"

Carefully, Mason withdrew the photograph of his wife from inside his battered coat. Though it had become well-worn over the years, all its edges rounded and a light crease running down one side, he still found its beauty and elegance without equal.

But as beautiful as the faded photograph was, Mason knew that it paled in comparison to memories of the real woman; the way that Alice's blonde hair grew curlier during the spring rains, the sweet smile that she gave him when he told her how much he loved her, the soft feel of her skin against his as they made love. None of this could be seen in the photograph, but he, her husband, knew that it was there just the same.

Or it was there . . . until I destroyed it . . .

Before Mason could further contemplate what he had done, a racking cough raced across his chest. A wet, sticky discharge rose from his lungs and he had to struggle to release the phlegm. Bent over with discomfort, he finally managed to spit the mucus out of the racing train. This sort of coughing seemed to be happening more and more often. As the days grew colder, a growing weakness settled in his bones; the life of a hobo was hard.

With his hands at his face, Mason ran a gentle touch over the black beard that covered his cheeks. When he was a younger man, when he was courting Alice, he'd kept his face clean-shaven, but the beard he now wore wasn't for fashion; it was necessary. Though he could no longer touch what lay beneath, he knew that it was there nonetheless . . . a burden that he could never erase and never share.

Closing his eyes, Mason remembered the fateful day that had changed his life at once and forever. There had been mud and blood and then an explosion and then . . .

All his memories since then had been about running, running from his past, as far and as wide as the rails could take him. He'd been to Paris, to Bordeaux, New York, California, and even the swamps of Louisiana. He had dug wells, strained on the end of a chain uprooting tree roots, whitewashed fences, and even begged to get what he needed to survive. He'd lived a lie, allowing those who loved him to believe that he was dead, because he believed it was better that way.

But still, he couldn't completely erase the thought of Carlson . . . of Alice . . .

"A man is made up of his past, his present, and even his future."

Speaking the words that his father had told him so many years before sent a shiver up Mason's spine. Every day that he had spent running from what he had been was also a day spent running away from what he was meant to be, what he had been destined for. Much of what had lain before him the day he boarded that long train for the war, for France, was still there. As long as he drew breath, it would be there.

But I've been too ashamed, too afraid to go back for it . . .

Mason's back had already begun to ache from being tossed against the train car's wall. He'd managed to survive this time, but what about the next . . . or the next . . . or the time after that? Men such as Horace and Del lurked around every corner, their eyes eager for prey. This life was hard, in some ways even harder than being a soldier, and he was getting tired.

For the first time in eight years, Mason knew that the longing he felt for home and family, for Carlson, for Alice was so great that he could no longer ignore it. What harm would it cause to go and look upon the people whom he loved? What harm could come from staying at the edge of town and remembering, if only for a while, what he had once been? He would have to change a train or two, but he knew that he could be there within a matter of days. As the Wisconsin night sped by in a blur, Mason Tucker made up his mind.

He was going home.

Chapter Five

As HE HAD DONE nearly every day for the last eight years, Zachary Tucker stood at his office window and drank two fingers of whiskey, a silent toast to both his good fortune and his brother's death. Beneath his sill, Carlson was beginning to wake from another night's slumber. A pair of wagons lazily made their way down Main Street; a shopkeeper swept a scattering of leaves from in front of his door; a dog began barking somewhere in the distance. Zachary looked at his pocket watch, a quarter after seven o'clock in the morning, and smiled as if he were a proud parent.

Someday soon, I will own this town . . .

"I'm waiting for an answer, Mr. Tucker," a voice spoke from behind him.

Zachary turned slowly to fix his gaze upon Wilbur Stack, a representative of the Gaitskill Lumber Company of Minneapolis, freshly arrived on the earliest morning train. A short, balding man with just the smallest hint of a chin, Stack was immaculately dressed, his dark suit of the latest fashion and without a single wrinkle or out of place crease from his trip. Beady eyes peered out from a pair of round spectacles precariously perched atop his bulbous nose. His face seemed utterly devoid of good cheer. Zachary had the impression that the man was a lawyer of some sort; it seemed that when money was involved, particularly big money, men of that stripe could be found scurrying about like insects on an overripe fruit.

"I'm sorry, Mr. Stack, but it seems that I was somewhere else for a moment," Zachary apologized. "What was it that you asked?"

Sighing irritably, Stack said, "I was explaining to you that while the Gaitskill Lumber Company has done all that it had set out to do with regard to the new mill they planned to construct east of town, it appears to the board of directors back in Minneapolis that things are . . . lacking on Carlson's end. I was asked to come here to give you an opportunity to explain your point of view, but for that, I'm still waiting."

Instead of answering, Zachary asked, "Would you mind if I smoked?"

Stack nodded. "If you must."

From the moment he received the telegram that told him to expect a visit from the lumber company's representative, Zachary had dreaded his impending arrival. In his experience, meetings such as this could easily degenerate into shouting matches, spiteful accusations, and often the collapse of a carefully prepared deal.

Plucking a thickly rolled Spanish maduro from the silver box on the edge of his enormous oak desk, Zachary took his time in snipping the cigar's end and striking the match to light it. Puffing heavily, he soon had the end blazing red and bluish tendrils of smoke rising toward the ceiling. Fresh tobacco smoke burned in his throat.

"Where are my manners?" he said in sudden awareness. "Would you like one?"

"No thank you," Stack answered curtly.

Zachary's desire to smoke, as well as his offering a cigar to his guest, was not born out of a longing for tobacco; it sprang from his desire to avoid showing weakness. Making Stack wait for him to proceed, while infuriating to the man, also served to remind him that his host was not without power of his own. Too often in situations such as this, whoever was on his side of the desk bent over backward to please his benefactors.

But that is something I will not do!

Weakness was not an attribute that many would ascribe to Zachary Tucker. Well over six feet tall, he was a thick man who was drifting toward fat; like his father, his ability to consume drink and large meals was something of a local legend. His coal-black hair, pomaded smartly, had begun to show just the faintest hint of a silver-gray at his temples. He often ran his fingers through the bushy thickness of his mustache. While his cheeks were ruddy, a color associated with good cheer, the blackness of his eyes, as well as the dark circles that surrounded them, suggested something far different. Many a man had been broken under the stare of those eyes.

"I'm afraid I don't see the problems you so clearly do," he finally said.

"You must be joking," Stack replied impatiently.

"Everything is going exactly as we intended," Zachary explained, cutting the man off while absently flicking a half-inch of ash from his buttoned coat, one of a seemingly endless wardrobe of the newest fashions.

"Not according to the papers you've shown me," Stack argued, holding up a sheaf of documents. "Everything indeed does seem to be in order, save for one property," he continued, peering down his nose at a particular sheet, "owned by one Eliza Watkins and Otis Simmons."

Simply hearing the names of his late brother's in-laws sent shivers of disgust running down Zachary's spine, a reaction that he hoped had not been betrayed by his face. To have his financial future so intimately connected to those people was an insult he wouldn't be able to stand much longer. But every time he tried to speak with Rachel Watkins . . .

God damn Mason and that damn family!

"They'll come around," Zachary assured his visitor.

"You said the same thing four months ago," Stack snapped back. "Or have you already forgotten that visit?"

"My associates and I are doing everything in our power to ensure that all will go exactly as planned," Zachary explained, pointing over Stack's shoulder to the quiet man standing in the corner. Travis Jefferson had worked for Zachary Tucker for the last four years, usually doing jobs of an unsavory nature. Thin, but wiry and strong as a wildcat, he was apt to let his bony fists do his talking. It was a brave man who willingly faced him. Close-cropped brownish-blond hair framed an oval face. An angry scar, white and fat, ran diagonally from his hairline down to his tanned brow. He didn't acknowledge Tucker's gesture, nor did Stack turn to look at him.

"You'd better be," Stack said. "You know how much is at stake."

"Oh, yes," Zachary answered. "I do."

Nearly one year earlier, the Gaitskill Lumber Company had come to Carlson with the intention of opening a lumber mill to the east of town. Large groves of cedar and oak covered that area, ideal for the growing needs of Minneapolis and St. Paul. With the railroad already an established presence, all seemed in place for a prosperous partnership. All it would take was a rail spur run from the lumber operation to the existing depot.

But then there had been a snag . . .

One of the conditions that the lumber company had placed upon the deal was that they wanted to buy up the properties located around the depot. Newly constructed offices would coordinate traffic from the mill to and from the Twin Cities. Company executives could come to view the enterprise's progress without having to camp out with the laborers. The amount they offered for the properties was generous, far above true value, and all those who first had been approached had jumped at the deal. But then Zachary had spoken with Eliza Watkins and everything had gone to hell.

Standing in the darkened room on the

second floor of the boardinghouse, her eyes had filled with tears as she recounted all of the wonderful years her beloved daughter, Alice, had spent growing up under the building's gabled roof. She'd told him of birthdays, skinned knees, her girls sliding down the banisters to the front door, and of the first time Alice had brought Mason to visit, until Zachary had been ready to pull out his hair! Eliza told him that selling the house would be nothing short of a betrayal to those memories. Though he had offered to raise the buying price higher than any building in Carlson, she told him no amount of money would change her mind.

The worst part for Zachary was that he knew she and Otis needed money. Any fool who stood outside and looked at the property could see that the owners weren't financially secure; worn and chipped paint, a sagging roof, and cracks in the windows were only the most obvious of their problems. Boarders in these parts were few and far between. Eliza had given up her birthing practice and Otis was a drunk. Even Rachel . . .

What future did these people have?

"A great deal of work has gone into making sure that this deal actually comes off," Stack explained, his eyes never wavering from Zachary's. "A considerable amount of . . . greasing the wheels has occurred, if you know what I am saying. For it to come undone now would be a grave disappointment . . . indeed, nothing short of a *grave* mistake," he added pointedly.

"As I explained," Zachary assured him, "they'll eventually sell."

"For your sake, I hope you're right, otherwise . . ."

"Otherwise what?"

"While it's certainly too late for the company to turn its back upon the town, considering all the preparations made, it might well revisit its intentions of doing further business with you." Stack smiled sardonically. "If word were to get out that you were unreliable, who's to say what future opportunities would ever be presented? After all, the Gaitskill Lumber Company is one of the pillars of Minneapolis's business community. It is not an enemy one would wish to have."

Without any doubt, Zachary knew that this was the true reason for Wilbur Stack's visit, to give him a warning. Failure to do as he had promised would have undeniable consequences. The lumber company would make him pay for his failure by blacklisting him from any further contracts. With the right amount of pressure, his dream of owning Carlson, of being the most powerful man in the area, could go up like so much smoke.

"There is another matter," Stack explained with a delicate cough.

"Yes?" Zachary asked curiously over the end of his cigar.

"There are some members of the company's board who would prefer to work with your father, Sherman Tucker, on this particular matter," Stack said with caution, clearly weighing each of his words, watching for Zachary's reaction. "His is a name well known in business circles. Many remember his efforts to bring the railroad to Carlson in the first place. I've been instructed to ask if it might be possible to bring him into our negotiations."

Zachary smiled inwardly. This request was something he'd long anticipated, and had expected to be made much earlier. His father had been a lion, one of several founders of Carlson, and through sheer will had built the town into a successful community. When he opened the Carlson Bank and Trust, he'd done so with the belief that fairness always bested greed, that by helping a neighbor through difficult times the whole of the town could be strengthened. He'd taken pains to raise both of his sons to believe in the same principles, all in the hope that they would one day succeed him. But Zachary had always known differently . . .

The truth is that I was never supposed to be the successor!

Mason had always been their father's favorite. As the elder brother, he had clung to Sherman's elbow, following the older man around like a puppy. For that obedience, fortune had smiled upon him. Mason had been the one of the two blessed with the looks of a leading man in the theater, the brains to master any task put before him, the grace and wit to charm anyone he met, and the hand of the most beautiful girl in Carlson. *He* was the one who had always been meant to carry the mantle of the bank; *he* was the one who would be expected to lead Carlson into the twentieth century; *he* had always been the one . . .

But then he had gone off to war.

Though the news of Mason's death had shaken all of Carlson to its very core, Zachary had been privately elated. There had always been a simmering rivalry between them that grew with every passing year, but hostility existed mostly on Zachary's end; after all, he had nothing Mason could have wanted. If he had a penny for every time he'd been told to act more like Mason, he wouldn't have needed the rotten bastard to die in order to inherit the bank; he'd have already been rich!

And suddenly it all belonged to me!

Mason's sudden passing had aged Sherman Tucker a decade in what seemed little more than a blink of an eye. More and more, the older banker withdrew himself from public life, retreating to the library of his home on the northern edge of town. By the time Alice Tucker died giving birth to Sherman's granddaughter, he'd fallen so ill that he needed round-the-clock care. It was undoubtedly only a matter of time until he joined his beloved son in heaven.

Sherman's exit had left Zachary in complete control of the bank and the future of Carlson. His philosophy of business was nearly the exact opposite of his father's; he felt nothing mattered but the money. He didn't give a damn if a farmer was going through tough times or a merchant was still waiting for a shipment of goods from Duluth. If the money he was owed wasn't paid in time, he had no qualms about seizing whatever he could as payment. Was it his fault if businessmen had bitten off more than they could chew? Money was power . . . and that was what he coveted.

"I'm afraid that my father's illness is so severe that he will be unable to be of any help in this matter," Zachary explained patiently. "The doctors all say to expect the worst, but I prefer to be more of an optimist. Perhaps if he makes a recovery, he might be able to aid us in the future."

"I see," Stack answered, clearly disappointed.

"But make no bones about it, Mr. Stack," Zachary said with just the slightest touch of steel in his voice, "my father has often expressed the utmost faith and confidence in my abilities. After all, he taught me everything he knows. If he were able to join us, I'm certain that he would have made the very same choices I have."

Stack stared at Zachary for a moment longer, looking as if there were things he wished to say, but instead began shuffling papers into his briefcase. "I believe our business is concluded," he said finally. "Good day, sir."

"Good day, Mr. Stack."

"God damn it all!" Zachary swore angrily after he was certain Wilbur Stack was out of earshot. Snatching up his empty glass, he generously refilled it with whiskey and sent the contents burning down his gullet. He poured even more, but he was so agitated that instead of drinking it, he tossed his still smoldering cigar into the glass, ruining it all.

"What are we gonna do now, boss?" Travis Jefferson said as he stepped from the shadows toward Zachary's desk. He had been around enough of the man's rages to know to stand back respectfully.

"What can we do but keep on, you simpleton?" Zachary snapped.

"How about movin' the lumber company's offices farther up the line? There ain't no reason that they gotta be next to the depot, is there?" Travis suggested. "Maybe we could find some other folks that'll snap up the money that you're offerin'."

"It's far too late for that," the banker answered dismissively. "Gaitskill has already made plans that they won't want to change, no matter what sort of explanation I give them. The consequences of simply asking them to do so would be disastrous.

"I've made a promise to them that I believed I could keep," he continued. "It's just proving a bit harder to do than I had expected. No, we will just have to make things work . . . even if we have to force them a bit."

"How much force are you talkin' about?" Travis asked, the hint of a smile curling at the corners of his mouth.

Zachary took a good long look at his lackey. Travis Jefferson was absolutely not one to shy away from violence. In the past, he'd proven to be valuable beyond measure: a late-night visit here, a guttural threat delivered there, and, on one memorable occasion, a bone-breaking. All it would take was one word and he would set upon Eliza Watkins and her drunkard brother as if he were a starving wolf.

"We're not at that juncture yet," Zachary said. He walked over to the window and stared back down the street. The boarding-house was just visible from the rear, a reminder of the sizable obstacle that lay in his path. "I'm going to try to have a word with Rachel. She always struck me as the reasonable one. If I can get her to understand the predicament she is in, offer some extra money, maybe she can succeed in getting her mother to finally see reason."

"And if she can't get it done?"

"That, my friend," Zachary said, smiling, "is where you come in."

Chapter Six

RACHEL TOSSED a freshly laundered sheet over the wire clothesline and paused, the sun's faint warmth pleasant on her up-turned face. Overnight, the weather had begun to change; there was a crispness to the air that spoke more of the coming winter than the last remnants of fall. Wispy clouds spread across the autumn sky, as thin as gauze. A formation of ducks, head-ing south to warmer climes, beat their wings furiously, quacking noisily at each other. Still, this day was beautiful.

And here I am working yet again!

The small courtyard behind the boardinghouse was framed on either side by the adjacent buildings, the rear by a narrow alleyway. Three lines of wire were strung from wooden poles driven deeply into the ground. Facing toward the south, the courtyard spent much of the day in sunlight and was ideal for drying wet laundry.

Rachel had risen early—dawn had just broken—and set about the first of her morning chores. After breakfast, she'd been to visit the Wickers, declaring that newborn Walter was in tip-top shape. Though the baby was drowsing soundly on a newly knitted blanket, it was clear from the bleary-eyed look on his parents' faces that he had caused a sleepless night, with many more surely to come. After accepting her payment, she'd headed back to the boarding-house and resumed her work.

Hefting another sheet, Rachel pulled one of the clothespins free from her lips and fastened the laundry to the line. Laundry, laundry, and more laundry! It was every bit as backbreaking as it was time-consuming. Late spring, summer, and early fall it went out on the yard line. In late fall, winter, and early spring she labored in the stone-walled basement where the coal furnace dried the wash, albeit a bit more slowly. She reckoned that it was only a matter of weeks before she would begin hanging sheets downstairs.

This particular morning, she had tried her best to persuade Charlotte to help her, but the girl had laughed and run off to play with Jasper. Watching her, Rachel had wondered how Charlotte had managed again to get away from Eliza's watchful eye.

What am I ever going to do with that girl?

The previous day's disastrous trip to her sister's grave sprang back to Rachel's mind. Nothing had gone as she had hoped. She'd taken Charlotte there because the girl needed to acknowledge her mother, but Rachel had been left to speak to Alice by herself.

The sudden slamming of a door at the rear of the boardinghouse roused Rachel from her unpleasant reverie. For a brief moment, she thought that her uncle Otis had come to help her with the laundry, but between a break in the wet sheets she was dismayed to see that it was Jonathan Moseley striding toward the line.

"Rachel," he called. "Are you out here?"

Holding her breath and standing completely still, Rachel hoped that he'd fail to notice her and let her be, but a poorly timed gust of wind raised a pair of sheets so high into the air that she was left in plain sight. When their eyes met, his face brightened just as hers fell.

"Ah, there you are!"

When Rachel first laid eyes upon Jonathan Moseley, he'd reminded her of a scarecrow. Tall and thin, stoop-backed and awkward, he appeared to be made up of nothing but knees and elbows. Mostly bald, he insisted upon combing what few wisps of straw-blond hair he had over his barren pate. His thin nose was crooked; his eyes were large and buglike, and his small mouth was filled with stained teeth. He had an unpleasant habit of darting his tongue out and running it over his dry, cracked lips. There was simply nothing attractive about the man.

For the month that he had been a boarder, he had represented himself as a traveling salesman making his way across Minnesota. His shabby and battered case contained every sort of item that could possibly be hawked: brushes of all sizes, shoelaces of varying length, Bibles, and a hair cream that he claimed would cure baldness. For the life of her, Rachel couldn't imagine who would buy such a product from a man with so little hair.

Jonathan boasted that he was successful; he was always rambling on about a mansion he had his eye on in Chicago. But from the shoddy state of his clothing, such declarations were hard to believe: his white shirt was shoddily made and splotched with food stains, the dark pants he wore looked nearly an inch too short, and the bow tie wrapped around his neck was poorly tied and ridiculously out of fashion.

"What a lovely day this is," he declared, spreading his bony hands wide, "but it is all the more beautiful because you are in it, my dear Rachel."

"Thank you for such kind words, Mr. Moseley," she replied as dismissively as she dared.

"How many times must I tell you?" He grinned. "Call me Jonathan."

Rachel cringed inwardly. The last thing that she wanted was for this man to have some degree of familiarity with her. Whenever he had previously tried cornering her, she'd taken great pains to escape, listening politely for a moment before excusing herself to take care of other matters. But try as she might, she could not get him to understand that she was not interested; at every opportunity, he came back for more.

"The work never ends around here, from the look of things," he declared, his hands on his bony waist. "Every time I turn around, there you are, busy with some task or other."

"There is certainly much to be done."

"Would you mind if I helped you?"

"No, no, no," Rachel replied nervously. Her mind raced over every excuse she could think of, settling upon, "My mother insists that things be done a particular way and if I were to come back with it done incorrectly, I'd have to wash it all over again."

"Well, we can't have that, can we?" Jonathan answered with feigned disappointment; it was clear to Rachel that such feelings were contrived; he was obviously relieved that he wouldn't have to do any actual work.

For a few minutes, they remained silent, Rachel continuing to put the laundry on the line and Jonathan watching her as if she were a pupil doing mathematics at the chalkboard and he the teacher waiting for the first sign of a mistake. It took all of her will not to just dump the basket and run. She was so intent on finishing her chore that when Jonathan finally did speak, she nearly jumped in surprise.

"I suppose you might be wondering why I was looking for you?" he asked.

"I . . . I hadn't . . . thought to ask," Rachel muttered.

"I was wondering if you might like to accompany me on a picnic," Jonathan explained pleasantly. "I found the perfect spot on the north side of the lake, a clearing surrounded by tall elms and more wildflowers than you could count in a week! When I first saw it, I couldn't think of anyone I would rather share it with than you."

Momentarily taken aback, Rachel was struck mute. Previously, Jonathan had only made subtle hints of his romantic feelings for her, certainly nothing so forward as this!

Romance was something that Rachel had never found much time for; she'd had her fair share of men attracted by her looks, but nothing serious. With all of her responsibilities, particularly with Charlotte, she did little to encourage them. Besides, if she did ever decide to pursue a relationship, it wouldn't have been with Jonathan Moseley. "I thank . . . I thank you for thinking of me," she stammered, "but I'm afraid I just can't! I have all of this laundry to finish hanging and then I have to—"

"Surely it doesn't all have to be done this instant, does it?"

"But my mother," Rachel struggled. "She insists that—"

"If there's any insisting to be done here, I do believe that I should be the one doing it." He laughed. "It would certainly be no trouble to gather a picnic basket. Two people like ourselves need some time to be away, to be alone, and to let . . . things . . . take their natural course."

"I beg your pardon?"

"Why it's only the normal way of things that an unattached, successful man such as myself would wish to find companionship with an equally single young woman as lovely as you," Jonathan explained as he slowly stepped toward her, his tongue licking across his lips. "That's how all good romances begin, don't you think?"

Rachel could feel the flush of embarrassment color her cheeks and she turned back to her laundry. Revulsion at Jonathan's suggestion roiled her stomach. Bending over, she grasped for another piece of laundry, anxious to do something, anything, to lose his interest. But just as she gripped a sheet corner, she felt the hem of her skirt being lifted, followed by the sensation of a finger running across the bare skin just above her boot. There could be no doubt what was happening.

What in the hell does he think he's doing?

Spinning around and snatching her skirt back toward her, Rachel caught Jonathan straightening up, a patently false look of innocence plastered across his ridiculous face, his hands clasped behind his back. The remnants of a smile still played across his chapped lips.

"Have you lost your senses?" she shouted at him.

"You misunderstand my intentions, my dear," Jonathan explained, his green eyes dancing with mock offense. "It was quite innocent. I saw that your hemline was about to be snagged in one of the broken wickers of the laundry basket and I thought to save you more work. If there had been a tear, who knows how many hours it would have cost!"

Rachel didn't believe a single word of his explanation. All of the irritation she felt came boiling out in an instant. Angrily, she stepped toward him, ready to give him a much-deserved piece of her mind. With his meek exterior, she expected him to retreat as she advanced, but he surprised her by closing the gap between them. His thin fingers painfully grasped her wrists, pulling her closer.

"This is the spirit I find so attractive in you," he declared.

"Get your hands off me!"

"Why would I want to do that?"

As she tried to break his grip, Rachel could see that Jonathan had no intention of letting her go. From the mischievous gleam in his eyes, she was horrified to realize that he intended to kiss her. As quickly as she could manage, she turned her face away from his.

"You need to get away from a place

such as this," Jonathan said, his voice no more than a deep whisper in her ear. "Beauty and talents like yours are wasted here. You need to be somewhere, with someone who appreciates you for what you truly are. Run away with me . . . let us start a new life together far away from this godforsaken place."

"Let go of me this instant!"

Just as Rachel was ready to scream out for help, the door to the rear of the boarding-house again slammed shut. Her earlier hopes were finally answered; her uncle Otis stumbled down the short steps and out into the yard. The dark whiskey bottle hanging from his listless hand gave every indication of his condition; he was already three sheets to the wind, his cheeks burning as red as his nose. Though he was drunk, Rachel had never been happier to see him in her life.

Looking over his bony shoulder, Jonathan released his grip on Rachel so quickly she would have thought her blouse had burst into flames. He was once again the traveling salesman, his face as innocent as newly fallen snow. Rachel moved away from him, gently massaging her arms where he had grabbed her.

"Just the fella I was lookin' for," Otis said gruffly when he'd reached them.

"Me?" Jonathan asked in surprise. Briefly, a shadow of worry crossed his face, a fear that maybe he had been caught doing something he shouldn't. "Whatever for?"

"For the four bits you been owin' for rent on that there room," the drunken man said before taking yet another swig of his liquor. "Seems like every damn time I been up a-poundin' on your door, there ain't nobody there. Thought I heard your voice out here . . ."

Jonathan looked from Rachel to Otis, expecting her to tell him all that had occured, but she held her tongue. She knew that he'd understand her silence to be some sort of returned affection, but the truth was much simpler; times for her family were tough, and kicking out one of their few boarders would only make them tougher.

"How . . . how much did you say I owe you?" Jonathan muttered.

"Four bits," Otis repeated.

"I might have that much on me," the skinny man said, checking his pockets.

"You best be knowin' that this here ain't no charity house, Mr. Moseley." The words fell out of Otis's mouth as slurred as if they themselves were drunk. "What with all the work poor ol' Rachel here is doin', it just wouldn't be right of you not to pay what you done agreed to. The way some of us is headin', why, our word's gonna be all we got left!"

"Quite right, Mr. Simmons," Jonathan agreed.

For a moment, the salesman looked hopeful that Otis would let him bring the money to him later, but the large man didn't budge, fixing a determined yet unfocused stare upon him. "I guess I'll need to fetch my money purse, then," Jonathan finally said with a huff. His eyes lingered on Rachel for a moment longer before he set off back toward the house.

As she watched him go, Rachel knew that she would have to keep a close eye on Jonathan Moseley. He obviously had bolder plans for her; but if he put his hands on her again, she would be ready.

*   *   *

In his room on the top floor of the boardinghouse, Jonathan Moseley seethed. All of
his many intentions for the day seemed to
have been going well until that obese
drunkard had come out and ruined everything! If it hadn't been for him, why, he
could have been down on the lakeshore
frolicking with Rachel instead of digging
for money he didn't have.

"Damn that man and his poor timing!"

Cluttered and cramped, Jonathan's room
looked as if it had been struck by a tornado
and earthquake all rolled into one. Cascading piles of books, bundles of brushes,
and bottles of hair tonic vied for whatever
space could be found on the floor and the
small table near the window. His lone chair
and bed were both covered in clothing;
shirts and dirty socks were tossed willy-
nilly and shoes were underfoot.

**Even if I had any money, I wouldn't
know where to find it!**

Though he portrayed himself as a
man of great prospective wealth, the fact
was that Jonathan Moseley was nearly
penniless. He had attempted many enter-
prises: investing in a "surefire" Oklahoma

oilfield, selling insurance outside of St. Louis; he'd even traveled with a circus as a carnival barker.

But all had ended in failure . . .

Now he was attempting to ply his trade as a traveling salesman, but he could already see that this was headed in the same direction as all of his other careers. The fact was that people didn't want the junk he was selling. With winter coming, his prospects seemed bleak.

Not that he considered himself above stealing. He'd needed occasionally to break into a home or business. He felt no shame, no regret. He'd learned long ago that there were moments a man had to take what he wanted. He might need to do so again.

Part of his interest in Rachel Watkins was that she had a secure roof over her head for the coming winter. If he were to become romantically involved with her, it seemed unlikely that he would be expected to pay for his room. But that was hardly the end of his interest.

The truth was that he lusted after her. Even in the plain blouses and skirts she wore, he could see that she had curves in all the right places. His loins positively ached to be between her legs! She had once smiled at him and the burning desire it had caused had lasted for days! While Jonathan had no illusion that he was the best-looking man in the world, he also knew that in Carlson, Rachel had little room to be choosy. If he were to play his cards right, if he were to display his ample charms at just the right time, he had no doubt that she would fall for him.

That was why today was so important!

He'd finally managed to get Rachel alone, away from that poorly behaved brat and the thin walls of her mother's flea-ridden boardinghouse, and then everything had been going as well as he could have hoped. It had been a risk to reach up under her skirt as he had, but the defiant way she had spoken had been well worth it and nothing short of arousing. Though she protested, Jonathan had known that she was only moments away from accepting his offer of a picnic.

But then Otis had come along and ruined it all!

Thinking of the fat, drunken man gave Jonathan a sudden idea . . .

Maybe if he were lucky, Otis would have

already wandered off to the bottom of whatever bottle he was currently nipping on and Rachel would again be by herself.

Hurrying over to his small window, Jonathan stared down into the open area behind the building. Wiping away a layer of dust, he arrived just in time to witness Rachel finish hanging the last of her laundry, snatch up her basket, and return inside.

He was too late . . . his chance was missed.

As he collapsed onto his clothes-strewn bed, anger simmered in Jonathan's heart. Everything had run off the rails! Too much was riding on his pursuit of Rachel for him to give up the hunt; on the contrary, he knew that he would just have to try that much harder.

He smiled to himself. "Whether she likes it or not."

Chapter Seven

MASON TUCKER LEAPT from the moving train about a quarter mile from the outskirts of Carlson, just as the engine began to slow on its approach to the depot. Choosing a spot that had been cleared of trees, he slammed hard into the ground before tucking his head and rolling through, his momentum carrying his satchel up and over his head. It was a well-practiced move, an action that left him ready to run quickly if necessary.

Leaving the train short of town had been an easy decision; he was not certain how close to town he wanted to get, and either

way, the last thing he wanted was someone to identify him. From where he had
exited, it would be a short walk to the first
houses.

"And then I'll be home, I reckon," he
muttered to himself.

But just as Mason straightened, a wave
of dizziness washed over him. With a trembling hand, he steadied himself against a
tall oak tree, his feet buried in an impressive drift of fallen leaves. Ever since his
encounter with the two assailants in Wisconsin, his bouts of queasiness seemed to
be coming more and more frequently. Closing his eyes tightly, he waited for the world
to stop spinning and was finally rewarded.

Slowly at first, then gaining stride, Mason
made his way toward Carlson. The densely
packed forest on the outskirts of town soon
gave way to gently rolling farming fields
already stripped of their recent harvest.
He passed a farm where a man and his
son were both atop ladders, picking apples from trees and dropping them into
baskets hung from their shoulders. Somewhere in the distance, someone was burning brush.

Eventually closer to the town itself,

Mason was surprised to see that houses had sprung up much farther from Carlson's center than he remembered. Sturdy homes covered with fresh coats of paint were aligned in orderly blocks with new streets spurring toward Main Street. Trees he recalled as saplings were taller, their branches reaching ever higher. Much remained that he recognized, but much was different.

Easily jumping over first one fence and then another, Mason cut across yards as he headed toward the northern end of town. He kept his head down, moving quickly, not wanting to be noticed and ever watchful that he not draw too much attention.

The last thing I need is a barking dog!

When he had finally decided to return to Carlson, he had known in his heart where he would go first; the loving house that he and Alice had shared in the days just after their wedding. Dashing from the cover of a tree to the safety of a woodpile and then across yet another fence, he found himself close enough to see the house clearly and his heart began to pound furiously.

Back when the house was built, Mason

hadn't been particularly comfortable working with his hands; he was much more within his element in his father's bank. But a wise choice had been made in hiring out the home's construction; even eight years later, it was still a work of beauty. A two-story Victorian with a gabled roof and large, multipaned windows, it looked almost exactly as he remembered it. He smiled as he recalled the nights he and Alice had spent on the wraparound porch with its latticework runner and sparkling white columns.

Crouching in the deep shadows, Mason was suddenly filled with doubt about his decision to return. He felt nervous, fearful that Alice would see him and be disgusted by what he had become. A shaking hand reached up to touch the scarred side of his face. The memory of what had once looked back at him from a cracked mirror sent a shiver of revulsion racing down his spine.

No matter what, he would never let Alice see the truth.

Movement at the front of the house shook him from his unkind thoughts. The front door swung open and a well-dressed man stepped down from the porch and momentarily reveled in the sunshine. Whistling to himself, the man shot his cuffs and smiled confidently. Just the sight of him caused Mason's heart to sink like a stone.

What did you expect to find, you fool?

During the long years that he had been traveling, Mason had often wondered what had taken place when Alice had learned of his passing. As a young widow, she would have had no shortage of suitors. After so many years, she would have moved on . . . found a new husband . . . found a new life. Though he had wanted her to be happy, the sight of her new man was like a blow to his chest.

But as surprised as he'd been to see the man step from the door, Mason was even more shocked when a young woman followed her husband outside. She wasn't Alice. With her dark hair cascading down over her pale yellow blouse, the woman rose up onto her tiptoes to plant a tender kiss upon the man's cheek. They both laughed before heading down the street toward the center of town. In moments, they were lost to his sight.

What . . . what is going on here?

Mason was utterly perplexed. Stepping from the shadows out into the middle of the street, he stared at his former home, then back down the street, returning his gaze again to the house. At that moment, he was no longer the least bit concerned whether he was seen or not. Questions raced through across his mind. *Who are the people now living in my and Alice's home? Why doesn't Alice live there anymore? Where in heaven's name did she go?*

Before he could set about finding answers to his many questions, another wave of dizziness washed over him. This seizure was worse than the last, strong enough to drive him down to one knee in the road. Pulsing pain assaulted his senses and he had to squelch the urge to vomit. He touched his forehead with the back of his shaking hand; it was hot. He was sick, but he refused to allow his illness to keep him from the answers he so desperately needed. Gritting his teeth, he pushed to his feet and breathed deeply, settling his racing head.

"Hold yourself together," he commanded himself.

Once he was sure that he wouldn't pitch face first into the road on his first step, Mason set out for the only place he could think of to get the answers he wanted; Eliza Watkins's home across from the train depot. While he knew he couldn't just go up and pound on the door demanding answers, he could watch and hope he might learn something. Going there would be a risk—there was really no way to get there other than by crossing through the center of town—but it was a risk he was willing to take.

Mason stuck to the shadows of the buildings along Main Street, taking great care not to be noticed. Still, it was hard for him not to stare at the way Carlson had changed in his absence; there was a new lawyer's office next to Hamilton's Grocery, a new steeple atop the Lutheran church, and even a new balcony running the length of Carlson Bank and Trust.

Struck by all these changes, Mason was also prompted to recall old incidents from his youth: chasing after his father as he made his way about his business, sloshing through mud puddles with his brother, and painstakingly choosing which candy he would purchase from Laurson's Mercantile with his shiny new penny. Carlson remained a part of him, no matter how many miles he'd traveled or how many years he'd been gone.

He had just stepped down from the boardwalk, gawking at all of the changes, memories swirling about his dazed head, when he collided with a man so violently that they both nearly fell to the ground.

"What in the name of—?" a gruff voice spat.

Quickly straightening himself, Mason was horror-struck to find himself only inches away from Samuel Guthrie, a man he had known since birth. With his hawkish nose and unruly brush of a mustache, the man was unmistakable, even with the wrinkles that lined his face. Mason clearly remembered running into his father's office at the bank and being greeted by Samuel's quick smile.

"Why don't you watch where you're going?" Samuel snarled.

"I'm sorry Mr. Gu—" Mason caught himself, rapidly adding, "sir . . ."

Watch your tongue, you fool!

"No-good, worthless bum!" the man snapped before walking away in a huff.

Watching the man go, Mason realized that he hadn't been recognized. Though Samuel Guthrie had once held some hope that Mason would wed his own daughter, he hadn't known who had collided with him, even at a distance of inches. In Guthrie's eyes, he'd been nothing but a destitute fool, a blight upon the town.

Catching his reflection in the nearest window, Mason had to admit that there was reason for Mr. Guthrie's assumption: his coat and pants were both dirt-streaked; his satchel was a littered mess of patches and temporary stitch jobs. His unruly hair and beard, his skin worn by the elements, and the wildness of his eyes were all frightening.

The realization of just how far he had fallen struck Mason like a thunderbolt from a stormy sky. Before he'd set foot on that train bound for the European war, he'd had everything: admiration, an adoring wife, a future . . . Now he was lucky to have what was in the bag slung over his shoulder. He had gone off to fight for his country and had been changed forever. Now he was unrecognizable. He had lost everything.

"No one will remember what I once was . . ."

As well as he could manage, Mason continued toward Alice's mother's home, this time paying more attention to those around him. He was only a couple of blocks from the depot, from turning the corner to his destination, when what he saw stopped him cold; crossing the road in front of him, a cigar clasped between his teeth, was his brother.

Zachary had also changed in the eight years since Mason had last seen him; considerable weight had been added to his frame and his hair had begun graying. But much about his brother seemed the same. His dress was still expressive of his belief that he was better than everyone around him; nothing but the best had ever been enough for Zachary Tucker. His look was still angry; his brow was furrowed and his hands clenched into fists as he walked.

Mason knew that if there were anyone in Carlson who would have benefited from his disappearance, who would have even welcomed it, it would have been Zachary.

The financial responsibilities that their father had been grooming Mason to assume would have gone to his brother. He'd always been a greedy child and had in turn grown into a greedy man. Without Sherman Tucker's steadying hand, he couldn't imagine what Zachary would become.

"You're someone I don't want to run into, brother," Mason mumbled.

While he could write off part of Samuel Guthrie's failure to recognize him to the man's advanced age, Mason knew that he couldn't take that chance with Zachary. He had no doubt that if they were to come face-to-face, there would be no mistaking his true identity.

Before he could make up his mind what he should do, Mason was struck by another wave of sickness, this one greater than all of the others put together. For an instant, his vision went black and his world was turned upside down. His satchel fell to the ground and he crashed down onto his knees beside it. Vomit poured from his mouth as his stomach heaved, the nausea threatening to overwhelm him. Wild panic raced through his mind, panic that his condition would attract unwanted attention, and he struggled to rise to his feet, running from the street. There was no hope that he could wait outside Eliza Watkins's house. He had to get away.

Any hope of seeing Alice would have to wait.

Slowly and as carefully as he could, Mason made his way among the tall trees on the far side of Lake Carlson. He wasn't sure how he'd been able to walk such a distance, but he refused to allow himself to fall again too close to town. Even with such determination, he nearly toppled as another shudder raced through him and his knees nearly went out from under him.

I feel as weak as a newborn kitten!

Blots of sunlight dappled the leaves that swayed above him, but Mason was thankful to be in the shade. Though the October day carried with it a coolness remembered from his childhood, he felt as if he were burning up with a fever. He'd somehow managed to strip off his heavier coat, but sweat poured freely from his body.

The other thing that burned at him was shame; it had embarrassed him to run away to the woods. Ever since that fateful day eight years earlier, whenever he'd been hurt, whenever he had been threatened, his first instinct had always been to run for safety. If he were ever to change, he would have to stay and hold his ground.

Once he had crossed the edge of town, Mason knew exactly where he'd been headed. Picking his way through the trees and underbrush, he tried to examine the ground for faint signs of the path while his head continued to throb painfully. He passed a lightning-struck evergreen, its needles brown and long dead, skirted a depression filled with muck, mire, and the occasional rotting tree branch, climbed a low rise that almost took his meager breath away, and then came to a clearing he recognized. A surprised squirrel skittered away noisily as he stumbled to the far side of the open space. And there it was.

"The old shack," he said aloud.

Leaning against a majestic elm tree was a rough hut. No more than ten feet wide and an equal amount in depth, the building had obviously seen better days. The roof sagged at its crown, an indentation that was clearly deep enough to let in rain. The glass of the lone window had long since fallen out. The white paint that had once been proudly slapped on its sides was now peeled and chipped away until only a few flecks remained to cover the graying wooden planks. Still, the shack was a sight for Mason's eager eyes.

As a child, he had come here often, as had nearly every child in Carlson. For a moment, worry at being discovered played across his thoughts, but he knew that it was already far too late for such concerns.

Another spasm of sickness assaulted him and he had no choice but to once again vomit. Even though his stomach was empty, he continued to dry-heave, noisily retching on his knees. Summoning all of his remaining strength, he rose and stumbled toward the shack.

He pushed open the door and entered on unsteady feet. The cool darkness of the inside was as welcome to him as the musty, fetid odor was unpleasant. The furnishings were meager; an uneven table and the rotten remnants of a mattress. Mason didn't mind the squalor; all he wanted was shelter and to be out of sight.

Wandering over to the corner farthest from the door, he collapsed into a heap on the warped planks. Darkness once again rose to overwhelm him and he knew he would be unable to resist any longer. His last thought before slipping into unconsciousness was of Alice.

I . . . just need . . . to get some . . . rest . . .

Chapter Eight

WITH HER BROW KNIT in determination, Rachel ran a rag over the dusty top of the oaken bureau in the boardinghouse's sitting room. Over and over again, she polished the worn surface until she was finally happy with the glassy sheen. Even as she finished, she knew that it would soon have to be done again. Nothing in the house stayed clean for long.

Though it was still early in the day, Rachel was thankful that she had not seen any sign of Jonathan Moseley since their encounter at the clothesline the afternoon before. She doubted that it had been any sense of shame at what he had done that kept him away from the dinner table the night before, and she kept a wary eye open, half expecting him to jump out and accost her from some shadowy hiding place.

All through the day and night, Rachel had pondered her decision not to speak to her mother or uncle about what had happened; Eliza would be horrified if she knew. If Rachel did tell, she had little doubt that Jonathan would be evicted from the boardinghouse, probably after receiving a beating at Otis's hands. But in the end, she had decided that her first instinct was the right one; to make him leave would do nothing but take money out of her family's pocket. He would remain dangerous, but now she would be wary.

If he bothers me again, he'll pull back a stump!

Suddenly, there was an insistent rapping at the front door. Tossing down her rag, Rachel hurried to answer, hoping that it might be someone seeking a room; but she was instantly disappointed to find Zachary Tucker waiting for her. On his face was a lopsided grin.

"What do you want?" she asked curtly.

"Now is that any way to talk to someone that was once part of your family?" he replied in mock indignation. "Why, there was a time when you and I were practically brother and sister."

"We both know that time has long since passed."

"Indeed, it has," Zachary said, acknowledging Rachel's harsh words with a chuckle. "May I come in?"

From the very first time she met Zachary Tucker, Rachel had found the man to be nearly insufferable. Loud and obnoxious, unwilling to extend any generosity without attaching a price tag to it, he acted as if everyone he met was beneath him. Even though he was undoubtedly the richest man in Carlson, the townspeople had no wealth of affection for him. She and Alice had wondered if Mason and Zachary were even related; no two brothers had ever been more different.

Still, her mother had taken great pains to instill manners in her, so she held open the door and let him enter, even if the thought of being near him repulsed her.

"If you've come wanting to speak to my

mother, I'm afraid that you'll leave without getting what you want." When Rachel had ventured inside her mother's room before dawn, a tray of food in hand, she'd found Eliza Watkins to be in a particularly foul mood, even for her. She'd been worried, more preoccupied than normal about some unknown danger. Nervously wringing her hands, her mother was so fearful that something bad might happen to her daughter that she had pleaded with her to stay in her room, and had been irritated when Rachel had refused.

"Actually," Zachary explained, "I came to see you."

"Me?" Rachel responded in surprise. "Whatever for?"

Zachary wandered over toward the window, pulling the lace curtains aside so that he could look outside for a moment. Rachel was beginning to wonder whether he had heard her question when he said, his back still to her, "Do you enjoy living this way?"

"What do you mean?"

"Do you enjoy living like this?" Zachary asked with a wide sweep of his arms around the sitting room. "Making a living from a boardinghouse in a town as small as Carlson, working day in and day out for strangers. Well, that just doesn't seem like smart business to me. To be quite honest with you, Rachel, it seems rather foolish."

"We make do," she answered defiantly.

"Do you?" Zachary replied with skepticism. "I can tell you that from outside appearances, that is certainly not the case. Hell, I would be willing to bet that whatever meager profits you manage to eke out of this place are most surely washed down Otis's gullet!"

"It's not . . . that way . . ."

"We both know that it is," he answered bluntly. "While I certainly respect your desire to stand up for your family's good name, it cannot be denied that you're hanging on by the thinnest of threads."

The truth in Zachary's words stung Rachel; though it pained her to admit it even to herself, the boardinghouse hardly managed to provide them enough to feed themselves. Every day seemed a greater challenge than the last. That Mason's brother chose to remark on their difficult circumstances only reminded her of what they had all lost.

"Things would have been different if Mason were still alive."

"For the both of us, Rachel, my dear," he replied with a malicious smile.

But you're the one who's glad about it, she thought.

Much had been spoken around Carlson about how Zachary Tucker had gained from his brother's death, although it had all been carefully whispered for fear that the man would hear. With Mason gone, all that Sherman had built had gone to his younger son, for better or for worse. Rachel could see that it was clearly the latter.

"Why did you come here, Zachary?" she asked, the anger rising ever higher in her breast. "If it was to tell me about how my life hasn't amounted to much or to have a laugh at my expense, I have better things I could be doing."

Zachary sighed, fixing her with a steady, serious stare. "I came here because it has always been clear to me that you've been the intelligent one in your family," he explained. "Because while your mother hides away in her room, reliving her daughter's death over and over again, and while your uncle drinks himself into a stupor, you're the one who knows what terrible trouble you're all in."

"Trouble?" Rachel echoed the banker.

Turning his heavyset body from the window, Zachary slowly walked toward Rachel until he stood very close to her. He was a large man, much taller than she, and he seemed to tower over her. With an ample stomach and piercing, menacing eyes, he had the look of someone who could more than hold his own. For a brief moment, she was reminded of her encounter with Jonathan Moseley, but she refused to allow herself to shrink before Zachary; the truth was that she wasn't frightened by him, nor would she ever show any hint of weakness.

"What are you talking about?" she asked again.

"How much longer do you think you can keep this up?" Zachary asked with carefully measured intent and a syrupy tongue. "How many more long years will the burden of this boardinghouse's upkeep be yours and yours alone to bear? When you're your mother's age, will you still be here, still just doing what is expected of you? Without help, and without the large sum of money that will be needed to fix all of the many things wrong with it, I wouldn't be the least bit surprised to learn that it had all fallen down about your ears. If you let it, this place will be your grave!"

"Why are you telling me this?"

"Because I am the one person who can change your future."

Excitedly and in great detail, Zachary explained the deal that he had struck with the Gaitskill Lumber Company. Patiently, he explained the tremendous benefits that would be brought to Carlson: the countless number of jobs, the boon all of those men would be to the livelihoods of the town's businessmen, and even of a pledge made to build a brand-new schoolhouse at the lumber company's expense. He also told her of the one condition placed upon him by the deal, that he acquire all of the build-ings located around the train depot so that they could be converted into offices for the lumber company. And that was where her family came in.

When he told her about the generous offers that were made to purchase all of those properties, particularly the price that he had been asked to give for the boarding-house, Rachel at first thought he was joking, but upon realizing that he was not, she found her breath taken away.

"You made . . . this offer to my mother?" she asked hesitantly.

"I did." Zachary chuckled, a deep rumble that would have unnerved her if his words hadn't already done so. "But she wouldn't hear of it. She'd rather continue having you slave away as if you were nothing but the hired help than leave this place with all of your problems solved."

"What reason did she give for turning you down?"

Instead of answering, Zachary regarded her with a keen interest. "Are you telling me that she didn't even bother to tell you about it?"

Confusion reigned in Rachel's thoughts. While she didn't expect to know everything that went on around the house, what Zachary had explained to her sounded important enough that it hurt her that she had not been told, that a way out of their troubles existed.

Why wouldn't Mother tell me about such an offer?

What reason could she possibly have for turning it down?

"Is the offer still good?" she asked.

"It is," Zachary answered with a gleam in his eyes. "And it's one that I think you should grab. After all, there's more than just the three of you to worry about . . . There's Charlotte as well."

The mere mention of Charlotte's name angered Rachel; every bit as clearly as on the day on which it was given, she remembered the promise that Sherman Tucker, Mason and Zachary's father, had made to Alice after her husband's unfortunate death. He had pledged to support Charlotte, always to make sure she was cared for, even if it cost him all of his wealth. But that aid had never been forthcoming.

"Your father swore that he would—"

"And that is a pledge that I give you my word I intend to keep," Zachary said, cutting her off before she could say any more, "as long as you can persuade your mother to sell this place."

"I don't know if—"

"Think about it, Rachel," he kept on, his hands gripping her shoulders. "No more days wasted cleaning up after others you hardly know, your mother and uncle no longer living in shameful surroundings, and, most important, Charlotte will finally have everything she would ever need. Everything you've ever wanted can be yours, and all I ask is that you persuade Eliza to do what you know is for the best, not only for you, but for each and every person in Carlson."

Though it pained her to admit it, Rachel knew that what Zachary offered was very appealing. The thought of leaving her chores behind, of not having to worry about rainwater pouring in through a hole in the roof, of endless days spent hanging laundry on the line, of ensuring that Charlotte was properly cared for, was as enticing to her as anything she could remember.

But could she accept Zachary Tucker's word as the truth? Clearly, he had a lot riding on the deal with the lumber company. In his current position, wouldn't he say anything in order to gain what he wanted? With his reputation as something of a snake in the grass, how far could she take him at his word?

I need to speak to my mother!

Sensing that he had said enough, Zachary released his grip on Rachel and made his way to the door. Before stepping out, he turned back to her, seriousness written across his face. "Whether you choose to continue living from hand to mouth"—he sneered as he looked back around the house—"or to take advantage of my offer . . . it's up to you."

Zachary Tucker was very pleased with himself. Hurrying back toward the bank, he could scarcely contain the wide smile that kept creeping up at the corners of his mouth. Even in his wildest of dreams, he had never imagined it would go so well.

There was little doubt that he had made an impact on Rachel; the way she had blanched when he'd told her how much was being offered for that decrepit boarding-house had pleased him no end. She was pragmatic, a realist, someone who would recognize that there was a better way to be had. His instincts to go to her had proven true.

Now all I have to do is wait . . .

Zachary didn't feel the least bit guilty for having lied to Rachel; the mere thought of a company as successful as Gaitskill offering to rebuild Carlson's schoolhouse was enough to make him laugh. But he had simply followed a strategy that had served him well in the past; tell the other person whatever she wants to hear. He hadn't been lying when he said there were many who would benefit from the railroad's arrival . . . not the least of whom would be him and his bank.

What did bother him was the mention of Charlotte Tucker. His father had been nothing short of a fool when he had made the offer to care for the girl; undeniably distraught with grief at Mason's death, he had not been thinking clearly. He'd even mentioned a ridiculous idea to send her to some sort of woman's college. But once illness had taken hold of Sherman, Zachary had chosen to forget the promise.

But Rachel had never forgotten.

Having never taken a wife or had children of his own, Zachary could see Charlotte as exactly what she was; a threat to all that he had taken pains to accomplish. As Mason's child, she could make legitimate claims to the empire her father was set to inherit. Just by right of birth, she could cut a piece from Zachary's pie, and that was something he could not allow.

Over the years since Mason's death, he had made a show of concern for his niece's welfare, without actually doing anything of substance. Now, as a condition for the sale of the boardinghouse, he knew that he would have to give her something, but he would maneuver to ensure that she received little more than she had now. No matter what, Charlotte would never be allowed to grow into a thorn in his side.

"At least I didn't have to see the little bitch!" he muttered.

Quickening his stride, Zachary took comfort in the fact that Rachel was almost assuredly talking to her mother even as he walked. That Eliza had never spoken about his offer was especially good news; he had seen the pain written on Rachel's face as clearly as words printed on a page. That hurt would only intensify when they argued. If Rachel were as persuasive as he hoped she would be, it would only be a matter of time before the Watkinses came to him, begging to sell the boardinghouse for what was offered. All he needed was time and a little patience, and all of his dreams would come true.

But what if Eliza said no?

Though he doubted it could happen, Zachary knew that there was a chance that Rachel would be unable to persuade her mother. By staying in her darkened room for all of these years, Eliza Watkins had shown herself to be more than a bit unstable. Even when faced with reason and a pile of money so large that she could drown in it, she could still prove to be as stubborn as a mule. Besides, she'd already turned him down once.

If that were to happen, then he would have no choice; Travis Jefferson would have to be unleashed. On that day, people would be hurt, blood would be shed. There would be no telling what the final fate of his dead brother's remaining family would be.

In the end, all that mattered was that he got what he wanted. Who got hurt was not his concern.

Chapter Nine

RACHEL PUSHED OPEN the door to her mother's room without a knock and stepped inside. The interior was as gloomy as always, darkened by the heavy curtains draped across the windows. If it weren't for the meager light thrown off by the small lamp on top of Eliza's bureau, it would have been hard to see much of anything.

Eliza was in her usual place, peering out of a sliver of space between the curtains to see outside. Her face was drawn in concentration and worry and her hands wrung nervously. Deep wrinkles, the result of many years spent in dire expectation of

the worst, were etched across her forehead. When Rachel brought her breakfast, it had been clear that this was a day
when her demons were getting the better
of her.

"What's the matter, dear? Are you sick?"
Eliza fretted, taking Rachel's hands in her
own. "Oh, I just knew that this was going
to be a dreadful day!"

"I'm fine, Mother," Rachel said quickly.

"But that doesn't mean you'll stay that
way!"

When her mother was like this, worked
up into a frenzy of worry, Rachel knew that
it was hard to talk to her about the most
trivial matters; broaching a subject so important would be next to impossible. Still,
she knew that what Zachary Tucker had
told her could not be ignored for long, and
that therefore there was much for her and
her mother to discuss. She couldn't wait
for Eliza to calm down.

"Zachary Tucker was here," she said
simply.

"Did something happen to Sherman?"
Eliza asked in a panic. "He's been dread-
fully sick. But he was always such a kind
person, I'd hate for something horrible to

have occurred! Oh, it would be such a tragedy! When you get to be my age, you'll know how painful it is to watch everyone around you pass!"

"That's not why Zachary came."

"Then what on earth did he want?"

Rachel sighed, fearful about confronting her mother, but determined and desperate to know the truth. "He told me about the lumber company's offer, about the plans that they have made for Carlson, and about how he'd come to you and inquired about buying the boardinghouse. He told me what they had offered and that you'd turned them down."

"He came around about that old thing again?" Eliza snorted derisively. "I certainly hope that you told him the same thing I did! The nerve of that man wanting us to give up our home!"

As surely as if she had been struck in the chest, Rachel knew that Zachary had told her the truth; he had come to her mother with a very generous offer and she had turned him down, leaving the family in their financial predicament. She wondered if everything else he told her was equally true.

"Why didn't you take his offer?" she asked, her face flushing bright red.

"Do you . . . do you want to sell our home?" Surprise was written across Eliza's face.

"It would make life easier for all of us," Rachel pressed. "There'd be no more having to clean up after others, providing rooms for strangers. We wouldn't have to constantly worry about making ends meet or paying our bills. It would be hard to leave, but with the kind of money that Zachary is offering, we could make a new start!"

"Would you have taken the money?"

"I would have," Rachel said, swallowing the lump in her throat.

Without uttering a word in reply, Eliza stepped away from her daughter and crossed the room to the scarred bureau. Picking up a silver picture frame, she stared intently into the eyes of her lost daughter, into the photograph that she had had taken of Alice right before her wedding. Rachel waited for her mother to speak, but Eliza remained silent; it was as if she were waiting for Alice to say something.

"Why wouldn't you take what was offered?" Rachel asked again.

"Do you still remember the day that you and Alice spent the whole afternoon sliding on rags down the staircase banisters because you thought that you could clean them faster that way?" Eliza asked, her eyes never wavering from the picture. "I can still hear your laughter carrying through every nook and cranny of the house."

Rachel remembered how they had raced each other back up the steps before once again sliding down, laughing until they were almost out of breath. She recalled how on one particular trip she had crashed violently at the bottom of the stairs, but before the tears could well up and come pouring out, Alice had been by her side, kissing her scrapes and calming her fears. "I do," she answered simply.

"How about the day that Alice spent in the kitchen making apple pies for the Fosters after their barn burned from a lightning strike? She said she was worried that they would be too busy to remember to eat. She spent half of the night making sure things were just right."

Unbidden recollections of how Alice had proudly walked down the long road to the Fosters' farm carrying a tray of fresh, still cooling pies sprang up in Rachel's mind. It always seemed as if her older sister were leaping from one good deed to another; from knitting mittens to be sent to an orphanage in Minneapolis to giving singing lessons to some of the less well-off girls at church. There were so many selfless things Alice had done out of the goodness of her heart.

"As much as I might have complained about it, I even have fond memories of that rainy April day she brought home that wounded, mud-caked, mangy dog and nursed it back to health in the sitting room. Then, just as it was nearly ready to be back on its own, it went and had a litter of puppies! Until my dying day, I'll never forget the way that Alice's face lit up at the sight."

"Me neither," Rachel admitted.

Because mine did exactly the same thing!

"What I am trying to tell you," Eliza continued, finally turning back to face her daughter, "is that every one of those memories happened here . . . they all happened right here in this house. They're in the cracked walls and the floors, they're right there in every corner and every closet, they are in every window and doorway and even out around the washing line, all of them waiting for one of us to rediscover them."

"Mother," Rachel began gently. "Alice is . . ."

"Dead," her mother finished for her, the first wetness appearing in her eyes even as a smile spread across her face. "I know that," she agreed. "I know that there are no new memories to be made, but each and every day that I spend here in this house, I feel as if these older memories, these recollections of happy times, are with me, as if Alice were still with me.

"If we were to agree to sell this home, if I were to just accept all of the money that Zachary is offering and move, we could take the memories with us, but no matter how badly we wished things wouldn't change, they would never be the same. Wherever we went, to whatever new home, we could never manage to bring Alice with us."

Rachel knew that much of what her mother was saying made sense; there were days that she had spent walking around the boardinghouse, remembering special times she and Alice had spent together. Not only was there the ever-present burden of Charlotte's uncanny resemblance to her mother, but there was also simply nowhere in the house to go without some memory, some glimpse of a much happier time, coming back to her.

Still, Rachel wondered if by so desperately clinging to the past, they were denying themselves the opportunity to live. The truth was that Alice was gone, and while her death had been so devastating for them all, there was nothing that could be done to change it. While Rachel didn't want to let go of her treasured memories of her sister either, choosing to wallow in their past wouldn't ever completely assuage that loss, nor completely erase the pain.

"Besides," Eliza argued, "Zachary Tucker cannot be trusted."

"I know that."

"You don't know the half of it," her mother snapped, cutting her off. "For as long as I live, I'll never forget what Mason told me . . . about how his brother had ruined Archie Grace's life."

Momentarily confused, Rachel could only echo, "Archie Grace?"

Everyone in Carlson knew the sad story of the town's blacksmith. Ten years earlier, heartbroken over the recent loss of his wife to influenza and despondent over money troubles, he'd gone out to his workshop one summer night with a bottle of whiskey and a length of rope and hanged himself. The whole town had turned out to pay their respects; there hadn't been a dry eye at his funeral.

"What did Zachary have to do with Mr. Grace?"

"While there was no denying that Archie was devastated by his wife's death, the truth was that he was pulling himself together," Eliza explained slowly, her green eyes as flat and cold as a Minnesota plain in winter. "There were rumors that he'd come into some money, something about an aunt back east who had always been fond of him, and that he would finally be able to pay off some of his outstanding debts. The way that Mason explained it, Archie had been so wound up when he'd received the money, he'd run off down to the bank around closing rather than wait until morning."

"And Zachary was there?" Rachel asked.

"He was . . ."

A sickening feeling began to spread

across Rachel's gut; she had thought Archie Grace to be a nice man, always ready with a cheery smile or laughter. The insinuation that Zachary had something to do with his death was repulsive, but she wanted to know more, to learn the horrible truth.

"As a matter of fact," Eliza continued, "Zachary was the only person there, just locking up for the night. Archie came upon him on the front steps, a bit breathless from running over, and said that he wanted to make a deposit. Zachary told him that he would take care of it, and so Archie just handed over the money . . . It was the last time he ever saw it."

"Zachary took it?" Rachel blurted incredulously.

"Not according to him, but yes, he did." Her mother sighed. "The next time Archie went to the bank, he found that there was no record of any sizable deposit. Confused and growing angrier by the moment, he confronted Zachary, but the bastard acted as if he had no idea what the poor man was talking about. Even when the matter was brought to Sherman's attention, Zachary clung to his lie, swearing on his late mother's grave that he had never taken Archie's money. Behind closed doors, he suggested that maybe Archie had been drinking or was a bit confused."

"But . . . but that's not right," Rachel protested. "Surely someone saw Mr. Grace giving Zachary the money!"

Eliza shook her head. "Remember, it was a late February night and Zachary had been alone at the bank. Besides, you know how quickly the sun sets come winter. Since it was so cold and dark, not a soul was around to see him rob that poor man."

"But who would have believed him?"

"Sherman had no choice." Eliza shrugged. "When he demanded the truth of his son, Zachary sat there and lied to his face every bit as slick as rainwater running off a duck's back. You also have to recall that Archie had been going through a tough time and he'd been known to tie on one or two at the tavern. What with those two things working against him, poor Sherman had no option but to accept Zachary's take on the event."

"And then . . ." Rachel began but couldn't finish.

"And then Archie took himself out to his workshop and hung himself," Eliza explained with a heavy heart. "There weren't many folks that knew what had happened at the bank. Sherman made sure that tongues didn't wag, so most all of Carlson figured that Archie couldn't take the loneliness any longer and saw only one way out of it."

"But Mason told you the truth?" Rachel asked.

"He did."

"He believed what Archie had said? That his own brother was a liar?"

"I'm sure that he's always known that Zachary was no good," Eliza sneered. "Living with him for all of those years had to have taught him something, but I think even Mason was surprised by the depths of Zachary's deception of Archie Grace. When he told Alice, she was so horrified that she burst into tears and, to the best of my knowledge, never spoke to her brother-in-law ever again. I doubt that Mason would have blamed her."

Rachel shivered at the thought of Zachary stealing Archie Grace's money. There was little doubt that he was a greedy, overbearing man who treasured the pursuit of money over nearly everything else, but the man her mother had just described was nothing short of evil. Still, she knew there was little that would've led her to believe that Zachary had been misunderstood. That Mason hadn't swallowed his own brother's story was particularly damning.

How can I believe a word he said about the boardinghouse?

"Would you place Charlotte's future in the hands of such a man?"

Her mother's question struck Rachel mute. When Zachary had first made the offer to follow up on his father's pledge to provide for Charlotte, she had had reservations, but wanted to do what was best for the girl. Now, in the face of the accusations made against the man, she wished to keep her niece as far away from him as possible.

"He told you that he'd provide for Charlotte, didn't he?" Eliza asked.

"Yes . . . yes, he did."

Her mother nodded solemnly, moving back toward the window and peering onto the street below. "Zachary Tucker does not give a damn about that child . . . never has," she finally said, her voice low with a barely restrained anger. "All she is to him is a reminder of a brother he couldn't stand. If she were in trouble, he would be the last person I would ever turn to for help, and that's God's honest truth!"

"But what about the money his father promised?" Rachel prodded. "He said that if we sold the boardinghouse to the lumber company, he'd ensure she got what was rightfully hers."

"That money is gone forever, child."

"But what about—"

"Just put it right out of your head!" Eliza snapped, her voice as raw as any open wound. "That bastard wants you to have hope, to believe it was somehow possible, but you'd have as much luck getting that money as you would snatching the sun from the sky! I want us to stay in our home and reject what Zachary is offering as much for Charlotte as I do for you or myself. I need her to grow up in this house surrounded by childhood memories."

For the first time in the many years Eliza had insisted on Charlotte's visits to her mother's tombstone, Rachel recognized that she and her mother did not have as many differences as she had imagined. While she wished that Eliza would leave her room from time to time, she could clearly see why her mother never wanted to sell the boardinghouse. For all that she had lost, this was where her family was, and that family was centered around her granddaughter.

Though she still hated being responsible for so many of the chores needed to keep the boardinghouse running, Rachel felt a slight flush of shame begin coloring her cheeks. In the face of all they had lost by Mason's death, what still remained after all the years was the strength of family. Her mother, Charlotte, herself, and even her uncle Otis all depended on one another to make ends meet. Though Zachary's offer was tempting, it would be dangerous to accept it; heeding the cautionary tale of Archie Grace was the wise thing to do. Besides, her mother was right; memories of her sister lingered in the old house. Maybe she should explain that to Charlotte.

"I want her to be happy," Rachel said simply.

"So do I," Eliza agreed. "We each have our own ways of going about it, but in the end, we both want the same thing for her."

Listening to her mother, Rachel knew that never would she sell the boarding-house to Zachary Tucker, even if he were to increase his offer to ten times his original price.

And that is just fine with me!

Chapter Ten

CHARLOTTE RAN through the tall grass along the shore of Lake Carlson, happy to be out of school. If she'd had to spend five more minutes at her desk reciting times tables in arithmetic class, she would have been tempted to run screaming from the room! It was so boring that it was all she could do not to fall asleep. The only thing worse than waiting for the end of the day was thinking about having to go back tomorrow.

While the other kids laughed and played together, Charlotte stood in the background by herself. Always surrounded by adults, she was shy around other children. She had no real friends because she used her sassy mouth to cover up that shyness.

The big black dog ran along beside her, panting, his tongue lolling out his mouth. Bounding from one clump of wild grass to another, Jasper seemed not to have a care in the world save having fun, a feeling that Charlotte shared. In particular, she cared little about the burrs and thorns that kept snagging her blouse and skirt, even tugging at her long blonde braids, although she knew she would receive a tongue-lashing from her grandmother as soon as she got home.

I'm not gonna worry 'bout that today!

Pushing any thoughts of her grandmother's nagging out of her head, Charlotte set about enjoying what was left of the day. The autumn sun provided some degree of warmth, even as a cool breeze rustled the few brown and burnt-orange leaves that still clung to their branches. Only a scattering of fluffy clouds marred an otherwise clear blue sky. In short, with winter only a couple months away, this day was one to savor.

Suddenly, a rabbit darted from its hiding

place and bounded out ahead of them. Jasper was off like a shot, a flurry of barking and churning legs, darting deeper into the woods in pursuit. Charlotte came to a quick stop, her chest heaving from both running and laughter. "Go get 'im, Jasper!" she yelled as the dog's barking faded into the distance, leaving her alone among the trees.

Being alone in the woods was not frightening to Charlotte; she loved exploring. Out among the thickened knots of trees and bushes around the lake was particularly inviting. Here, she and Jasper could do as they pleased. She laughed out loud thinking of prissy Ethel Phelps who never ran and played at all for fear of getting her fancy dresses dirty. Here, Charlotte could do exactly what she wanted without having to worry about being constantly fussed over by her grandmother, as if she were as fragile as an egg.

Charlotte knew that her grandmother loved her, in her own way. But all of her constant worrying was too much! *Make sure you take your mittens because otherwise you'll catch cold! Don't run down the stairs . . . what do you want to do? Fall and hurt yourself? You shouldn't go out today . . . it's supposed to rain and Lord knows you'll catch your death of cold!* Her grandmother's hand-wringing knew no end! She'd made it her life's goal to make sure her granddaughter didn't have any fun at all. Even as Charlotte disobeyed day after day after day, the worrying kept on. After a while, it just sort of went in one ear and out the other.

And then there was Aunt Rachel . . .

Every year it was the same thing; Rachel dragged her out to the cemetery to visit her mother's grave. Usually she went, mumbled a few things, and everyone was happy, but this year had been different. She and Jasper had been dragged away from their playing, she had been miserable; she really wasn't sure why she hadn't run away right then and there. The long walk to the cemetery felt as if it took hours. Even after they arrived, she had been unable to understand the point of it all. *Why do I have to try to get to know my mother? Can she really even be my mother if I don't remember her face or the sound of her voice?*

A pair of butterflies danced in front of

Charlotte's face, grabbing her attention away from thoughts of her long-dead mother. Monarchs, their beating wings speckled a bright orange, fluttered by. The sight of them was surprising; butter- flies were usually long gone by such a late autumn date. As they made their way away from the lake, Charlotte followed, jumping up to try to catch them, laughing because they managed to stay just out of her grasp.

This is better than school any old day!

Following along behind the dancing butterflies, Charlotte moved from along the lakeshore deeper into the forest. She weaved between tall oaks and elms, stumbled down a gentle depression, and fought her way through a wild rosebush, all to keep the beautiful butterflies in sight. Finally, the tangle of underbrush opened out before her and she entered into a clearing well shaded by the overhang of branches from the surrounding trees.

Ahead of her lay a decrepit old shack, leaning precipitously against a big elm tree as if it had been drinking like Uncle Otis and needed the support. Rotted planks

seemed to cling to the frame out of desperation. Only jagged fragments of the window remained from long-ago smashed
panes. Charlotte figured that one good
wind or snowstorm would bring the whole
thing crashing down into a heap on the
forest floor.

In her adventures through the woods,
Charlotte had come across the shack before and avoided it. Her grandmother had
warned her to stay away from it. She had
told her that hobos and tramps used it
and would carry little girls away if they
caught them.

She had been scared until her aunt
Rachel had explained that not all hobos
were bad men; some were just down on
their luck. Whatever that meant.

Apparently there was still somewhere to
discover! The broken-down building sat
before her eyes like a present at Christmas. She was still marveling at her luck in
finding the shack again when one of the
butterflies gently flew through the slumped
frame of the door. Without a moment's
hesitation, Charlotte followed.

The inside of the shack was dark; the

scant light that managed to penetrate the tree's cover did little to illuminate the small space. As she waited for her eyes to adjust, Charlotte wrinkled her nose at the dank, sour smell that assailed her. Momentarily, she wondered if this wasn't a place where animals came to die; she had come across her share of dead raccoons, squirrels, rabbits, and even deer during her explorations. Pinching her nose shut, she knew she'd have to remove whatever carcass there was if this was going to be her new special place.

She was just about to go back outside and call for Jasper when she heard a faint rustling sound that froze her in her tracks. Her breath caught in her throat as she waited, listening, hoping that it had been nothing more than a figment of her imagination.

Is there something here, with me, inside the shack?

With her eyes nearly adjusted to the gloom, Charlotte looked for some sign of a wild animal. In the corner farthest from the door, a pile of ragged cloth lay in the deepest shadow. As she watched, the rustling noise came again, and this time the rags moved!

Could it be coons . . . or possums . . . ?

Though her heart was hammering like a rabbit's caught in a trap, Charlotte edged a bit closer to the pile of rags. She wanted to lift the rags up and steal a look. She'd be careful not to be nipped. Grandmother had explained that some animals in the woods were sick with something called rabies. But Otis always said, "Them darn animals is much more scared of you than you are of them . . . Just don't give 'em a reason to bite you!"

But just as she was about to reach out and touch the pile, Charlotte let out a gasp. A man's face appeared in the gloom! Though his eyes were sunken and his face heavily bearded, she knew that he was looking right at her. Even as she stood there staring, he lifted one trembling hand and held it out to her as if he thought she would take it.

"Alice . . ." the man mumbled. "Help me . . . Alice . . ."

Mason Tucker was undeniably sick, his body burning up with fever. He had no idea how much time had passed since he had first entered the shack in the woods; days and nights went by in a dizzy blur of illness. His limbs felt weak, as if his strength were being drained out of him like water from a jug. Even the simple task of stumbling out behind the shack to relieve his bowels was an exercise in both perseverance and futility.

He was just about to try to raise himself up off the floor and once again make his way outside when he heard the faint creaking of a floorboard. Holding his breath, Mason waited, hoping that he had imagined the sound. When it persisted, another squeak and then a shuffle, his worry was that it was a wild animal come in search of food. If it were an inquisitive squirrel or raccoon, he figured that he would have enough strength to scare it away. But if it were a coyote or a wolf . . .

Opening his eyes, Mason peered toward the door, but his vision swam and he was unable to see clearly. Blinking rapidly, he strained to make out something, anything, of his visitor. Slowly, the room began to come into focus, and he discovered that it wasn't an animal but a girl!

Initially, he was fearful that he'd been found trespassing by the shack's rightful owner or that he'd run afoul of the law. His instinct was to run away, even though he knew his present condition made that impossible.

Mason watched as the visitor drew closer. But with each step, his vision grew clearer until he finally saw the person's identity, a realization that lifted all of heaviness from his heart.

"Alice . . ." he said through cracked lips. "I'm sick, Alice . . ."

She was every bit as beautiful as Mason remembered; her long blonde hair hung in tight braids, and her bright blue eyes pierced him all the way through to his heart. Even the look of surprise on her face was as familiar to him as his own reflection in a mirror. Even though her blouse and skirt were simpler than he remembered her liking, the joy he felt at seeing her again after almost nine long years sent tears of joy streaming down his face.

Mason wondered why she was here in the shack with him. Maybe she had noticed him in Carlson and followed him. Maybe Samuel Guthrie had recognized him after all and had gone to his father. His father had told Alice . . . and she had sworn that she would find him . . .

Or maybe the life that he had been forced to live for all of those years hadn't been real but instead a nightmare from which he couldn't manage to awaken. Maybe he'd never climbed on that train, maybe he'd never gone off to fight in France . . . and he and Alice still lived in their home . . . and he was still following in his father's foot-steps at the bank . . . Maybe he had instead been far sicker than he'd ever imagined.

"Oh, my beloved . . . Alice . . ." he mut-tered.

Gathering what strength he had left, Mason pushed himself up off the rotted floor and onto unsteady feet. His sudden movement seemed to startle Alice, who quickly stepped back toward the door. Worrying that she would once again dis-appear from his life, he moved to hurry after her, but the room began spinning and suddenly it was all he could do not to fall to the floor. Desperation pounded at his heart.

"Don't . . . don't run . . . from me . . . Al-ice," Mason pleaded.

"Why do you keep calling me that?" she answered.

"I can't . . . lose you again . . ." he said through stiff lips.

Just as he was about to grab her and pull her back to him, a thunderous barking exploded around the tightly cramped space of the shack. In Mason's twisted vision, it looked as if a humongous black wolf had leaped between him and Alice, its hackles raised and its teeth bared in a snarl. But even in the face of such a ferocious beast, he refused to cower in fear, to be denied the reunion he so desperately wanted.

"Alice . . . I . . ." he stammered.

"Jasper, hush!" he heard before the darkness that lingered on the edge of his vision closed in and the room turned upside down.

Before Mason could take another step, the floor seemed to rise up and smack him in the face. All around him, the darkness that had sat at the edge of his weakening vision swarmed closer, blotting out much of what he could see. But before he could be completely taken, he saw Alice grab the still barking animal by the thick hair of its coat and pull it back toward the door. When she returned, she knelt down beside him and began to brush his sweat-slick hair away from his eyes with a touch as gentle as a feather.

"Mister? Are you sick?"

"Oh, my sweet . . . Alice . . ." he managed before the darkness swept over him again.

Charlotte ran headlong through the trees and bushes of the woods as fast as her legs would carry her. Branches whipped by, striking her in the face, but she couldn't have cared less. Her heart pounded in excitement at her discovery and a smile curled the corners of her mouth.

Jasper ran alongside her, leaping over downed branches and skirting past the thorniest bushes. Charlotte was proud of him. He had been trying to protect her. While he had protested being dragged back outside, Jasper had finally relaxed when he realized the man posed no danger to either of them.

The strange man was sick; while the halting way that he spoke and the fact that he could hardly stand would have been enough, one touch of her hand up against the blazing heat of his forehead told her all she needed to know. He needed help . . . and she was the one to give it to him.

There were things that she could get him from the house: some water, a bit of food, blankets, maybe a pillow. But Charlotte knew that she would have to be careful. This would be her secret. She wouldn't tell anyone at school, and she especially wouldn't tell her grandmother or Aunt Rachel; she could practically already hear her grandmother's warnings. No, she would have to make sure that no one saw what she was doing.

If someone were to see me . . .

Charlotte knew that there was something special about the strange, sick man. She didn't know his name, or where he had come from.

Maybe he is my fairy godfather . . .

Chapter Eleven

NOW WHAT IN THE WORLD is that girl up to?" Eliza asked.

Rachel placed the serving tray that held her mother's breakfast on the table and stepped over to the window. Dawn had only recently broken on the day, but the sun already warmed the slowly awakening town, though the fall chill in the air had certainly grown more pronounced. Peering over Eliza's shoulder, she watched as Charlotte ran around the far corner of the depot and hurried toward the lake, a pair of woolen blankets clutched under her arm. As always, Jasper trotted along behind her, giving the occasional bark. In seconds, they were lost to sight.

"This is the fourth time I've seen her do something like this in the last week. If it's not a blanket, it's an old woolen coat or a covered basket," Eliza explained, her face a mask of concentration, her hands wringing with worry. "And that's only the times I've seen her! Who knows how many times she managed to avoid me! What do you suppose she's up to?"

"It's probably nothing." Rachel shrugged, turning away from the window and setting her mother's plate of biscuits and gravy and cup of coffee on her favorite table. "Although I have to agree with you that it is awfully early for her to be up and about."

"She's up to no good!"

"What would make you say such a thing?"

"Because that child is always getting into one form of trouble or another!"

"She and Jasper are probably just playing house in the woods."

"The woods!" Eliza exclaimed with fright, her eyes growing wide and her hands rising to her cheeks. "What if she were to run into some wild, rabid animal? What if she wasn't looking where she was going and carelessly tripped over a log and broke her arm in the fall? All this is to say nothing of bug bites, poisonous plants, snakes, or any number of other things that could hurt her!"

Inwardly, Rachel winced; she should have known much better than to put the idea of Charlotte traipsing around the woods into her mother's head. Now she would be beside herself with worry until the girl finally returned home, and then would only get better once she had given her granddaughter a proper scolding laced with warnings of all the terrible accidents that could happen to her when she was out of sight.

Rachel knew that her slip of the tongue had come about because of all the many things swirling around in her head. It had been a little more than a week since Zachary Tucker came to her with his offer to purchase the boardinghouse, and every day she expected to find him once again at their door, demanding an answer. Her nights were filled with worry about the reaction she felt certain to receive when she told him that they would not sell their home;

she wondered if he would set about ruining all of their lives the way he had destroyed Archie Grace's.

While there was still a part of Rachel that daydreamed about all that they could do with the money being offered, she knew that her mother's decision remained the right one. It was clear from what Eliza had told her that Zachary could never be trusted.

The other matter still playing on her mind involved Jonathan Moseley. Since the afternoon he had made his repulsive advances she had managed to stay far away from him, or at the very least made certain that there were other people around. At meals, he was as talkative as always, regaling anyone who would listen about his success as a salesman and his grandiose plans for the future. But in between the ever-present smile and witty banter, she occasionally saw him looking at her with an eye that told her his intentions were far from wholesome. He would approach her with his lewd remarks and grabbing hands yet again; it was only a matter of when.

"You should follow her," Eliza said, breaking into her thoughts.

"What?" Rachel asked in confusion. "What are you talking about?"

"The next time that Charlotte heads off to wherever it is that she's taking all of these things, I think you should follow her. It's the only way we would know without any doubt that nothing is the matter."

"You're overreacting!"

"I am not!" her mother answered defensively. "You said it yourself that her being out at such an early hour isn't normal. What's wrong with being absolutely certain she's safe?"

"She's just a child, Mother." Rachel sighed. "This is the sort of thing that a girl her age would do . . . just as Alice and I did. We ran around in those same woods. Why can't you let her have the same fun . . . the same freedom?"

"Because I know all too well what it feels like to lose a child."

"Alice wasn't a child anymore. She was a grown woman."

"And I lost her all the same," Eliza said as tears came to her eyes. "Isn't the fact that Charlotte isn't a grown woman—that she isn't capable of truly knowing right from wrong—reason enough to find out what she's up to?"

With all her heart, Rachel knew that this was an argument she couldn't win; her mother always seemed to have an opposing answer. Her own worries and insecurities had grown so great in the years she'd locked herself in her room that she couldn't help projecting them onto others, particularly Charlotte. She would be so worked up over what could be befalling her granddaughter out in the woods that Rachel was certain she wouldn't eat even a forkful of her breakfast.

She can worry all she wants . . . but she'll worry alone!

"If you want to know what she's doing," Rachel said, "follow her yourself."

"You know that I can't do that," Eliza answered in exasperation.

"The reason you can't follow her is that you won't," she declared as she picked up the empty breakfast tray and headed for the door. "Because you choose to stay in this room."

"This isn't about me," her mother said

just before her daughter shut her door. "You never know what she might have found in those woods."

With the door to her mother's room closed behind her, Rachel hurried down the hallway toward the staircase. The second floor of the boardinghouse contained four small bedrooms whose doors all opened onto the hallway, which began at the head of the stairs, wrapping around until it reached her mother's room at the end. A railing guarded the inside of the hallway that opened to the foyer below.

Other than her mother's room, only one space was currently occupied; the third door from her was Jonathan Moseley's room. With the empty tray clutched in hand, she stepped quickly down the hallway, eyes on the carpet runner at her feet, hoping beyond hope that she would make it to the staircase undetected by him.

But just as Rachel was halfway down the hall, having made the first turn that would lead her to the stairs, the door to Jonathan's room was suddenly flung open and the loathsome man practically leapt into the hall, blocking her path.

"My dear Rachel!" Jonathan cried with clearly fake surprise. "What a lucky coincidence that I would run into you just as I was about to head out and attempt to sell some of my wares," he explained as he gave a hearty slap to his worn traveling case. "But as my mother used to say, luck often has a way of smiling upon the truly blessed."

Rachel doubted that luck had anything to do with their encounter; it was far more likely that Jonathan had heard her earlier arrival on the stairs and had waited for her to return, one ear pressed tightly against the door in an attempt to hear her coming back down the hallway. The thought of his conniving made her sick.

"I was just taking my mother her breakfast," she said simply as she tried to step around him but, as she moved toward the wall, Jonathan took it as an opportunity to get even closer, coming so near to her that she uncomfortably stepped back.

"I must say," he said, giving his lips a lurid lick, "that you look every bit as lovely as usual today."

Rachel found it impossible to return the compliment. Although Jonathan was dressed in his finest clothes, a checkered wool suit with a primly knotted bow tie, he was anything but handsome. With his heavily pomaded hair and the nearly over-powering scent of flower water mixed with unwashed body odor, he was disgusting. Considering his other physical flaws, Rachel figured that it would be a miracle if he managed to sell anything.

Memories of their encounter at the wash line came unbidden to Rachel's memory; the vile way his lust-filled eyes had roamed across her body, the nauseating things he had said to her, and particularly the feeling of her skirt being lifted and his hand running up her leg.

If it hadn't been for Uncle Otis . . .

In the week since Jonathan had ha-rassed her, Rachel had made a promise to herself that she would avoid being caught alone with the man. But trapped in the hallway, far closer to him than she ever wanted to be again, she knew she had made a mistake.

"Good luck with your work," she said flatly. Once again, she tried to maneuver around him, but she hadn't moved but a step when his hand shot out and snatched her by the arm. His grip was tight, his fingers hurting as they dug into the soft flesh.

"Not so fast," Jonathan warned.

"Let go of me," Rachel snarled, angrier than a stirred-up hornet's nest.

"Never, my dear." He smiled with a mouth of ugly teeth.

Furiously, Rachel tried to shake her arm free, but her protests only made him clamp down harder. Desperately, she tried to hold back the tears that began welling in her eyes.

"I do hope you've had time to reconsider my offer from last week," he said.

"There's nothing that would ever make me change my mind!"

"Oh, how I do love that defiant streak in you," Jonathan crowed, his eyes as cold as any wolf. "But there is no argument that can be made strong enough to prevent us from being together. Quite frankly, you would be a fool not to see that a woman of your humble beginnings could greatly benefit herself by being with a man such as myself."

With surprising strength, Jonathan tugged at Rachel's arm and pulled her crashing into his chest. So close to the man, his face mere inches from hers, his beady eyes dancing in their shallow sockets, she couldn't help but feel a revulsion far greater than she had ever known before. He was so near, so uncomfortably against her that she couldn't even crane her neck in the almost impossible hope that Otis would once again intercede.

This time, I'm all alone . . .

"Why must you always be so very difficult, my darling Rachel," Jonathan whispered, his fetid breath warm upon her face. "Though I am a patient man by nature, there are limits even to a man of my stature. Do you get some perverse thrill out of making me wait?"

"Jonathan, I—" she began, hoping that she might somehow be able to dissuade him from his ardor and escape his clutches, but his eyes narrowed to little more than slits and his grip tightened upon her.

"Because there is a limit to how long I intend to keep playing our little game. If you continue to reject our future together," he explained, his voice suddenly as threatening as a knife's blade, "then there will be consequences that you will inevitably regret . . . painful consequences . . ."

Rachel's eyes widened at the full import of Jonathan's words. Where before she had believed that merely rejecting his advances would be enough, that he would finally, if not a bit slowly, come to understand that she had no romantic interest in him, she now knew that she was mistaken. He was obsessed not only with her but with a future he had conjured in his own mind. To obtain that vision, there seemed nothing he would not do.

Horrified, Rachel prepared to scream. But just as she drew breath, Jonathan abruptly let her go, strode past her, and made his way down the stairs. He moved confidently, as if he didn't have a single care in the world, pausing only when he reached the front door.

"Remember what I said, Rachel." He turned around to face her, his eyes boring holes with a menacing stare. "The last thing either of us wants is for me to lose my temper."

Without another word, Jonathan left the boardinghouse.

Rachel draped another damp sheet over the clothesline and paused, wiping the sweat from her eyes. The noonday sun hung high in the sky above her, but the heat it provided was slight; it was the exertion of her task that caused her discomfort. Rachel paid little attention to her work; instead her mind was racing as she thought about Jonathan Moseley, even as her eyes kept close watch for any sign of his approach.

While a few hours had passed since Jonathan had accosted her in the hallway of the boardinghouse's upstairs, Rachel still felt as if the trauma had just occurred. *I cannot believe the boldness and shamelessness of that man!* Every time she blinked, she saw the way he had looked at her, felt the uncomfortable touch of his hand upon her, and even smelled the stench of his breath. Regardless, she knew that her troubles were only beginning.

After Jonathan approached her at the laundry line, Rachel had been able to put his advances out of her mind for the sake of her family. But while they still needed to eke whatever living they could out of the boardinghouse, she had begun to doubt that it was worth the danger of providing a room to the salesman. As soon as she finished her task, she was going to march into her mother's room, demand that Jonathan Moseley be thrown out on his ear, and then . . .

The sudden slamming of the boarding-house's rear door startled her. She turned quickly, expecting to see Jonathan coming toward her, a ridiculous smile plastered across his thin face, eager to resume their earlier discussion, but instead it was Charlotte.

She was in a hurry, running down the short steps before jumping off the last one into the yard and beginning to dash toward the alley. Her dark skirt billowed out behind her skinny legs and her thick blonde braids bounced with every step. Rachel could see that she was awkwardly carrying something in the makeshift pouch she had made out of the front of her blouse. As always, Jasper ran playfully along beside his constant companion.

"Charlotte!" Rachel shouted. "Charlotte, wait!"

Charlotte skidded to a stop, every bit as startled as Rachel had been at the slamming of the door. For a long moment, it looked as if she was torn between resuming her mad run and actually listening to her aunt. She stood teetering, an unsure look on her face.

"Come here for a moment," Rachel said.

Still uncertain, Charlotte looked back over her shoulder to the alleyway beyond. Jasper stood with his two back legs in a mud puddle and gave an insistent bark; it was as if he was trying to cajole her into joining him, into a return to whatever fun they had planned.

"We were just gonna go and play," the girl complained. "We weren't doin' nothin' wrong . . ."

"Don't make me come over there," Rachel warned.

Reluctantly, Charlotte did as she was told and trudged over to where her aunt stood; Jasper gave a short whine before joining the girl. As Charlotte walked, she kept her face toward the ground, her small shoulders slumped, but the contents of her blouse remained out of sight.

"What are you hiding in your blouse?"

Charlotte shrugged. "Nothin'."

"Then why do you have your hands bunched up like that?"

There was no answer.

Exasperated, Rachel reached down and tugged one of Charlotte's hands away, revealing a strange treasure: the leftover biscuits from that morning's breakfast, one of which fell to the ground. Hurriedly, the girl snatched the morsel from the ground and put it back with the others.

"What are you doing with these?" Rachel asked.

"I was . . . I was just a bit hungry," Charlotte mumbled, her eyes never rising.

"Didn't you get enough to eat this morning?"

"It . . . it isn't that . . ."

"Why can't you eat them here?"

"We just want to go play," Charlotte said, finally looking up into her aunt's face as her eyes began to grow wet with tears. "Jasper and me were gonna go explorin' and I wanted to make sure we had somethin' to eat. That's all it is, honest!"

Rachel stood with her hands on her hips and weighed the meaning of Charlotte's words carefully. While much of what the young girl said made sense, and it was possible she was telling the truth, Rachel couldn't help but hear her mother's words from that morning, a worry that Charlotte was behaving strangely. Though prone to senseless fretting, her mother may have been right, but then there was only one way to learn the truth . . .

"All right, Charlotte," she said. "Then you can go."

The last word was barely out of Rachel's mouth before Charlotte was off like a shot, Jasper at her heels.

But instead of returning to her chores, Rachel waited until Charlotte had just passed beyond the end of the alley. With more than half of her wash still waiting to be hung, she hastened off to follow.

Chapter Twelve

HURRYING AFTER CHARLOTTE, Rachel did her best to keep the child in sight. Cautious lest she get too close to the running girl and accidentally be seen, she waited behind the depot, darting her head around the corner. The October day had grown colder and she wrapped her shawl closer around her shoulders before once again stepping out and continuing her pursuit.

Charlotte ran swiftly while holding tightly to her bundle of biscuits. Rachel found herself breathing heavily as she struggled to keep up. If worse came to worst, she thought, she would be able to follow the sound of Jasper's barking.

After rounding the corner of the depot, Charlotte plunged down a well-worn path at the edge of the woods; Rachel recognized it as a trail that hunters traveled in search of wild game. Tall oak, poplar, and pine trees crowded out the sky, their branches swaying in the gentle breeze. Thimbleberry, sweet fern, and honeysuckle bushes were bunched together on the forest floor, their leaf cover already browned in the face of the coming winter. Rachel moved carefully, more than a bit worried that she would stumble upon a snake among the twists and turns of the path.

Where could the child be going?

All around, birds chirped and squawked, calling out from high in the forest canopy. Squirrels ran furiously about, frantically burying nuts and assorted other tidbits for the winter and spring. Rounding a corner in the path, she startled a pair of rabbits who darted from her into the safety of the underbrush, a rustle of fallen leaves the only sound to mark their passing. So far, she'd been lucky enough to encounter only the most harmless of creatures, but what if she met a rabid skunk or wild dog?

Circling around a solitary boulder wedged into a low gulley, Rachel followed the path as it neared the lake. The surface of Lake Carlson was as undisturbed as glass, save for the gentlest of ripples caused by the autumn breeze. It reflected the orange, red, and purple leaves from the trees on the opposite side. Straining her neck, Rachel caught sight of Charlotte farther ahead, with Jasper frolicking around her.

It had been a long time since Rachel last ventured into these woods. When she and Alice were young girls, surely not much older than Charlotte was now, they had spent hours running about between the trees, playing hide-and-seek with other children. In those days, she remembered being immune to the unseen dangers lurking in every shadow, the pain of a scrape against a tree's rough bark, or the worry of encountering a pack of snarling wolves. Now she nervously looked about, her heart hammering, ready to bolt at the slightest hint of trouble.

Maybe my mother isn't so paranoid after all . . .

Recklessly hurrying so that she wouldn't fall any farther behind, Rachel caught her foot on an uncovered tree root and came crashing down painfully onto the rocky path. Somehow she managed to use her hands to keep from going facedown, but her body landed hard. Wincing as a burning ache flared up the length of her leg, she rubbed at her knee, aware the skin was scraped and bleeding.

"Damn it all," she cursed through clenched teeth.

Gingerly rising back to her feet, she felt woozy with pain. Steadying herself against a maple sapling, she tried to focus on the path, to find some sign of Charlotte, but she couldn't see anything of the girl through the thick foliage of tree and bush branches. She heard the sound of Jasper's barking, but it was more distant than she would have expected, as if she'd fallen to the ground for minutes instead of seconds.

"Oh, Charlotte, you little dickens," she muttered to herself.

Moving as gamely as her tender knee would allow, Rachel plowed through the underbrush of the trail, parting the remaining leaves of an elderberry bush. Sweat glistened on her brow and plastered her blouse to her skin. She hurried, concerned she might have fallen too far behind to know where Charlotte was headed.

Rachel's bruised knee would only permit her to go so far before she had to stop to rest. Every time that she halted, she tried to find the highest ground possible to look for any sign of Charlotte, but she never caught a glimpse. Worry began to gnaw at her that she would have trouble finding her own way out of the dense forest. *If I were to be caught out here at night . . .* Pushing the thought out of her head, she pressed on deeper into the woods on the opposite side of the lake. She hoped fervently that Charlotte knew her way out of the dark woods. Carefully making her way down a depression and up the steep incline on the other side, she once again paused to catch her breath.

Suddenly, the sound of voices was carried in the air, so faint that she first thought they might have been the wind. Straining, Rachel caught the unmistakable sound of Charlotte's voice, but then heard another, deeper, that of a man. Listening a bit longer, she also heard the whine of a dog.

Confused by the second voice, Rachel hurried forward as quickly as she could. She pushed past a couple of rotted tree trunks and jumped across a narrow creek leading toward the lake. The thorns of a wild rosebush snared the hem of her skirt and she yanked so hard on the caught-up clothing that she heard the fabric tear. Finally, as the voices grew still louder, she stepped between a pair of elms and entered into a small clearing.

There, tucked unsteadily against the trunk of an enormous tree, was a shack. From its dilapidated look, it had long ago been left to rot. Somewhere in the recesses of her memory, Rachel recalled having been there before; she remembered crawling inside during one of her and Alice's games of hide-and-seek and not being found.

Before she could recall any more, she heard a voice coming from inside.

It was Charlotte's!

Charlotte tucked the wool blanket closer to the sick man's neck and made sure that he was completely covered with the three other quilts she had taken the first day she'd returned to the small shack. A small pillow snatched from one of the boarding-house's extra rooms cradled his feverish head. Together, she hoped that they made the stranger more comfortable.

Carefully, she broke up the leftover biscuits and fed them to the man one at a time, watching out for any crumbs that might want to lose themselves in his scraggly beard. Weakly, he took what was offered to him, chewing more slowly than a newborn calf taking its first grass. When he had finished eating, Charlotte gave him water she had collected from the lake, scooped into a china cup she had taken from her grandmother's cabinet.

Hungrily, Jasper whined in the corner of the shack.

"Just hush yourself," she scolded him. "You'll get your share!"

Charlotte couldn't believe that only three days had passed since she had first come across the sick man in the broken-down shack. Ever since that fateful encounter, she had been caring for him as best she could manage, stealing whatever clothing, coverings, and food she could find. Once, she had even managed to avoid going to school to come to the woods instead.

Still, the stranger didn't seem to be getting any better. During most of her visits, he shivered violently no matter how many blankets she piled on him. Often he moaned or rolled around feverishly, staring at her with a far-off look in his glassy eyes. He never said much, usually some clipped words spoken through chattering teeth. Gently, she touched his forehead and felt a burning heat that managed to frighten her.

"We need to get you to a doctor," she said.

"No . . . no, Alice . . ." the man mumbled. "I'll . . . I'll be better tomorrow . . ."

"But we need to—"

"Just stay . . . with me, Alice . . . and I'll be . . . just fine . . ."

From that first encounter in the darkened shack, the stranger had insisted on calling her Alice, her mother's name. Once, she'd told him that she was called Charlotte, but he was too sick and confused to comprehend. Every time he said the name of her long-dead mother, a chill ran down her spine; somehow, she felt closer to the woman she would never know, had never even met, than she had at the cemetery. No matter how many times she asked, he had never been willing to tell her his name.

"When I'm sick," she argued, "I have to go to the doctor."

"I just . . . just need to . . ." he said before once again slipping into unconsciousness, something he was beginning to do more and more often.

Charlotte frowned. At first she had hoped that she could keep the strange man all to herself, hiding him from her grandmother, and Aunt Rachel, and especially from the other kids at school. But as the days passed, she had begun to realize that if she hid the man much longer, there was more than a fair chance he would get sicker and die. Though she didn't know anything about him, that was something she wouldn't allow to happen.

The inside of the shack, even with all of the things she had taken from the boardinghouse, was practically bare; there wasn't even a door for her to shut! Other than the dilapidated table, there was no furniture. There was no lamp for her to light. There was no bed for him to lie on, only the damp, rotting floorboards covered in mouse droppings.

Luckily, it hadn't rained during the time he had been there, but that was something Charlotte knew she couldn't count on for long; with the gaps between the boards above her, any water would come pouring inside. Besides, with the coming change in the weather, it would be getting much colder, especially at night. Soon even the blankets wouldn't be enough to keep him warm.

"So what am I gonna do to make sure you get well?" she asked.

Not for the first time, Charlotte wondered if she might be able to light a fire. She had watched her uncle Otis do it many times, usually with a shot of whiskey and a match, but it had always been in a chimney. The shack didn't have a chimney or a stove and she was much too afraid to try to light one inside. Maybe she could get him outside, but he hadn't had the strength to go outside and relieve himself and she doubted she was big enough to move him on her own. Still, she wondered if she had a choice.

Just as she was about to get up and

look for a place to build a fire, Jasper came alert, a low growl rumbling deep in his throat and the hair on his back standing on end.

"What is it, boy?" she whispered.

As if in answer to her question, Jasper began to bark. Suddenly, there came the sound from outside the shack; the noise was as clear to Charlotte's ears as when Otis rang the dinner bell. Her heart hammered with the fear that a fox or a wolf was approaching, or that someone had discovered what she was hiding in her special place. Either way, she knew she was in trouble.

Rushing over to where the stranger lay, Charlotte cowered beside him, bringing her knees up to her chest and staring fearfully at the door. Yet another noise came from outside. Jasper's growl filled the tiny room.

Someone is out there.

Charlotte didn't really know why she wanted to be closer to the man; in his current condition, unconscious with fever, there was nothing that he could do to protect her, and for that matter, she knew that there was little she offered to defend him. Still, something about the man called to her, and she wanted to be near him.

And then, before she had time to worry any more, a shadowy figure darkened the shack's door. Even in the gloom of the small shack, Charlotte could tell that it was a woman, her skirt billowing over booted feet. Purposefully, the stranger strode into the shack.

Aunt Rachel!

Rachel stood in the shack's crooked doorway and peered into the deep gloom inside. Jasper continued barking in the corner nearest the door, but she paid him little heed; her attention was riveted upon Charlotte. The girl knelt on the floor in the far corner, her small body shaking and her eyes wide with fear. Next to her lay a makeshift bed, piled with blankets just like the ones Rachel had seen her taking earlier that morning. Undoubtedly, this was where she had brought the biscuits, too.

"What's going on here?" she demanded.

"I'm just trying to help him, Aunt Rachel!" Charlotte cried. "Honest I am! He's sick."

For the first time, Rachel noticed that there appeared to be someone lying among the pilfered blankets. This was why she'd been coming out here!

Rushing over to her niece, Rachel grabbed Charlotte by the wrist and hauled her to her feet. Confused, frightened, and more than a bit angry, she began to pull the girl toward the door, to get her away. Charlotte began to fight against her, straining to stay by the man, tears streaming down her flushed cheeks. In response, Jasper's barking intensified.

"Don't make him leave!" Charlotte pleaded.

"I've had just about enough of this, young lady! Come along this instant!"

"But he's sick! He needs me!"

Looking down at the man, Rachel was surprised that Charlotte was so worked up; the stranger looked like nothing more than a down-on-his-luck bum. His scraggly beard was full of snarls and knots, his closed eyes looked ready to sink down into his skull, and his skin was weatherbeaten. She'd seen men like him passing through town, looking for a rail car to hide in, and she had always felt pity for them. She was amazed that Charlotte had been coming into the dark woods to care for the man, and had been bringing him blankets and food.

The realization that her mother was right all along struck Rachel like a lightning bolt. Eliza had warned her, had pleaded with her to follow Charlotte into the woods and find out what she was doing, but Rachel had ignored her mother's admonitions as usual. This time her mother had been right.

"You shouldn't be here," Rachel warned the girl. "He could have something contagious."

"I just wanted to help him!"

"This sort of man could be dangerous," she explained. "He might be an outlaw or a jailbird."

"Don't . . . don't be mad at . . . your sister . . . Rachel," the man suddenly spoke from the makeshift bed. "Alice . . . Alice was . . . helping me. She knew I'd not . . . hurt her."

Rachel's knees felt weak as she looked at the stranger, his words echoing in her head. Releasing her grip on Charlotte, her mouth fell open as her heart thundered in her chest. Even as she stared at him, the man's eyes fluttered and he once again descended into the darkness of unconsciousness. For the briefest of moments, she thought that she must have imagined the man's words, but in her heart she knew that it was all startlingly real.

He called me by my name!

He said "Alice" . . . he thinks that Charlotte is Alice!

Staring at the strange man's face, Rachel felt a gnawing in her stomach, a slow realization beginning to dawn upon her. Parts of the man's face, of his damaged features, began to take on some degree of familiarity. But it wasn't possible . . .

"It . . . it can't be . . . He's dead."

Chapter Thirteen

TRY AS SHE MIGHT, Rachel couldn't keep the strange man's words from echoing over and over in her mind. *Don't . . . don't be mad at . . . your sister . . . Rachel.* Shaking her head, she hoped that things would begin to make sense, but she couldn't help but feel more confused than ever. *Alice . . . Alice was only . . . helping me . . .*

Cautiously, Rachel knelt down beside the makeshift bed and took a closer look at the stranger. She could see that, once again unconscious, he was utterly ravaged by illness; his breathing was ragged and sweat beaded on his weathered forehead.

Still, it was there around his eyes, and maybe the nose, that she recognized him . . . or thought she did. It had been so long, so many years since the last time, since . . .

Was it possible . . . could it be that this was . . .

"Who is this man?" she asked Charlotte, her eyes never leaving his agonized face. "Did he ever tell you his name?"

"No," the girl answered, her eyes as wide as saucers. She inched closer to her aunt, still rubbing her wrist where she had been grabbed. "Every time I asked him, he said nothin'. Most times he didn't even talk."

"Where did you find him?"

"Jasper and I were playing and we ran inside the shack and he was here. He was sick. Don't be mad at me!"

"I'm not," Rachel answered soothingly. It was clear to her that Charlotte had become attached to the man. Even in the midst of her own confusion, she couldn't help but admire what the child had done, though she knew that her own mother wouldn't think kindly of things being taken from the house without her say-so.

"Do you know who he is?" Charlotte asked.

"I . . . I'm not sure . . ."

"He knows who you are," the girl persisted. "He said your name."

Rachel could only nod. Even with all of the evidence she was beginning to gather to the contrary, she still had trouble believing that the man lying on the blankets was Mason Tucker. There had to be another reason, another explanation for the stranger's identity. Still, she couldn't deny that Charlotte was right; he had spoken her name . . .

But not just mine!

Turning back to Charlotte, she asked, "Did he call you Alice?"

The words practically raced themselves out of Charlotte's mouth as she explained the things that the man had said since she had discovered him; about how he had called her Alice the first time they met and about how, even when she tried to explain that she wasn't who he thought she was and to tell him her real name, he still persisted in calling her by another name. "I don't think he knows who I am. Why doesn't he believe me when I say I'm Charlotte?"

Looking at her niece's questioning face, Rachel wondered if she didn't already know the explanation: there was so much of Charlotte's mother in her that, if a man were incredibly sick, a bit delirious, he might manage to confuse them. With her blonde hair, her sparkling blue eyes, and even the sly purse of her lips, Charlotte looked so much like her mother.

"Why does he call me that?" Charlotte asked. "Did he know my mother?"

Unable to answer the girl's questions, Rachel turned her attention back to the sleeping man. She couldn't be sure that he was really Mason. So many years had passed since she stood beside her sister on the depot platform, watching the men head off for war. She remembered that she had always found him handsome; with his black hair and broad shoulders, he would have been a catch for any woman. It wasn't that she had been jealous of Alice . . . maybe a bit envious. But this man, in his current condition, was so very far from being handsome . . .

Suddenly, the absurdity of Rachel's thoughts became apparent. It was utterly ridiculous of her to believe that this could be Mason! The truth was that Mason Tucker was dead and had been for more than eight years! He went off to fight the Germans and had died in France, just like thousands of other men!

How can this man possibly be Mason?

"He's sick, Aunt Rachel," Charlotte said softly.

"I know that."

"What can we do?" Charlotte kept on as a fresh batch of tears began to slide down her cheeks. "We can't leave him. If we do, a wolf will get him."

Rachel found it hard to argue the point, as she had heard wolves howling in the night. She had also felt a growing cold in the air over the last several days. Winter in Minnesota came quickly; one day might be nice, a warmth still in the air, but the next could be the one that signaled the coming of chilling rains and, eventually, crippling snow. In his condition, the stranger couldn't hope to last long. As bad as his illness was, it would only grow worse in the days to come. If she were to turn her back on him, to walk away from his desperate plight, she had no doubt that he would die a miserable, painful death.

"We have to do something," Charlotte implored.

In her heart, Rachel knew that she didn't have a choice; she knew that she had to take the man back to the boardinghouse. Even if she were to come to the shack every day, bringing him food and water, she knew that it wouldn't be enough. It also wasn't possible for her to bring Dr. Clark with her; she was certain that all it would accomplish was to cause even more questions to be asked, questions that had answers she wasn't ready to share with anyone.

If this man was really Mason Tucker, if he had somehow managed to survive the war all those long years ago, Rachel needed to find out on her own. She already knew that she would have to keep him secret from her mother and, for that matter, the rest of Carlson. Once she had nursed him back to health, she would ask him his name, and if her suspicions proved correct, she would ask him much, much more.

And he will answer me!

"We have to take him back to the house," she said simply.

"Oh, goody!" Charlotte clapped her hands.

Before the girl's excited voice had faded from the cramped inside of the shack, Rachel grabbed hold of her, fixing Charlotte with a stern stare. "You can't tell another person about any of this," she explained. "This has to be our secret, just yours and mine."

"But if we don't tell anyone else, how are we going to get him home?"

Rachel knew that Charlotte was right; she knew that she wasn't strong enough to take the stranger back to the boardinghouse on her own. In his weakened condition, there was no way she could hope for him to help.

But then she was struck with a bold idea. There might be one other person that they could trust, someone who might not ask any questions. This person just might be able to get the man back to the boardinghouse.

If he wasn't too drunk . . .

"I know what we need to do," Rachel said.

"What's that?"

"Let's get Uncle Otis."

Otis stood just inside the shack's door, his hands on his knees, breathing as heavily as a mule that had just been forced to plow a hundred acres. Rivulets of sweat poured down his round face, and his skin was flushed a bright red. The front of his shirt was soaked through and his hands, as they fished a small flask of whiskey from his pocket, were damp.

"Now . . . this here . . . is just what . . . a fella needs," he panted, unscrewing the lid and bringing the liquor to his lips. Straightening his stooped back, he drank greedily, wiping his mouth with the back of his hand as he finished. "That's more than a bit better!"

Rachel paid her uncle little notice. As soon as she was back inside the shack, she hurried over to where Charlotte still knelt by the sick man. Touching his forehead with her hand, she frowned; his skin was still incredibly hot even though he seemed to be shivering in his sleep, both sure signs that his illness was getting worse.

"Did he wake up at all?" Rachel asked her niece.

"Not once," the girl answered with a shake of her blonde braids. "He moaned a bit one time, but his eyes never opened."

"Shoot and tarnation, Rachel," Otis exclaimed as he waddled over to the makeshift bed and looked down. He took another swig of drink before adding, "You didn't say nothin' 'bout me comin' all the way out here to dig a grave!"

The truth was that Rachel hadn't told Otis much of anything. She'd discounted the idea of concocting a lie when she had raced back to the boardinghouse; even though he was a drunk, her uncle had a way of knowing when people weren't being honest. Instead, she'd kept things vague, telling him only that she was in a spot of trouble and that he was the only person who could possibly help her. The small bit of flattery had worked much better than any lie or, for that matter, the truth.

Though Otis had complained about the quick pace Rachel had kept while hurrying back to the shack, he had done his best to keep up with her. Occasionally he'd asked what the trouble was, or why she needed him, but she'd remained silent and gone even faster. Now that he knew why she had brought him out into the woods, Rachel could only hope he would do as she intended.

"Who in the hell is that fella?" Otis asked.

"I don't know," Charlotte answered simply, just as she had been instructed. Before she left the shack, Rachel had taken pains to make it clear to the girl that she should tell Otis as little as possible about the man. Charlotte truthfully didn't know much, but the last thing they needed was for her to tell her uncle that the man had called her by Alice's name.

No one can find out until I know the truth . . .

"He's just a stranger," Rachel added. "Charlotte found him here."

"Then why should we be helpin' him?"

"Are we supposed to just let him die?" she asked her uncle. "He's sick, terribly sick, and he needs to be cared for."

"If he's as sick as he looks, then we should be gettin' the doctor. The only thing you know 'bout medicine is birthin' babies, and he sure don't look pregnant to me." The heavyset man guffawed. "As for me, all I know is what my grandpappy taught me 'bout sick cows, and even if he's on death's door, he ain't gonna take too kindly to me stickin' my hand up his backside!"

"Dr. Clark is still out of town," Rachel answered, ignoring her uncle's attempt at humor, "and it might be too late by the time he returns. Besides, the nights are getting much colder now, and in this shack, we can't be certain this man will survive until morning."

"So what do you reckon we're supposed to do?"

"We need to take him back to the boardinghouse."

"Please, Uncle Otis," Charlotte added.

Otis seemed to be weighing all the things they had told him, looking from each face to the other, and then back again. He brought the flask of whiskey back to his lips, but before he could take a drink, he thought better of it and screwed the lid back on. With a sigh and then a chuckle, he said, "Sure don't look like he's gonna be able to pay for a room."

"When he gets better he can," Charlotte suggested.

"Do you think you'll be able to help me get him back?" Rachel inquired.

"Shoot, darlin', this old fella might not be much to look at," Otis explained, with an odd sense of pride, patting his enormous stomach, "but I still got a fair share of fire in this here belly!"

Instead of trying to fashion a makeshift travois out of two long sticks and the blankets Charlotte had taken, a method once used by local Indians to transport their sick and wounded, they settled upon simply carrying the sick stranger back as best they could. Otis felt confident that with Rachel's help he would be able to manage the difficult task, provided that they were able to stop once in a while so that he could wet his whistle. If they didn't have too many obstacles, they would be back at the boardinghouse by dusk.

With a groan, Otis leaned the man forward at the waist and, with one limp arm slung over his shoulder, heaved the stranger from the floor. Rachel immediately took the other arm and they soon steadied themselves. Charlotte retrieved the blankets, pillow, and other things she had brought in order to care for the sick man, as well as the worn satchel that seemed to be the man's only possession, and they were off.

They had no more than shuffled outside the shack when Jasper began to dance around them, barking playfully; clearly, the sight of the stranger being carried unconsciously along excited him.

"You hush!" Charlotte scolded him. "We don't need any of that!"

With Charlotte leading the way, they traveled in a different direction than the one Rachel had taken on either of her earlier treks to the shack; it was obvious that the girl had spent a great deal of time in the woods and knew her way around. After a difficult passage through a clump of honeysuckle bushes, they found themselves on a worn, rocky path that skirted around the western shore of the lake.

Even on the path, the going was harder than Rachel had expected. Since he wasn't awake and able to help them, the stranger's limp body felt as heavy as a load of bricks. Occasionally, she or Otis would stumble under their burden, tripping over a rock or a gnarled tree root and threatening to fall, but they never did.

Charlotte stayed ahead of them, moving any fallen branches she could manage to lift out of their way or warning them about upcoming areas of standing water or mud.

After her turbulent thoughts back in the shack, it was strange for Rachel to be so close to the sick man. Part of her discomfort was from his smell; his body odor was that of a man who had spent a great deal of time away from a washbasin and a bar of soap. But the sound of his moans, a weak mewling escaping through his slack lips, tugged at her heart, something that surprised even her. Once again, she couldn't help but wonder if she were mistaken, if this man was Mason Tucker or not.

How can it be possible?

"I wonder what your mother is going to think of such a mess," Otis said.

"We can't say a word about this," she answered quickly.

"Why in the hell not?"

Panic gripped Rachel's heart at her uncle's pointed question. This was just what she had worried about from the moment she had decided to take the stranger back to the boardinghouse; how to keep Otis from telling his sister what was taking place.

"You know how Mother is," she explained carefully, weighing every word. "She already is nervous about all of the other boarders. If we were to tell her we had brought a sick vagrant back to the house, she'd be liable to be up half the night with worry that he had some terrible disease, or that once he got better he'd steal her good silver."

"He isn't gonna do either of them things, is he?" Otis asked.

"No, he's not," she answered with certainty. "But that won't stop her from worrying herself into a tizzy."

"Yer right 'bout that," he agreed. "And I reckon she won't never know nothin' 'bout it unless we say somethin'. After all, it ain't like she's gonna come on out of her room to help us haul him up the steps!"

"You can't say a word to her about him," Rachel pressed again.

As they continued walking, Otis looked across the stranger's still unconscious face at his niece and gave her a wink. "You ain't gonna have to be worryin' 'bout your Uncle Otis flappin' his gums." He chuckled.

"This here secret's safe with me, long as you don't mind me slippin' out back of the house once in a while to take a pull or two off of my flask. A fella my age gets thirsty every now and again!"

Rachel gave him an easy smile. Until she found out the truth, until she figured out why this man had called Charlotte by her mother's name, she would be happy to look the other way.

It was nearly dusk by the time they reached the boardinghouse. The sun hung low and orange on the horizon, its heat having long since left the day. Rachel rubbed her free hand against her arm for warmth; she couldn't imagine how the strange man had spent so many of these October nights outdoors.

Taking the back door, they cut through the kitchen and then up the long flight of stairs to the second floor. On the way, they had decided to put the sick man in the room directly at the head of the staircase; while it was the easiest to reach from downstairs, it had the added bonus of being as far from Eliza's room as possible.

Gently as they could manage, they put the man into the bed, making sure he was well covered with blankets. While Rachel pulled down the curtains on the setting sun, Otis lit an oil-burning lamp, and the flickering flame sent shadows dancing across the walls. With the man safely in bed, Rachel knew there was nothing more they could do but let him sleep.

"Let him get his rest," she said to Charlotte, shooing her toward the door.

"But I want to watch him," the girl protested.

"You can watch him tomorrow."

Just as she was about to close the door behind her, Rachel stopped and looked back into the room. She held the sleeping man's profile in her gaze, wondering for the hundredth time if he was who she thought he might be. Was it truly possible that this man was Mason Tucker? How could he have survived the war? If he had, why had it taken so many years for him to return to Carlson? The questions she had to ask seemed never to end, racing through her mind like comets across the sky.

Once you are better, all of these questions will have answers.

Unknowingly safe, Mason twitched and turned in his bed, sweat glistening on his forehead, his dreams lost in a hazy memory of a time he had spent the last eight years of his life trying to forget:

THE SOMME RIVER VALLEY, FRANCE— MARCH 1918

Mason Tucker pressed his body into the wet mud at the base of the trench, his bones rattling from the force of the explosions erupting all around him. Showers of earth rained down on him as if sent from heaven above. The noise was deafening. Each blast felt nearer than the last, and he struggled to keep his rifle in his shaking hands and his helmet on his head.

Dozens of other men shared his fate, heads bowed in the hope that they would be spared the shells that had already taken the lives of so many of their fellow soldiers. Not a soul dared move an inch in the midst of the chaos.

Drizzling rain fell from the ashen sky, the normal pitter-patter of its arrival lost in the grisly sounds of war. Behind the rear edge of the trench, a lone tree stood silent vigil over them, its leafless, gnarled branches pointing skyward accusingly. No bird, no rabbit, no other living thing stirred.

This is a living hell on earth!

Hardly a month had passed since Mason and the other men of his unit had first set foot on French soil. The Great War had been raging for almost four grueling years, but with the arrival of the Americans, talk had begun to suggest that the conflict would soon be over. Though he had enlisted full of equal parts daring and excitement, he had still allowed himself the hope that he would soon be able to return home to Minnesota.

The Germans had other ideas.

From the first time Mason fired his rifle in combat, any illusion he might have had was quickly proven wrong. All around him, men died. Bodies were broken as easily as if they were twigs stepped upon by a booted foot. Faces that he noticed one moment were simply gone the next. The first time he had killed a German soldier had been difficult, the second time only slightly easier. Days slowly bled into weeks. Towns and cities drifted by as if they were smoke borne upon the wind; names such as Amiens, Creil, and Beauvais were as difficult to pronounce as they were to identify. Even the weather seemed to be set against them; torrential spring rains turned the earth into an unmanageable quagmire of mud and set long trains of rats scurrying the length of the flooded trenches. When the sun did manage to shine, its meager warmth did little to assuage the chill that filled him. The food was barely tolerable and bouts of influenza stole as many lives as German bullets. Mason Tucker knew one simple truth: going off to war was nothing like what he had imagined when he enlisted.

Suddenly, the German guns fell silent. Though his heart pounded heavily in his chest, Mason couldn't hear it over the continued ringing of his ears. He was about to move, to cautiously peer up over the lip of the trench, when the relative silence was broken by the opening up of American artillery. This was to be the opening stage in his unit's offensive; the orders had come down for them to cross the no-man's-land of barbed wire, shattered trees, and broken bodies in an effort to take the enemy's position.

"It won't be long now, lads," Mason's captain shouted in encouragement, his voice little more audible than a whisper over the roaring guns. "Once they're good and softened up, then we'll overrun the damn Huns!"

"Just like the last time, I bet," a soldier beside him said sarcastically, though carefully out of his commanding officer's earshot.

"They keep sayin' that this time'll be the one that gets the Krauts to quit, but it don't seem to me like they're payin' attention," another answered to a few sporadic fits of forced laughter.

Mason's hand strayed to press down upon his breast pocket. Inside, tenderly wrapped among the soft folds of a handkerchief, was the letter he had just received from his wife, Alice. He'd devoured every word, reading her flowery script over and over again until he could recite it by heart. It was almost as if she were speaking to him, the sweet sound of her voice as clear to his ear as the gently lapping waters of a lake in springtime. Alice's loving words kept him moving forward, buoying him against the horrors of the war. Without her letters, he wondered if he would have the strength to go on.

"Hope they know where they're firin'," another soldier said as the heavy guns continued to roar.

"If they don't, we're gonna know soon enough."

"Damn machine guns'll cut us to ribbons!"

"Not if we get them first!"

Struggling to keep his thoughts from lingering over the deadly machine guns he was about to face, Mason focused his mind on Alice. They had known each other since childhood and he couldn't remember a day when he hadn't been in love with her. When she had agreed to become his wife, it was as if the Good Lord had reached down and given him a star from the night sky. They had been married only five months when he enlisted, boarded a train, and left their home in Carlson, Minnesota, for the United States Army. The sight of her waving good-bye to him from the platform, her curly blonde hair blowing in the breeze, tears running down her soft cheeks, was one that returned to him often. Though she was without him, he was thankful she had her family, particularly her younger sister, Rachel, for support.

"Damn Krauts will be waitin' for us!"

"Then we'll just have to show 'em what we came over here for!"

Though he had been gone for only months, Mason wondered if he wouldn't already be unrecognizable to his young wife. Before he arrived in France, he knew that there were many who considered him to be quite handsome: a tall frame that was broad across the shoulders; piercing blue eyes he had inherited from his mother; a firm, square jaw topped by a thin nose; coal-black hair. But now, in the face of brutal conflict, he knew that he had changed: he always felt filthy, covered in mud and the blood of his fellow man; on the rare occasions he caught a glimpse of himself, his eyes looked haunted, his face an unruly mess. Would Alice be horrified to look at him? Would she recognize her husband or think him a stranger?

May the Lord help me return the man I was when I left! And return I must!

"Just a bit more!" the captain shouted above the din.

"Like he's lookin' forward to it," a man joked, but this time no one laughed.

When Mason left Minnesota, he'd made a vow to Alice; he would return to her safe and sound. He'd given his word truthfully, confident in his ability to fulfill his promise. More important, Alice had believed him. Though death was all around him, he felt certain that he would escape its cold embrace; he would do his duty, but do it carefully, cautiously. After all, he and Alice had their whole future ahead of them; the joy of bringing children into the world, stepping in to take over his father's thriving business, a life filled with love and affection. They had their entire lives . . .

Once again, the guns fell silent. All around Mason, men appeared to rise out of the muck and mire, edging toward the front of the trench, rifles clutched in muddy hands. Though several had joked during the thunderous firing of the artillery, now all held their tongues, their faces determined yet grim. The soldier beside Mason made the sign of the cross.

"This is what you have prepared for!" the captain bellowed. "Go get 'em, boys!"

Once again patting his breast pocket, Mason reassured himself that his wife's letter was with him. Though he knew that Alice was safe in their home in Minnesota, he believed that some small part of her was beside him; regardless of whether they were simply words written on paper, the feelings and emotions they shared with each other were real enough to pierce the darkness of war.

I will be true to you, my beloved! I will return!

The near-silence of the trench was broken by the shrill sound of the captain's whistle as he gave his men the order to engage the enemy. As one, they began to clamber up the ramparts, their hands and feet struggling to find any purchase in the muddy earth. One after the other, they disappeared over the lip of the trench, moving forward to fight for their country.

Mason Tucker crested the trench and trudged forward, his rifle at the ready.

Chapter Fourteen

CHARLOTTE SAT IN A CHAIR in the bedroom at the head of the stairs, watching the man sleep. Brilliant rays of afternoon sun streamed through the curtains, holding out the promise of an October afternoon of fun, but she wasn't about to spend her day outside, even if it were one of the last nice days she might see before spending the winter cooped up indoors. She had run home from school as fast as she could, all so that she could sit and stare.

The stranger lay perfectly still, his eyes closed and his chest gently rising and falling with every breath. Rachel had washed his face and hands with a washcloth, removing the dirt and grime, and Otis had stripped him of his tattered clothing, dressing him in a nightshirt a former boarder had left behind. Though he seemed awfully thin of face, even with his unruly mess of a beard, Charlotte thought that he looked somewhat peaceful, at rest even though he hadn't awakened even once.

Two long days had passed since they brought the stranger to the room in the boardinghouse, and the secret of his existence was burning a hole in Charlotte's proverbial pocket. Never in her life had she wanted to talk about something more, to run screaming through the streets of town, shouting her news to anyone who would listen. Even though she knew that this was the last thing she should do— Rachel had warned her against it more times than she could count—her silence was no easier to bear.

"We can't tell anyone he's here, can we, Jasper?" she said to the dog.

Jasper raised his head from his paws in answer, staring at her from his resting place next to the door. His ears rose expectantly, betraying a wishful hope that they were finally going to end their self-imposed exile indoors and resume their normal routine of exploring and playing, but when Charlotte remained in her seat, he dropped his head with a sigh, defeated.

When she was alone in the room with the stranger, Charlotte sometimes found herself talking to him, telling him about her day at school or about some ordinary goings-on around the boardinghouse. She wasn't sure why she did it; she supposed that it was either because she detested the silence of the room, or maybe that she would have wanted someone to talk to her if she were in his position. Either way, he never answered.

But she kept on talking anyway.

Lazily, Charlotte moved one of the checker pieces across the board she'd just been given for her birthday. She had promised the first game to Uncle Otis. He had taught her how to play last winter as they sat next to the wood-burning stove and the board had been his gift, but she had brought it into the room in the hope that the man might want to play if he ever woke. So far, the game remained untouched. Frustrated, she took one of the pieces and flung it hard against the wall, where it fell with a clatter to the floor.

Waiting for anything, whether it was a sunny day after a week of rain or Christmas morning, was every bit as painful to her as the time she had fallen and chipped a tooth. Her grandmother and Rachel always preached the benefits of being patient, that all things would arrive in good time, but Charlotte couldn't bear it. Passing the time until the man woke up, as well as keeping the secret of his existence, made her want to shake him and try to wake him up.

What's the point of having a secret if you can't tell anyone about it?

Keeping silent about what she knew wasn't the only thing weighing heavily on Charlotte's mind; it was only two weeks until the performance of the school's annual play. Every fall, all of the citizens of Carlson jammed themselves into the school's tiny auditorium to watch the children sing songs, act out comedy skits, and even shed an unintentional tear or two. This year's theme was in honor of the recently finished harvest. While this would be the first time she had been forced to participate and had a small part as an orange leaf being blown across the stage, it didn't make it any less traumatic.

Dancing across the stage and making a general fool of herself would have been just fine for Charlotte if it wasn't for the preening of Catherine Nichols. Three years older than she, Catherine had the lead part in the play, the farmer's wife preparing the bountiful dinner to be attended by the whole town. She had been crowing as loudly as any rooster about how she was the star of the show and how everyone in town was coming to watch her.

Charlotte knew that all the girl wanted was attention, but she couldn't stand her just the same. She desperately wished she could tell everyone about what happened in the woods, about finding the stranger, just so that no one would pay any attention to Catherine anymore; she would gain a lot of satisfaction from knocking the girl down a peg or two.

But all that would really do is upset Rachel!

Ever since Rachel had followed Charlotte out to the shack in the woods, she had taken a particularly strong interest in the stranger, going often to the bedroom and looking at the man with a curious as well as impatient eye. Once, Charlotte had crept up the staircase in the middle of the night, to find Rachel already inside the darkened room!

"Have you been talking to her?" Charlotte asked aloud.

"No . . . I've been sleeping . . ." a voice answered.

Charlotte's eyes flew to the bed, where the stranger's eyes fluttered, one hand rising weakly from the sheets to rub at the sleep in his eyes. After days of uninterrupted rest, he was awake.

The stranger was finally awake!

Mason's eyes fluttered as sleep finally released its grip on him. Slowly, he came out of a foggy dream of riding on the gently rocking rails of a train as a cool wind rushed through the open door, ruffling his hair and carrying with it the scent of freshly cut pine. For a moment, as the vision retreated from his mind, he had no idea where he was.

When he was finally able to see clearly, Mason's gaze wandered over the tiny room in which he lay. The furnishings were meager: a nightstand with an oil lantern stood next to the bed, there was a chipped dresser topped with a washbasin in the far corner, and a coat tree leaned awkwardly just inside the door. Sunlight poured through the thin curtains of two windows, falling on the golden hair of a little girl sitting in a chair at the foot of the bed.

Even as he struggled to awaken from his stupor, Mason found that there was something familiar about the girl. Much of the child's face was in the shadows, and most of what he could see was fixed in a frown of concentration, but there was something there he knew that remained just out of reach. Absently, the girl pushed a checker piece across the black-and-red surface of its board.

Suddenly, the memory of what he had been doing before he collapsed into a black darkness came back to Mason. He remembered jumping off the speeding train outside Carlson, making his way to the house that he had shared with Alice and finding another man and woman living there, running into Samuel Guthrie, and the illness that had nearly felled him where he stood. He recalled making his way into the woods on the far side of Lake Carlson, finding the shack he had played in as a boy, and then . . . nothing.

I went out to the woods to be alone . . . What happened?

"Have you been talking to her?" the girl suddenly said, looking in his direction.

He wasn't sure what she was talking about, but the simple sound of her voice was as welcome to his ears as the first birdcall of spring. "No . . . I've been sleeping . . ." he managed.

The girl's face rose in surprise to the sudden sound, her eyes lighting up with delight, and she rushed from her chair over to the side of the bed. She was so excited that her small hands grabbed up fistfuls of blanket, clenching and unclenching without pause. Her mouth opened and words poured out so rapidly that Mason couldn't understand a single one of them.

"I need . . . I need some water," he rasped.

The girl obliged, fetching him a glass from a pitcher next to his bed. She had to help him bring the tin cup to his mouth, and water dribbled down his beard, but he drank greedily, doubting that he had ever been as thirsty in his life.

Up close, he was struck by just how much the girl resembled Alice. It wasn't just the blonde hair, but also the sparkling blueness of her eyes, the slightly upturned nose, and the way her smile curled a bit at the edges. Even her excitement at his waking was similar; Alice had an infectiously optimistic way of seeing the best in everything and everyone. Once again, he wondered where his wife was.

"Are you a hobo?" the girl asked when he had finished drinking.

"Sort of," he lied gently. It wasn't that he wanted to deceive the girl, but more that the answer was too complex, far too difficult for him to explain, including to himself.

"You were awfully sick."

"I was," Mason admitted.

"Jasper and I took care of you," she said proudly.

"Who's Jasper?"

His nails scratching against the wooden floor, a large black dog padded over to the bed and jumped up, placing his front paws on the edge of the mattress. He barked once, as if he were saying hello, and the girl gave his thick neck a scratching as he panted, his pink tongue lolling out of his mouth.

"I suppose . . . I should . . . thank you both." Mason smiled. He raised a fragile hand to the dog, and Jasper gave it a gentle lick, his wet tongue darting over outstretched fingers.

"That means he likes you," the girl observed.

Suddenly, Mason was aware that he was wearing a nightshirt instead of his familiar clothing. A tremor of panic raced across his heart, a fear that he had somehow misplaced his belongings, but most important, that he had lost his picture of Alice.

"I had some things . . . with me when . . . I got sick . . ."

"Don't worry none about your stuff, it's all there," the girl said as she pointed at another chair Mason had not originally seen. There, draped across his satchel, was his worn overcoat. Though he hadn't laid eyes on it, he felt certain that the photograph was safely inside.

"My uncle and Aunt Rachel brought you back," the girl continued.

The mention of the name Rachel sent Mason's mind to racing. *That's the name of Alice's sister!* Was it possible that the woman the little girl was talking about was the same person? If so, was he in Eliza Watkins's house? The room didn't strike him as particularly familiar, but it had been so many long years since he had been there, it was possible that he didn't remember.

"Who's Alice?" the girl asked, breaking his frantic thoughts.

"What?" he asked quickly.

"You called me Alice," the girl explained.

Mason realized that the first thought he'd had upon looking at the girl, that she closely resembled Alice, must have been the same reaction he'd had when encountering her in the woods. He must have been delirious, half out of his mind with fever, and had imagined that he was being cared for by his loving wife, not some small girl.

"What is your name?" he asked, ignoring the girl's question.

"Charlotte," she replied.

"It's nice to meet you, Charlotte," Mason said warmly. "My name is . . ." he began before hesitating. With Rachel's name having been mentioned, he'd absolutely no choice but to think that he had been taken in by Alice's sibling, his own sister-in-law. Was this girl Rachel's daughter? Since Charlotte had mentioned an uncle having been involved in taking him from the secluded shack, he had to wonder if it was Otis Simmons, or . . .

Or was it Alice's new husband . . .

Before Mason could give Charlotte any kind of answer, the door to the room opened and he found himself staring at Rachel Watkins. As she strode inside, he tried desperately to hide his surprise; with his worries about her identity now confirmed, he felt filled with a mixture of happiness at seeing her again after so many long years away and an impending dread at finally being discovered.

Rachel had changed during the eight long years he had been gone. She was far more beautiful than he remembered; gone was the attractive yet awkward younger girl. In her place was a woman with striking coal-black hair, piercing greenish-brown eyes, and luxuriously full lips. Even though she had only been in the room for

a moment, he also noticed that she carried herself proudly. Forgotten was the
bashful girl he remembered as Alice's
younger sister. Rachel appeared more confident, more certain in her bearing than he
remembered.

"I heard voices when I was passing by
and I hoped that our guest might be
awake," she said with a smile that was
more curious than inviting. "It seems I was
right."

"I wasn't bothering him!" Charlotte said
defensively. "Honest!"

"She wasn't," Mason added, unsure of
how he should mask his voice.

"Charlotte, will you leave us for a moment?" Rachel said, her eyes never leaving Mason. Even as he tried to remain
calm, to not betray his ever-growing anxi-
ety, his heart thundered loudly in his chest.
Even when he had been a soldier on the
battlefield or when he had escaped from a
trainyard boss by the skin of his teeth, he
had never felt so ill at ease.

"But he just woke up," Charlotte whined.

"You'll have plenty of time to talk his ear
off later. Right now, I want to check his
temperature."

The young girl groaned but nonetheless stomped out of the room, Jasper in tow. When the door had clicked shut behind her, Mason said, "I want to thank you for all you've done for—"

"All I want out of you is the truth," she said, silencing him.

"I don't . . . think I understand . . ." Mason offered as a feeble answer, but he did understand. The time had come. He owed her an explanation.

Rachel stepped forward. "I think you do." She gripped the oaken foot of the bed, her eyes full of determination. "It's really you, isn't it?" she said softly. "Mason Tucker has come back from the dead. But eight years too late."

Chapter Fifteen

MASON, IT'S YOU, isn't it?" Rachel asked, her voice nearly as soft as a whisper. *Has Mason Tucker come back from the dead?*

Rachel's gaze held the man where he lay in the bed in the tiny room at the head of the stairs. Intently, she watched for some reaction, anything that might betray his response to her accusation, but he only looked back at her curiously. With his unruly mop of dark hair, equally unkempt beard, and penetrating eyes, he had the appearance of a vagrant, a hobo, whose life was spent aimlessly traveling the rails. But she felt certain that it was only a façade, a curtain hiding who he really was.

During the two days that he had spent in their care, Rachel had taken great pains to nurse him back to health. After making sure that he was finally resting comfortably, she'd washed the rest of the dirt and grime from his body. Though he wasn't alert enough to eat, she had managed to coax him to take some water she squeezed from a cloth into his mouth.

While the stranger's well-being was important, she tended to him not entirely from the goodness of her heart; what she really wanted was the truth. From the moment he had spoken to her in the darkness of the cabin, calling her by her name, Rachel had longed to know his true identity. Even as she cared for him, she found her curiosity often getting the better of her. In the middle of the night, while everyone else in the boardinghouse slept, she had come into his room to silently watch him. Her eyes had raced over his features again and again, hoping to find something that would convince her that she wasn't imagining things, that he was who she believed him to be.

But she could never be certain. Either too much time had passed since she had watched him leave on the train for France, clouding her memories beyond recovery, or Mason had physically changed and no longer resembled the man that she had known, her sister's husband. Still, the thought that she was right incessantly nagged her, refusing to let go.

And that's why I'm here . . . to finally learn the truth!

"I'm . . . afraid that I don't know what you're talking about," the man finally answered.

Refusing to allow him a chance to so much as catch his breath, Rachel rushed from the foot of the bed to the man's side, her fists balled tightly in a growing sense of frustration. When she spoke, the words flew from her mouth like arrows.

"What about what happened out in the cabin?" she prodded, her voice rising with every word. "Why did you call Charlotte by Alice's name? How do you know me? How did you know my name?"

Her sudden barrage of questions seemed to utterly unsettle the stranger. His eyes darted quickly from Rachel to the open window, then to the door, and finally back to the window before settling upon a spot at the base of the bed. Clearing his throat, he hemmed and hawed, started and stopped, all without giving any sort of meaningful reply.

Rachel knew she was being unfair; accosting this man while he was still recovering from a severe illness was almost certainly treatment that he didn't deserve. But she also knew that she didn't have much of a choice. She needed answers, answers to the questions she'd been asking herself over the last two days, the very same questions she'd been tortured by for the last eight years.

And by God, I will have them!

"How did you know my name?" she prodded again.

While he still seemed unsettled, the stranger sighed and said, "I'm not . . . not entirely sure, the sickness has muddled my head so that I can't think straight, although I seem to remember meeting a man when I was in the army, when I was a soldier in France, who said he was from a town in eastern Minnesota named Carlson. He often talked about two women he cared for, two sisters named Alice and Rachel.

"It sounded like such a wonderful place that . . . I suppose I wanted to see it for myself," he continued, an easy smile crossing his face. "But when I got here, whatever sickness I contracted finally got the better of me. I suppose that when you found me, I was half delirious with fever and those two names were the only thing roaming around in my head."

"A . . . a man you met . . . in the army?" Rachel asked, suddenly unsure.

"That's right."

"And . . . you're just now coming here?"

The man's smile was suddenly gone, replaced by a grim frown. "I was . . . in a hospital for a great while . . . because of my injuries . . ."

Rachel scarcely heard a word that the stranger spoke; she was so momentarily shocked that she wouldn't have been bothered by the boardinghouse's roof caving in. Worry filled her heart that she had somehow been wrong, that as certain as she had been that he was Mason Tucker, she had been mistaken. Still, there was something about the man's story that nagged at her. Even now, his eyes refused to alight on her for longer than an instant, and she found that she couldn't help but entertain the idea that he was lying.

I can't have been wrong . . . I just can't be!

"I don't believe you," she declared, hoping that she sounded surer of herself than she felt.

"I'm not lying to you," he answered, but she felt his voice waver.

"What's your name?" Rachel pressed.

"William . . . William Martin . . ."

"You're telling me that you're not Mason Tucker."

"No . . . I'm not," the man hesitantly denied, but even as he spoke, he turned his face away from her, contenting himself with staring at the wall. Even after finishing speaking, he refused to look back.

Confidence that she was still right in her assumption began to swell in Rachel's heart. Clearly, the man was hiding something from her. *Is it shame at the lies he's telling me?* No matter what it took, she vowed that she would get to the bottom of it.

"That's really too bad," she began, trying

her best to sound disappointed with what he had claimed. "Because if you really were Mason Tucker, long removed from Carlson and finally returned to town, to his grieving family, I would have been able to tell you about everything that has happened, for better or worse, since you were gone."

"For . . . better or worse . . . ?" the man repeated.

"That's right," Rachel agreed. "If you were Mason, I would tell you what has befallen your father, about all of the horrible things your brother has gotten himself into, but most important, I'd be able to tell you about Alice and your . . . Well, that last part wouldn't be any of your business, would it, seeing as how you're not who I thought you were."

This time, the stranger remained silent, although his jaw tightened.

"I'm glad that you're feeling better, Mr. Martin. I'll leave you be so that you can get some rest." She smiled as she took a step toward the door. "I reckon that it will still be a couple of days before you're able to be up and about, so I'll bring you some supper to help with your recovery."

For a brief moment, Rachel thought that he might actually let her leave, but just as her hand found the doorknob, his voice called out, "Wait . . . wait, Rachel . . ."

Turning, she asked, "What is it?"

"I just . . . just can't . . ."

"You can't what?" she prodded him.

Right before her eyes, it seemed to Rachel as if all of the uncertainty disappeared from the stranger. Sighing deeply, his shoulders squared themselves and his eyes rose to meet hers unflinchingly. For the first time since she had followed Charlotte into the woods and come upon him in the cabin, the man truly looked like Mason Tucker.

"You're right, Rachel." He nodded gravely. "I'm . . . Mason . . . Tucker."

Mason's words hung in the air as he stared at Rachel. Even the slight breeze that had been rippling the curtains appeared to have quit in the face of his admission. For several long seconds, silence filled the room.

In the end, Mason knew that telling the truth was the only choice he had to make. Listening to Rachel talk about his father, about Zachary, but most importantly about Alice, was more than he could bear. Besides, lying to her the way he had, inventing a fictitious soldier's story, made him sick to his stomach. He'd spent seven long years running from the past; this moment was the time for him to face up to what he had done.

"What happened? You were reported killed in northern France," Rachel asked, her eyes growing wet.

"Rachel, I—"

"Why didn't you let Alice know you were alive?" she demanded furiously, her voice rising in a pitch of anger. "You're dead— they came and told us that you had died in the war—so how could you possibly be here?"

Mason knew that he had no choice but to tell Rachel the whole truth, even if that truth would likely hurt them both. After all the many long years he had dreaded this moment, refusing to come back to Carlson, to show his scarred and ugly face, to see the revulsion on the face of his wife. He had avoided this very thing, he knew that there would be no more running, and that realization calmed him.

Alice and her family deserve better than what I have given them . . .

"We were in France," he began simply, his voice hushed, his chest starting to tighten as he remembered the day that changed his life. "We'd only been there a matter of weeks, a month or so, fighting along trench after trench, town after nameless town. All around us . . . there was nothing but death, destruction, and mud. Then one day, just like so many others before, we were given the order that we were expected to take a German position, to go up over the trench and take it, so when our officer blew his whistle, we went . . ."

Mason paused, the weight of his tale pressing down on him. Holding Rachel's eyes, he noticed that while she still hung intently on his every word, she seemed to have softened, if only a bit.

"We hadn't gone fifty feet when the German machine guns opened up," he continued. "Right next to me, a man was nearly cut in half. In that sea of mud mixed with barbed wire, I fell to the ground and tried to crawl to safety, but before I could move, artillery shells began to fall. The sound was deafening. Each successive crash made me feel as if my very organs were being shaken. Closer and closer they came, the heat from the explosions rolling across my face. But then I had the sudden sensation of being thrown, tossed as if I was little more than a doll, and then there was only blackness."

"They told me that you died," Rachel explained as the first tear broke loose and rolled down her cheek. "They said that a solider saw it happen. Your father told Alice that all that was found of you was a bloody piece of uniform."

Mason nodded solemnly in answer.

"But you lived?" she asked.

"Somehow . . . by some miracle, yes," Mason answered. "I woke up in a hospital filled with row after row of beds, all containing men who screamed through the night, my face wrapped in gauze and bandages. I drifted in and out of consciousness, my vision filled with a haze of nurses, doctors, and pain. Once, I woke to find a nun sitting beside me, reading from the Bible . . . I was convinced she was giving me my last rites. I don't know how long I lay there, only that it seemed like forever."

"But then they should have known that

you were alive," Rachel argued. "As soon as you were able, you would have told them who you were and they would've told your family."

"That was exactly what I intended to do, Rachel." Mason sighed heavily. "I promise you that I'm telling the truth, but then they took my bandages off, handed me a mirror, and . . ."

"And what?" she prodded him tearfully.

Mason stared into the eyes of his wife's younger sister and knew that this was the moment from which he could never return. *This is the moment I have been frightened by for all these years!* It was the decision he made that day that had kept him away.

But at the same time, Mason had already come so far, had told so much that by falling silent now, he knew that he would have failed. As painful as these memories were to recount, he vowed not to stop until they were finished.

"Lying there in my bed, getting stronger with every day," he explained, "all that I could think about was Alice, about how I had been spared so that I could return to her, so that we could be together again and resume the life we'd planned for all our lives.

"But the explosion that had put me in the hospital had done more than just knock me unconscious, it had also badly burned the side of my face." Gently, Mason's hand rose to touch his beard covering his right cheek. "None of the doctors could ever be certain if it had been caused by a burning piece of metal or some phosphorous agent the Germans had added to the shell, but it smoldered on my skin long enough to blister, scalding until my face was raw. What I saw when I looked in the mirror was an abomination, a festering, ugly mess of pus and blood. Right then and there, I decided that I could never return to Carlson, that I could never allow Alice to see what I had become."

"Why?" she asked. "Why could you never return?"

"Because I was no longer the person I was when I left. If Alice were to have looked at me, she wouldn't have seen the man that she loved, the man she married."

"But . . . you have a beard . . ." Rachel said.

"It's taken me more than five years to grow this," Mason explained, running his hand through the coarse but still spotty hair. "The doctors said that with the extensive scarring, they wouldn't expect much, if anything, to grow. Patiently, I've somehow managed to grow this much. When I first came back to the States, I wrapped my face out of shame."

A flare of anger crossed Rachel's face. "How long ago was that?"

Bracing for the furious response he was certain would follow, Mason said, "I was discharged from the hospital in France several months after the war ended . . . and returned home early the next year."

"You . . . you came back . . . over seven years ago?" Rachel asked, her hands gripping across her chest and her body shaking uncontrollably. "Seven years . . . may God damn you for this, Mason Tucker!"

"What was—"

"You selfish son of a bitch!" she shouted, refusing to allow him to offer any word in his own defense. "You had to have known how much grief your death would cause back home! But even knowing that, you still ran away and allowed all of us to believe that we had lost you forever! How could you possibly have done such a thing?!"

"What did you expect me to do?" Mason demanded, his own temper rising, even if he understood Rachel's accusation. "Every single day that I was recovering in the hospital, days that stretched into months, I looked around me and all I could see were men who would be a burden to their loved ones, to their families. There were men who were missing legs or arms, had been blinded by German artillery or gas or, like me, burned by explosions. The last thing I wanted was to be looked at differently, to be seen as having changed. Just the thought of Alice looking at me with pity in her eyes was horrifying!"

"She would have understood! She would have loved you!"

Mason shook his head. "Before I left Carlson, I promised her that I would return to her just as I left. What would she have thought if I didn't keep my promised word? What if she no longer recognized me or no longer loved me because of what had happened? Because that was something I could not bear to witness, I stayed away."

"But because you ran away, you've lost everything!"

Rachel's words struck Mason momentarily mute. Though he couldn't begin to understand what she meant, the implication was enough to cause his heart to thunder and his stomach to roil. He could only stare at her as tears cascaded down her cheeks.

"You've lost everything," she repeated as sobs racked her.

Fear gnawed at Mason. Somehow, he managed to croak, "I want to see Alice. I went . . . to our house but . . . she wasn't there, so get . . . her for me, Rachel."

"Oh, Mason," she answered. "It's too late for that."

"What . . . what are you talking about?"

"You can't talk to her! No one can!" Rachel cried. "Alice is dead!"

Chapter Sixteen

HER FATEFUL WORDS had no sooner been spoken than Rachel could clearly see the painful hurt spreading across Mason's face. His still brilliant blue eyes widened as they searched her face for some sign, some explanation for what she had said.

"Alice is . . . dead?" he managed in a strangled whisper.

Rachel walked over and sat on the edge of the bed. Gingerly, she took his callused hands in her own. She had felt so much anger toward him, resentment for his having left them to fight a war when his draft number had not even come up. She had condemned him for refusing to come home as soon as he was released from the hospital, but the wounded way that he looked at her softened her heart, if only a bit. Telling someone such news as she needed to report to Mason was no easy task. She felt tension growing in her own chest; she knew that nothing she would say to him this day would make him hurt any less.

"Mason, there is something that you need to hear, something that is going to be very difficult for you to bear," she began, carefully choosing her words as she tried to prepare herself for the emotional battering that was to come. "Alice . . . Alice died in childbirth," Rachel explained as gently as she could. "Alice died . . . giving birth to your baby."

Immediately, Mason's hands clenched hers tightly.

"What . . . what are you saying?" he asked, his already confused face growing incredulous. "Baby . . . but . . . Alice and I weren't expecting a child . . ."

"Alice only found out about her pregnancy after you had already left," Rachel explained. "By her own count of months, she determined that she must have conceived just before you set out, but it was only after you had arrived in France that she knew for certain."

Even as she recounted the story, Rachel could not help but remember just how excited Alice had been. For her, the very idea that she and Mason would create a life, that she would be a mother, was as great a gift as she could ever have been given. When she had finally confided in her sister, tears of joy sliding down her soft cheeks, her smile had been brighter than the summer sun.

If only it had managed to stay that way.

"At first, she didn't know whether she should tell you about the baby or not," she continued. "She was afraid that you would have been distracted or would have worried about her. But in the end, she decided to write you a letter telling you that you were to be a father. Alice waited and waited, but weeks went by without a reply."

"The mail . . . was erratic . . . we were never sure when it might arrive," Mason haltingly explained. "I . . . I only ever received a couple of Alice's letters, ones she had . . . written in the first days . . . after I left." Wistfully, he looked over Rachel's shoulder at the worn coat draped over a chair in the corner. "I . . . never . . . received that letter . . . I never knew . . ."

"I know, Mason," Rachel answered, certain beyond any doubt that he was telling the truth; the pain in his voice was so real that she found herself agonizing right along with him. "And Alice knew it as well. Because she'd heard no reply, she concluded that the letter had been lost, but before she could even begin to write another, your father and a military man came to the house and told her that you were dead."

"No one knew who I was at the hospital. My identification had been lost . . ."

"From that day forward, it was as if you were really dead to all of us."

Waves of pity washed over Rachel as she told Mason what had happened in his absence. Even though she had endured the experiences firsthand, having to watch hopelessly as Alice spiraled ever downward, telling her sister's husband felt somehow worse. At least she had been able to try to reach Alice, to battle against the decline, even if it did no good in the end; all Mason could do was sit and listen.

"What . . . what happened to Alice?" he asked. "How did . . . she die . . . ?"

Carefully, Rachel told of how after Alice received the news of Mason's death, she began slowly to waste away, how without her husband in her life she seemed no longer to have a reason to continue. Rachel explained how she and her mother moved Alice out of the home she had shared with Mason and back into her old bedroom in the boardinghouse.

"After a couple of months, she began to talk less and less," Rachel said. "Her looks began to change. She always used to take such pride in her curly hair, but eventually she quit caring, leaving it unkempt. Even her eyes seemed to grow distant. No matter how much our mother fussed, she never lifted a finger to change.

"Even though she was pregnant, it was all I could do to get her to eat, to keep her and the baby's strength up. She lost weight, and we worried she wasn't gaining enough for the child. Through the spring and summer, nothing ever changed. In the beginning, she had visitors, friends and acquaintances who wanted to offer their condolences for her loss, but when word spread that she never responded, people stopped coming.

"Then came the day when she was to give birth . . . and . . ."

"Tell me, Rachel," Mason insisted, his eyes imploring her to continue. "I need to know . . ."

"There were some . . . complications . . . something was wrong," she began as her eyes once again filled with tears. "My mother had delivered countless babies, so we thought that even though it would be a difficult birth, she would manage. But we soon found that Alice no longer wanted to help, that she simply didn't want to live no matter how much we tried to persuade her. Your death had broken my sister's spirit so completely that even for the sake of her child, she couldn't find the strength to go on. So as she slowly bled to death, she never once cried out, never once asked to see the baby even as my mother coaxed out its first cry. No matter what I said to her, no matter what my mother tried, we were unable to save her."

Mason's broad shoulders began to shake

as the first tears fell from his downturned eyes. While Rachel recounted what had happened to Alice, to his beloved wife, he had kept his gaze fixed on their entwined hands, but now that she had finished he looked up at her, his face a mass of emotion.

Rachel watched as a spark of recognition raced across Mason's face. For an instant, he appeared to be having trouble believing what he had surmised, looking first to her, then to his hands, then briefly out the window before once again returning to her.

"Charlotte . . ." he said, his voice faint. "Charlotte is Alice's daughter. My daughter . . ."

Since the fateful day when he had been tossed skyward by an exploding German artillery shell, Mason had experienced several moments when he felt utterly helpless to control his own life. Lying in the room in the boardinghouse, reeling as he tried to absorb what Rachel had told him, he again felt buffeted by fate, unanchored to the life he knew. His heart raced and his breath seemed to catch in his throat. Even if his life had depended upon it, he knew that in that moment, he was utterly incapable of speech or movement, struck mute by the knowledge that his and Alice's daughter was still alive.

"Charlotte . . . Charlotte is my daughter," he repeated.

"She is." Rachel nodded solemnly. "Even if her mother no longer had the will to live, Charlotte fought on . . . I think she gets that stubbornness from you. Even though it's hard for her to share her birthday with the anniversary of her mother's death, she just turned eight. She is your and Alice's child."

"I should . . . I should have understood . . ."

"Oh, Mason, I'm sorry," she said as she squeezed his still shaking hands. "I thought that because of the way you had been calling her by her mother's name while you were sick, somehow you might have understood that she was Alice's daughter."

Even as Mason tried to make some sense of what Rachel was telling him, the faintest memory of seeing Alice enter the dilapidated cabin welled up in his disordered thoughts. With Charlotte's blonde hair and striking eyes, both traits of her mother, it was easy for him to believe that he had made such a connection given the power of the illness that ravaged him, that he could have mistaken her for Alice.

When he first awakened to find Charlotte sitting at the foot of his bed, Mason had been surprised to learn that he had called her Alice. In his embarrassment, he had apologized, but even then he recognized that she closely resembled his wife. While he didn't remember Alice at such a young age, he could believe they would be the image of each other.

"Does . . . does she know that I . . . I am her father?" Mason asked, suddenly worried.

"No," Rachel answered with a shake of her dark hair. "Just like the rest of us, she believes that her father is dead. All she knows of Mason Tucker is what she's been told over the years."

"What about now? Now that you know, will you tell her?"

Fixing him with a serious stare, Rachel said, "The only person to decide that is you."

Even as he nodded his head in agreement, Mason knew the decision would be difficult. That he had a daughter, a child who had no idea he existed, was daunting enough. To bring Charlotte into his life, at least the life he'd been living for the last seven years, seemed an impossible task. Questions raced around in his head.

Would my being in Charlotte's life make it better?

What will she think of me once she's learned the truth of what I've done?

Can I just walk away . . . leave without telling her?

Mason had no more than thought the last question when he came to the sudden realization that, with his and Alice's absence from Charlotte's life, someone had done his job for him.

"The burden of caring for her has fallen on you, hasn't it?" he asked Rachel.

"Caring for Charlotte has been trying at times, but it has never been a burden," she explained. "I've done what I can for her because I'm certain that that is what Alice would have wanted. There are days that are harder than others, but I've never regretted it. Besides, I don't have to do it all alone. I have my mother and Uncle Otis to help."

"Your mother . . . how is she?"

"Alice's death nearly killed her. After all of the children she'd safely delivered over the many years, it was hard for her to accept that she failed to save her own daughter. Ever since that day, she hasn't delivered a single child. Now her days are spent in her room at the end of the hall, staring out the window, so frightened that she never goes outside."

"After everything that's happened . . ."

"It's much more than that." Rachel sighed. "My mother worries for the sake of worrying, wringing her hands until they're chafed and raw. It's hard on everyone, but especially Charlotte. She's always being told to be careful, not to run about so wildly, even though she's no different from Alice or me at her age. Whenever Charlotte so much as skins her knee, my mother will work herself into hysterics and tries to protect her by locking the child in her room. Every year it gets worse. She's never been able to accept that what happened to Alice was beyond her ability to control."

Mason knew that Eliza Watkins was just

another victim of his disappearance, but her painful struggles tugged especially hard at his heart. He remembered the days he had courted Alice, when Eliza had struck him as a particularly independent woman. Outspoken as she was hardworking, brimming with confidence at her abilities as a midwife, as quick to laugh as she was to fight for those that she loved, it seemed impossible that she had been struck so low.

"With my mother in her room," Rachel continued, "Otis and I run things here at the boardinghouse."

"Good old Otis," Mason said with a weak smile. "Is he still a drinker?"

"Worse than before. Thank goodness he was sober enough to help get you back here the other night."

Another flare of worry raced across Mason's mind upon learning that Otis Simmons knew of his return. Fearful that every tongue in Carlson would be wagging with news of his unexpected appearance, all fueled by a certain man's love of liquor and the way a snoot full of whiskey could make a man blabber things he shouldn't, Mason asked, "Will he manage to keep it quiet? The fewer people who know of my arrival, the better."

"Otis might be many things," Rachel explained, "drunk, lazy, and quick of tongue among them, but he knows how to keep a secret. You don't have to be anxious."

Momentarily relieved, Mason once again began to reflect upon all the many things that had happened during his absence. Never in his wildest imagination would he have thought that so much could have occurred. As his own life had forever been changed, so had others, many of them belonging to those he truly loved.

Shock and surprise still tore at his heart at the fact that his beloved Alice was beyond his reach. For longer than he could remember, he'd comforted himself with the belief that he would, at the very least, be able to look upon her face one day, even if it were from a distance. That their love and union had left behind a child, a daughter so like her mother, filled him with both joy and trepidation.

While I was gone, for better or worse, life went on without me.

"I'm sorry for all the misery that I've caused, Rachel," he muttered.

"I won't sit here and tell you that I haven't felt my share of anger at you and all of the grief you've caused, Mason," she said curtly. "That Alice's love for you was greater than her desire to live still torments me. I know it's not right to place all the blame on your shoulders, but because she couldn't continue living, none of our lives will ever be the same. But now that you've returned, there are decisions that will have to be made."

Mason knew that what Rachel was telling him was right; now that his supposed death had been exposed, he would have many hard choices to make. He expected that she would want him to begin making them as soon as possible, particularly those that related to Charlotte and whether he would take a role as the girl's father, so he was somewhat surprised when she squeezed his hands, rose from where she sat on the bed, and made her way back toward the closed door.

"You still need to get your rest," she said simply. "You were as sick as I have ever seen a man, and that sort of illness isn't just going to disappear. I'll be back later with your dinner." Just as Rachel was about to step out into the hall, she turned back to him with a tender look in her eyes. "Welcome home, Mason . . ."

Chapter Seventeen

IF THERE WAS ONE THING that bothered Jonathan Moseley, it was a secret being kept from him. Even as a child, a birthday gift or the most innocent of schoolyard mysteries would gnaw at his thoughts, make him dizzy, taunting him until he had figured it out. In adulthood, he had changed little, which was why he was pacing around his cramped room like a caged animal.

Two days earlier, he had been coming back to the boardinghouse from another mostly fruitless attempt to peddle his wares when he'd come across Rachel and her uncle practically carrying a destitute man back toward their home. Carefully, he'd kept his distance so as not to be seen, and watched as they hauled the stranger up the back stairs. Later, when he finally returned to his room, he came to understand that they had placed their new guest in the room next to his own.

Who in the hell is he?

From that moment, Jonathan had been tortured by the fact that he had little idea what was going on, even if it were right under his nose. People had been coming and going from the stranger's room, but he was no closer to learning the man's identity than he had been out on the street. Worst of all was that Rachel was so concerned. Once, he'd tried to speak to her at the head of the stairs, but she'd just barged by him as if he weren't even there and had gone into the room.

"Don't make the mistake of ignoring me," he mumbled to himself.

With every passing hour, every tick of his pocket watch, Jonathan grew more restless. Every once in a while, he'd managed to hear the faint sound of voices, although he'd been unable to understand a word of what was being said, even after he'd pressed his ear against the wall. So great was his curiosity that he'd had trouble sleeping and hadn't eaten much. After a while, he realized that his mistake was in waiting for the information to come to him; he would have to find out the truth himself.

Heaven only helps those who help themselves!

After leaving his room and taking a long look at the closed door behind which the stranger lay, Jonathan made his way down the stairs to where Otis Simmons lounged in a rocking chair. With his feet propped up on a precariously piled stack of pillows, a half-empty whiskey bottle tucked into the crook of an arm, and his large hands folded over his ample belly, he seemed as hard at work as usual. Even as Jonathan stood watching the oaf, the first deep rumbles of a snore began to echo from him.

"Excuse me, sir," Jonathan shouted, giving the man a persistent shake.

Otis came to with a start, his feet plunging from their resting place and his body jumping so high that he nearly sloshed a bit of his liquor free from the previous safety of the bottle. "What the hell's the matter with you!" he bellowed in anger.

"Don't you know no better than to go 'bout wakin' a fella when he's in the middle of havin' his afternoon nap?"

"I'm sorry to have startled you," Jonathan answered with feigned innocence, "but I thought you might want to have this."

From the breast pocket of his shirt, he produced the rent money that Otis had been badgering him about; he'd been fortunate enough to come across a widow in desperate need of mothballs; she had bought two boxes. That sale had been one of few made for weeks and he was glad to get it.

"'Bout damn time," Otis grumbled as he snatched the money from Jonathan's hand and stuffed it into his own pocket. Without another word, he made ready to go back to sleep.

Jonathan cleared his throat before Otis could close his eyes; after all, the reason he had come downstairs, had initiated conversation with the fat slob, wasn't because he was dying to pay the money he owed, but rather to gain information. "I say, Mr. Simmons," he began. "I was wondering if you knew anything about our new boarder."

"Don't know what you're talkin' 'bout," Otis answered gruffly.

"Surely you know of whom I'm speaking," Jonathan pressed, his interest more than a bit piqued by the other man's initial denial. "The gentleman that was moved into the room next to mine . . . the strange man that you and Rachel placed there two days ago?"

"He ain't no boarder . . . just some sick fella that needs to get his feet back under him before he sets back out for wherever it was he was goin'. Where that is or, for that matter, who he is ain't none of your business."

Jonathan couldn't be certain, but he believed he detected the trace of a threat in Otis's words. Just as when he was a boy out in the schoolyard, threatened physically by the older bullies for sticking his nose where it didn't belong, the prospect of finding out about the stranger instantly became far more attractive.

"You mean to say that you don't know the man's identity?"

"Nope." Otis shrugged.

"And that fact sits well with you?"

Jonathan asked incredulously. "A stranger living among us and you don't know the slightest thing about him! Why, he could be a fugitive from the law, or a murderer or bank robber or swindler who's looking to take unfair advantage of all of us!"

"If he is, he's gonna be in for one hell of a surprise when he finds we ain't got enough to afford a pot to piss in." Otis guffawed, his belly jiggling as if it were a roiling sea. "Put it out of your head and go back to sellin' your trinkets, Moseley. I ain't no detective from one of them pulp magazines, but even a guy like me can plainly see that that fella upstairs is 'bout as dangerous to us as a cat that done got caught in a whirlwind!" With that, Otis took a long draw on his whiskey, rearranged his pillows, closed his eyes, and gave the clear indication that any further conversation would be unwise.

Not wanting to push his luck too far, Jonathan made his way to the courtyard at the rear of the building. He'd held the slim hope that he would once again come across Rachel as she hung laundry on the line, giving him the opportunity to resume his courtship, but the courtyard was empty save for that brat of a spoiled child, Charlotte, and her mangy dog.

Jonathan was about to go back inside, to retreat to his room where he would once again plot his eventual breaching of Rachel's defenses, when a sudden inspiration struck him. *Surely, inducing Charlotte to tell me what I want to know would be a simple matter...* Where Otis had been reticent, he assumed that the little girl would offer little resistance; she was a fish on the end of his line that just needed to be reeled in.

"Charlotte?" he called as sweetly as he could manage. "Charlotte, might I have a word with you, my dear?"

For a moment, Jonathan worried that the girl would run. She looked at him, surprise showing on her face at his having spoken to her, and then over her shoulder toward the alley and escape, but eventually she came closer, with the mutt at her side.

"How are you this fine day?" he asked gently, trying to be as nice as he could but knowing that it sounded forced. Being kind to children certainly wasn't something that came naturally to him; their dull-wittedness drove him half out of his mind and trying to understand their rambling prattle was nearly enough to make him pull his remaining hair out.

"All right, I guess," she mumbled, kicking absently at a pebble at her feet.

"Say, Charlotte, I was wondering if you knew anything about the stranger who is staying in the room next to mine."

"He's not a stranger."

"You know who he is?" Jonathan asked delightedly. "You know his name?"

"Nope," Charlotte answered with a shake of her curly hair, "but he's no stranger. I took care of him in the woods . . . well, Jasper and I did, anyways. He's as nice as can be."

"But . . . you don't even know his name?"

"Only Rachel does," the girl explained innocently. "But she told me that I wasn't allowed to ask what it was, all on account of his not feelin' well. She wouldn't let me ask no questions, but that's all right with Jasper and me. Even if we don't know what to call him, we like him just the same."

Jonathan didn't hear much after Charlotte mentioned Rachel's name; his mind was stuck on the fact that his beloved had somehow grown close to the stranger, had been taken into his confidence and learned his name. He began to see the man as a rival, another suitor for Rachel's affections, and, even worse for his dreams, she seemed to be falling for his attempt; she was nothing but a fly to be caught in the man's spiderweb of lies!

And that is something that will not do!

"Your uncle said that the man was sick," Jonathan pressed. "Is that why Rachel is spending so much time in his room?"

"She's the one tendin' to him, but I'm sure I could do it," Charlotte pouted. "I was doin' just fine out in the woods."

"I'm sure you were, dear."

Certain that he could learn nothing further, Jonathan sent Charlotte back to her playing, and she was only to happy to oblige. When she ran away, Jasper hung back, staring at Jonathan with the hackles on the back of his neck raised, unblinking eyes boring holes into the man for a moment, before he too headed off for more entertaining exploits.

Jonathan knew that something, some sort of secret, was being kept from him, and that was a state of affairs that simply would not do. Clearly, Otis had been reluctant to say much, but from what he had gathered from Charlotte, he finally had something to piece together. Rachel was complicit! Beginning with the way she doted upon the sick man and ending with the preventive way she had kept her niece from asking questions—all pointed to the fact that there was a reason to hide the truth.

But the worst part of all was that the stranger was allowed to be so close to Rachel; with his illness, he would see her nearly every time he woke and would hear her voice before all others. *No man other than myself should receive such luxury!*

Stalking back to his room, Jonathan knew that he couldn't allow Rachel's relationship with the man to go too far lest his own dreams and plans for the future be ruined forever.

Somehow, some way, I will get to the bottom of this.

*   *   *

Zachary Tucker crushed the butt of his still smoldering cigar under his booted foot with an angry zeal that would have shocked most of his bank's customers. His fists were tightly balled and his temple throbbed whenever he gave thought to being denied what he wanted by Eliza Watkins, her drunken brother, Otis, but especially by the woman's daughter, Rachel.

"Damn their stubbornness!"

Nearly two weeks had passed since he had set foot inside the dilapidated boardinghouse and made his case to Rachel that she induce her mother to take his generous offer and sell him their property. He'd walked away elated, sure that she would make Eliza see reason, realize that they would be so much better off with money rather than memories that would never pay their debts. He'd been confident that all of his problems with the Gaitskill Lumber Company would soon be gone, forgotten in the rousing success of his ever-growing business.

But something had gone wrong.

He had waited, first day after day and then week after week, hoping that Rachel would come to him with the news that they had agreed to accept his offer. But time had passed without a word. Slowly, his frustration had become anger.

"I told you they wouldn't take the money."

Zachary turned to look at Travis Jefferson. The man lounged easily in one of the chairs in front of the desk, his hat in one hand as the other absently combed through his thick blond hair. Travis's words could have been taken as arrogance, a smugness bordering on insubordination, but his face betrayed nothing. Besides, as much as Zachary was loath to admit it, his lackey was right; he had underestimated Eliza Watkins and her brood's resolve to retain their ownership of the boarding-house.

"It is unfortunate that you were correct," Zachary angrily agreed. He made no attempt to show Travis that he was unhappy with his speaking; he had found that every once in a great while it was advantageous to let his underlings believe that they were right.

"I reckon that the question facing us now is what to do about it."

Without answering, Zachary went to his

desk and picked up the latest telegram he'd received from the lumber company. In it, they had informed him of their growing impatience and had expressed just how much longer they were willing to wait to receive what they had been promised.

"Three weeks," he spat. "All we have left is three weeks."

"Ain't a lot of time."

"No, it's not," Zachary agreed. "So whatever it is we decide to do needs to get results."

Just the thought of his deal with the lumber company going sour was enough to make Zachary sick to his stomach. Not only would he have lost many long months' worth of diligent work, but the future loss to the bank, and therefore to his pocket, would be almost immeasurable. That he would be thwarted by his dead brother's family was simply adding insult to injury. **And that cannot be allowed!**

"We should do what I suggested a ways back," Travis said solemnly.

"Which is?" Zachary snapped.

"It's like I said when the company sent that highfalutin lawyer up here to rattle our cage," the man explained as he struck a match against the heel of his boot and brought the flame against his cigarette. "You leave me alone with them Watkins folks for a bit and there won't be no problem that can't be overcome. It's mighty amazin' what a little persuasion can accomplish."

"You mean hurt them . . ."

"Only if they're disagreeable."

Zachary sighed and turned back to the window. Though he had often used Travis Jefferson's propensity for violence for his own ends before, breaking a debtor's arm or silencing a loose tongue, he felt a sense of reluctance to use him this time. He wasn't sure from where this unwillingness sprang; maybe there were some lingering feelings for his brother lurking in the depths of his heart. The thought of Rachel at the man's mercy, defenseless and vulnerable, made him a bit squeamish.

Still, he had no doubts what was at stake. If he were to fail in this endeavor, he would never control Carlson. Ever since Mason had foolishly set off for the battlefields of Europe, Zachary had bided his time, made his plans, and ruthlessly followed his own self-interest until he had secured what was rightfully his. Now, on the cusp of getting what he had always wanted, was no time to get cold feet. That Eliza Watkins and her family refused to acknowledge what was for the best wasn't his fault, and he would be damned if he would be the one to suffer. If they couldn't see reason, then let them suffer the consequences.

"What would you do to them?" he asked.

"You know me, Mr. Tucker." Travis chuckled. "I'll do whatever it takes."

Spinning around, Zachary smashed his fist down onto his desk so hard that his cigars nearly jumped from their box. "Tell me what it is you plan to do to them!"

Even in the face of his boss's fury, Travis Jefferson showed no sign of being spooked by the outburst. Calmly, he took a drag of his cigarette and blew an undulating stream of smoke toward the ceiling. With eyes as flat and cold as stone, he looked at Zachary and said, "If they don't give you what you want, they will know pain. Whether it's a broken bone or bloodshed, that'll be up to them. Makes no difference if it's man or woman, ain't nobody gonna keep us from givin' them lumber-men what they want."

Beads of sweat stood out on Zachary's forehead as he contemplated what Travis had said. Agitated, he nodded a couple of times and said, "Good, good . . . that's just fine. But for now I only want you to deal with Otis Simmons and not any of the women. Maybe if some harm comes to him, the other two will be willing to make a deal."

"You sure you don't want it to be the little girl?" Travis asked. "Nothin' gets results like harmin' a child."

Zachary tried not to show his revulsion as he answered. "Just do as I told you and give Otis a reason to change his sister's mind. Hopefully it will be the only time you need to make an impression."

"Then I best make it a good one."

Before once again turning back to the window, Zachary took a cigar from its box, lit it, and drew deeply of the acrid smoke. Staring out at the bustling street beneath him, he knew that he was stepping over the line; by sending Travis to encourage them to sell, he was giving in to his desperation. But great men didn't wait for opportunity to come to them, they seized it by the throat and refused to let go.

And that is exactly what I will do!

Chapter Eighteen

RACHEL ENTERED THE ROOM at the head of the stairs carrying a tray with Mason's lunch and found him leaning back in bed, staring out the window. Sheets of rain pounded against the glass, making it hard to see outside. The fall days had grown much cooler as October turned into November, sending a wet chill down her spine every time she went outdoors. Browned leaves, cascading from the safety of their branches, were carried along by the insistent winds. Soon there would be snow.

When Rachel placed Mason's tray on the bedside table, he didn't offer a word in reply. For the last two days, ever since he had admitted his true identity to her, he had largely remained silent during her visits, offering little more than mumbled thanks. With this day seeming to be no different, Rachel started to leave, only to be stopped before she could reach the hallway door by the sound of Mason's voice.

"The rain reminds me of France," he said softly, his voice a whisper.

Turning around to face him, Rachel found Mason still staring blankly out the streaked window, his blue eyes fixed upon some distant point. Simply hearing him speak gave her heart a start, and though she wanted to say something, anything, that might keep him going, she feared that the sound of her voice would once again cause him to fall silent. So instead she waited, hoping that Mason would find the strength to continue.

"It rained almost every day when I was in France," Mason finally continued. "Gray clouds seemed to always cover the sky, sweeping out to the farthest horizon, always full of rain. Nothing was ever dry—socks, books, ammunition—and the mud crept into every crevice. You could get stuck with every step if you weren't careful. Even when I woke up in the hospital, the sun shone only once a week; but that was all right because the pounding of the rain helped quiet the other men's screams and moans.

"When I was a boy, I used to love the coming of fall," Mason continued as the faintest hint of a smile curled his lips. "I always looked forward to the changing color of the leaves, the smell of fields being burned, and even the feel of cold rain upon my face. No other season, even summer, could compare. It was so special that I insisted Alice and I be married in the fall . . ."

Rachel nodded. "I remember."

The afternoon that Mason and Alice had been married was as gorgeous a day as could have been hoped for. Without a single cloud to mar the September sky, the sun had provided a perfect warmth. Standing outside the church in her best clothes, Rachel remembered that every way she turned, the view was as pretty as any painting. Nearly the entire town turned out to rejoice in the wedding of two of its very best, and the celebration had stretched long into the night.

"Nowadays I can't stand the rain." Mason frowned, finally turning to face her with wet eyes. "All it does is remind me of that damned war and the treasured moments I've lost and can never get back. What in the hell did I have to come back to?"

"You have to go on with your life," she soothed. "Once you're better—"

"It will never be better!"

Watching Mason wallow in his own misery, allowing his many regrets and aching remorse to get the better of him, to simply give up without a fight, made Rachel furious. Still, knowing all that the man had been through, she tamped down her anger; she hoped that by letting him vent his rage, he might get better.

"Your life is waiting for you."

"Which life are you talking about, Rachel?" he snapped. "The life I left behind in Carlson? Do you think I can just go back to my father and all will be forgiven, the prodigal son finally returns, and that I'll just be given back my position at the bank? Can you even imagine the horror-struck look on my brother's face if I were to walk in the door?"

The mention of Zachary Tucker sent a chill down Rachel's spine. It had been two weeks since he had approached her about selling the boardinghouse. She wondered which situation would have made him angrier: that his offer for their property had been rejected or that his brother was still alive.

"Or are you talking about the life that I have spent the last seven years living, traveling around in the darkness of a freight car, occasionally fighting for my belongings if not my life, hiding from the police, and hardly managing to scrape up enough money for food?"

"So instead you're just going to give up," she answered. "Do nothing?"

Mason remained silent, his jaw locked tight.

"Don't you dare ignore me, Mason Tucker," she warned, her voice allowing her anger to seep in. "Because I never had the luxury of giving up. When my sister died, I couldn't stay in bed all day, watching the world go by. I had a child to raise, your child, a child who, as far as the world was concerned, had no parents, no one to watch out for her. So I took that responsibility and it changed my life, whether I truly wanted it to or not."

"It's not the same," Mason disagreed.

"The hell it's not!"

"I had everything I ever loved taken away from me!"

"You act as if Alice's death affected only you!" Rachel shouted in response. "I miss my sister just as much as you do! Living in this house where the memories of her lurk around every corner, seeing the pity on people's faces as I walk about town, and even watching Charlotte say something or have an expression cross her face that reminds me of Alice . . . all of these things are painful! But I have never quit, never walked away from the people who count on me to do what is expected, what is right."

"Rachel, I—"

"Whether you want to admit it to yourself or not, you have a responsibility to Charlotte," she barked; this time, she was the one who would not allow him to answer. "It makes no difference that you haven't been a part of her life for the last eight years, you are still her father! Eventually, you are going to have to own up to that fact for her sake, every bit as much as for your own. She needs to know that she has a father, that she's not as alone in this world as she believes. While you might worry that you're not ready, it makes no difference when it comes to Charlotte's life. None of these choices are going to be easy, they will probably be painful, but you are going to make them, Mason! Of that you should have absolutely no doubt!"

Having said all that she thought Mason needed to hear, Rachel once again turned to the door. This time, when he spoke, she pretended she didn't hear him, slamming the door behind her.

Carrying a wicker basket full of freshly folded laundry, Rachel entered her mother's room still angry from her confrontation with Mason. After leaving his room, she'd busied herself with washing clothes. With the rainy weather she'd had to dry everything in the basement, but no matter how much she tried occupying her day, she couldn't take her mind off the things he had said.

The booming rumble of thunder rolled

across the sky as Rachel set the basket beside her mother's dresser. Eliza stood in her usual place, peering between the curtains as the world went by without her. She flinched as another flash of lightning lit up the sky.

"I do hope you haven't let Charlotte outside in this horrible weather!"

"She and Jasper are down near the stove; she's drawing," Rachel answered; it had been nearly as hard as pulling teeth to keep Charlotte from pestering Mason. Nearly every chance the girl got, she wanted to be in the sick man's room asking countless questions.

"Oh, thank goodness," Eliza exclaimed, clasping her hands to her chest in obvious relief. "Anyone caught outside in weather like this is just asking for pneumonia or to be struck by lightning!"

With her bundle of clothes delivered, Rachel was ready to exit the room, to leave her mother to her many worries, but just as she was about to open the door, she turned back, a question on her lips. "Mother," she began, "what do you remember about Mason?"

"Mason," Eliza echoed, her attention

pulled away from the chaotic weather, and her eyes focused on some far-distant place. "What I will always remember about Mason Tucker is the first time Alice brought him home and introduced him to me."

"The first time?"

"He actually took me by my hand and gave it a gentle kiss." She smiled as warmly as the stove in the room below. "Well, Alice turned a shade of red brighter than any beet! Of course, I was flattered, who wouldn't be? When you are a midwife, even though your work is important, it isn't as if you're often treated as a proper lady."

"He was probably just trying to make a good impression."

Eliza nodded. "And at that he succeeded. But it was more than that. He hadn't acted in such a way to give false flattery, but instead because he had the God-given ability to genuinely charm anyone. He'd already done it with Alice, so why not her mother? How many other people felt exactly the same way when they first met?"

Rachel knew that her mother was correct; the first time she had laid eyes on Mason Tucker, as she carefully peeked through the curtains and spied on her older sister and her new beau where they sat talking on the porch, she had been mesmerized by both his good looks and personality. When she was introduced to him, she'd hoped beyond hope that she hadn't flushed with the excitement she had so clearly felt.

"But Mason was so much more than that," Eliza continued. "In his job at the bank, he had the unfortunate duty of having to speak to those families who couldn't manage to pay their debts. He had to make difficult decisions, balancing what his father expected of him with what was right. But in the end, he would never allow one of those men or women to give up hope. He kept urging them to work hard, never to give up, and assuring them that everything would work itself out. Stories like Archie Grace's never happened in those days."

Listening to her mother's words, Rachel contrasted the Mason Eliza remembered with the man lying in the room down the hall. In his former life he had never given up; now he struck her as a man no longer willing to fight for what he cared for or believed in. In many ways, it appeared that the man who had left Carlson all those many years ago actually *had* died on the battlefields of France.

But there was another part of her that couldn't help but wonder if her mother was also right. Maybe the optimism she re-membered in Mason, the refusal to sur-render even when things seemed their gloomiest, was still inside the man. Maybe in the face of the trauma he had experi-enced since returning to Carlson, he only needed time to find the strength he would need to carry on. Briefly, she worried that maybe she had been too hard on him.

"Oh, how I wish he hadn't died in that war," Eliza continued. "As much for Char-lotte's sake as for Alice's or my own. There is no doubt in my mind that he would have made an excellent father."

Rachel felt faint. Hearing Eliza speak about Mason as if he were dead made her realize just how great a secret she was keeping. Heretofore unasked questions raced around in her mind.

What will be the reaction when ev-eryone learns the truth?

Will my mother be angry?

When will be the right time to acknowledge that Mason is alive?

"Why did you ask about Mason?" her mother asked.

"No . . . no reason . . ." Rachel stammered. "It's just that . . . I was remembering the day that he and Alice were married . . . and how different the weather was compared to today."

"It was a beautiful day," Eliza agreed with a smile.

Back out in the hallway, the door to her mother's room shut behind her, Rachel felt guilty about lying. Though at that moment she had no choice but to keep Mason's remarkable return a secret, she knew that the occasion would soon come where she would no longer be able to hide the truth. For now, the consequences of her deceit would remain unknown.

Rachel also knew that she had to reconsider Mason's plight. Her own memories of the man closely resembled those of her mother; he had been kind, hardworking, and blessed with a charm few men possessed. While the years he spent away had hardened him, she didn't know if the man he had been still existed beneath the rough surface.

Only time would tell.

Mason sat silently watching the rain fall against his window. Lightning crashed and thunder roared as the storm gained in intensity, the strength of the wind enough to drive the branches of a nearby elm tree against the glass. Suddenly, the door to his room burst open and, as tempestuous as the outside weather, Charlotte came running in.

"Look what I did!" she shouted. "It took all afternoon, but look what I did for you!"

Rushing over to the side of the bed, with a smile that spread ear to ear, Charlotte thrust a sheet of paper into his hands. The paper was covered with many drawings: a house, several trees, and a large sun sharing the sky with a pair of puffy clouds. But what stood out was a gathering of people: a man lying in a bed, a woman at his side, a small girl with blonde braids, and, right beside her, a big dog with its tongue hanging out the side of its mouth. The drawing was crude, clearly that of a child, but there was no mistaking who everyone was supposed to be.

"That's you in the bed," Charlotte declared proudly. With one of her small fingers, she pointed out everyone else. "That's Rachel, and me, and that there's Jasper . . . he woulda been mad if he wasn't in it."

"It's lovely." Mason smiled weakly.

"I made it for you to have."

"Thank you, Charlotte."

Though he hated to admit it to himself, there was a part of Mason that found it uncomfortable to be around Charlotte ever since he learned that she was his daughter with Alice. Every time he looked at her face, heard her infectious laugh, or felt her hand against his own, he was reminded of his wife. It was hardly the girl's fault, but it made him uneasy all the same.

"Once you're walkin' around," Charlotte kept talking, "I'll make you another one, then at Christmastime, and then in the spring, and maybe even when you go and—"

"Wait, Charlotte, wait," Mason cautioned her. "I . . . I don't know how much longer I'll . . . be staying here with you . . ." Even as he spoke the words, Mason understood that they were true; no matter how much thought he had given to the decision facing him, he truly didn't know what course of action he should take. After his confrontation with Rachel, her accusations still ringing in his ears, he didn't know how he could possibly stay.

"You . . . you might be going?" Charlotte asked haltingly.

"Once I'm back on my feet I might need to—"

"Stay a little longer!" Charlotte cried. "Oh, please, stay a little longer!"

With that, she collapsed onto the side of the bed and buried her head into Mason's side. Her small hands found his, holding on tightly as her shoulders shook with sobbing. Even Jasper was taken aback by her outburst, backing away toward the door with his tail between his legs.

Mason was speechless. He placed one hand on Charlotte's back and tried his best to comfort her, but to no apparent effect. Suddenly Mason understood just what his daughter had been missing for all of the years he was gone. Though Otis undoubtedly did his best, Charlotte had no father.

Although she was growing up in a loving home surrounded by a family that did all they could for her, the void he had created in her life had never been filled.

"I don't want you to go!" she sobbed. "Why . . . why won't you stay . . . a little longer?"

And to that, Mason Tucker had no answer.

Chapter Nineteen

OTIS SIMMONS STUMBLED down the darkened streets of Carlson, whistling a nameless tune. His made-up song and footsteps echoed off shuttered windows, closed doors, and empty boardwalks. Although night had long since descended upon the sleeping town and the moon hung full in the star-laden sky, he traveled a route he knew well. Even given his current state, he could find his way home.

I'm drunk . . . and proud of it . . .

Many an hour had passed since Otis was able to count the number of glasses of whiskey he had poured down his throat.

One toast had followed the next, all blurring together into a swirling vision of raised glasses and forgotten words. When he first arrived at the tavern, he had found a few of his friends, but they had all left early. Not wanting to go home, he'd continued imbibing. He'd never been one to let a lack of company keep him from a good time; often he drank to his own loneliness.

"And I had me a helluva time," he assured himself.

Even with the crisp chill of the fall night, Otis didn't feel cold. With the more than ample blubber on his belly and the amount of whiskey he had filled it with, contented warmth spread across his body. Besides, it wasn't anywhere near the time of year to be worried; in the depths of winter he would be concerned, because not to make it home then could mean death.

Fortunately, he'd managed to fill his own flask before the tavern had closed; he had long ago learned how disappointing it was to go home empty-handed. Unscrewing the cap, he tipped the liquor to his lips and drank deeply. Suddenly, the urge to urinate overcame him, and he reeled over to a secluded corner, undid his trousers, and proceeded to relieve himself, all the while never stopping his drinking for a moment. **Might as well fill up as I empty out!**

Otis was just about to finish when a sudden clamor rose behind him. Scarcely managing to turn around without falling over, he stared into the dark but saw nothing. With a shrug of his shoulders, he dismissed the sound as that of a cat out rummaging for food or for another feline to cozy up with for the night. Taking another gulp from his flask before screwing on the cap, he fumbled to close his pants and headed on his way.

Turning down the alley that led to the rear of the boardinghouse, Otis thought about the stranger Rachel had installed in the upstairs bedroom. The way that she doted on the man struck him as odd, but though he had wondered a time or two whether he should tell his sister, he'd managed to hold his tongue. Whatever reason his niece had in keeping the man a secret from Eliza must be good enough; Rachel had always had a good head on her shoulders and there was no point in doubting her now. Besides, being able to needle that cheap bastard Moseley about it had been a hell of a thrill!

Reaching the boardinghouse yard, Otis wondered how he was going to manage to sneak back into the house undetected. The last time he had come home in a drunken stupor, bumbling and stumbling inside as he made enough racket to wake the dead, Rachel had given him a tongue-lashing every bit as harsh as it was well deserved. Knowing that he might need a bit of alcoholic confidence, he retrieved his flask from his pocket. Thus deep in thought, he hardly heard the sudden pounding of footsteps behind him before something struck him and a shooting pain laced up and down his left arm.

"What in the—?!" he barked.

Crashing to the ground in a heap, Otis let his flask fly from his fingers and slide into the cold grass far out of reach. Looking back, he saw a shadowy silhouette raise something he thought might be a metal pipe or a piece of wood, and then bring it down hard upon his wounded arm. The pain racing across his body was so great, so utterly overpowering, that Otis couldn't even manage to scream, the sound remaining stuck in his craw. Reflexively, his other hand groped for his wounded arm, but even that touch ached.

Over and over again, the weapon was smashed into Otis's flesh, each flare of agony worse than the last. After one solid blow, the fingers of his other hand throbbed painfully, and he gave up any hope of warding off further punishment. Weakly, he tried to roll away, to escape from the beating that seemed as if it would never end, when one last blow with an audible crack broke the bone of his arm.

It was then that Otis found the strength to scream out, but even as he was blinded by pain, only the very first strains of his suffering were heard before a strong hand was clamped down on his mouth, silencing him.

Though his eyes wanted to close, to try to erase the crippling ache by shutting everything out, Otis forced them to stay open. At first, all he could see was the starry night, but that vision was soon replaced by another; a face that he couldn't see clearly enough in the darkness to identify. It was then that a man's voice gruffly spoke.

"Let this be a warnin' to you," he said, "that you best get any idea of holdin' on to this house out of your head. There's only gonna be one chance to do what's right, and that's sell this shithole and take what's been offered.

"You understand what I'm sayin'?" the man asked, and to encourage Otis to respond, he shook the wounded man's head so hard that his jowls quivered.

Otis could only nod in answer.

"If you don't do what I've asked, I'm gonna come back and find you," the assailant continued, the heat of his breath only inches from Otis's face, "and if stupidity gets the better of you, I'm gonna do far more than just bust a bone in your arm, I'm gonna cut you from ear to ear."

For emphasis, the unknown attacker gave Otis's broken arm a solid punch, sending such pain racing through his body that he nearly fell unconscious. Stars fluttered not only in the sky, but before his very eyes as darkness steadily encroached, his scream unheard as it was muffled in the man's never-flinching hand.

"Mark my words," the man warned, "sell this house or it will be your life."

Without another word, the attacker let go of Otis and quickly raced down the alley, leaving his victim alone with his misery.

Travis Jefferson hurried down the alley, careful not to be seen. Behind him, the fat man's moans were soon lost in the night. Absently, Travis tossed his weapon into the deepest recesses of the alley; the sturdy piece of oak had done what he intended; it inflicted enough damage.

Zachary Tucker's request had been easy to fulfill. Watching his prey, waiting for the right moment to strike, had not required great effort; Otis Simmons had been far more interested in his liquor than in noticing that he was being followed. Waiting outside the tavern for the man to leave had been a bit boring, but once the oaf had finished his indulging, Travis had simply trailed along behind and seized the opportune moment to strike.

Beating the man had been as easy for Travis as it would have been for him to whip a dog; save for the whining and yelping, it was no chore at all. The halfhearted way Otis had tried to deflect the blows raining down on him had amused Travis. Over and over he had struck, only stopping when he heard the telltale sound of breaking bone.

A part of Travis wished he could have gone further; a broken arm was certainly a step in the right direction, but if he had been able to spill a little blood, well, that might have ensured that bitch Eliza Watkins and her family would do what Zachary wanted. After all, fear was an amazingly effective tool. But if there was one thing he had learned during the time he had worked for Zachary Tucker, it was that he was a man who should never be crossed. In the end, that trait was what he admired about his employer, his callous ruthlessness.

Just like me . . .

Another part of Travis hoped that the fool wouldn't heed his advice; Otis Simmons had long since proven that he wasn't the smartest man in Carlson. Maybe on the next trip he'd get his chance with Rachel Watkins. In his ample experience, if there was one thing an uptight, haughty young thing like her needed, it was a round or two with a real man, the sort of man who wouldn't take no for an answer. It angered him the way she had led Mr. Tucker on, apparently giving her word about the sale of the boardinghouse, then withdrawing. Such trickery needed punishment.

Still, he had done what he was asked. The next move was theirs, and depending upon the answer given, he might still have some mischief to play.

When he left the alleyway, Travis Jefferson was smiling.

Rachel awoke from a pleasant dream with a start, a feeling nagging at her that something was wrong. A sense of dread weighed upon her. Anxiously, she blinked her eyes as she tried to shake the cobwebs of sleep from her mind.

The inside of her room was pitch black save for the sliver of moonlight that eased in through a crack in her curtains. Located on the first floor and facing toward the courtyard, Rachel's room was sparsely furnished: a small bed, a scratched and chipped dresser topped by a warped mirror, and a rickety nightstand. Slowly, her eyes adjusted to the gloom.

She had heard a strange sound, a noise

that was out of place, but as she strained to listen, she didn't hear it again. Even in the later fall months, she often slept with the window cracked open; she liked to let the sounds of the night carry her off to slumber. Tonight, the curtains rustled with the softest of breezes, carrying with it the insistent chill that announced the changing of seasons. Just as she was about to give up, to turn her head back to her pillow and return to her dreams, she once again heard the faint cry.

". . . help . . . can't . . . arm . . ."

Rachel rose from her bed, threw a knitted shawl over the top of her nightgown, and moved toward the window. Though the words had been barely more than a whisper, she knew that she hadn't imagined them. Looking out into the gloomy night, she couldn't see much at first, but as her eyes continued to adjust, there on the ground . . .

". . . damn . . . arm . . ." came another moan.

"Otis?" she gasped, suddenly recognizing the voice.

Without a moment's hesitation, Rachel rushed from the sleeping house and out into the cool night of the courtyard. Otis lay flat on his back in the dew-dampened grass just off the alley. In the light shed by the nearly full moon, she could see that he was in great pain; air hissed through gritted teeth, enormous beads of sweat stood out on his forehead, and one arm seemed to be cradling the other. He didn't appear to notice her approach; his eyes were closed tight and his face a mask of agony.

Kneeling down beside her uncle, Rachel's hand hesitantly went to the man's left arm. She had no more than touched it when his eyes flew wide open and he bellowed, "God damn it!"

"It's me, Uncle Otis," she soothed. "It's Rachel."

"My arm's busted, Rachel," he answered, panic in his voice. "It's busted!"

"What happened?" she asked, unsure of what to do. "Did you fall?"

"Someone . . . someone jumped me and . . . and whacked my arm . . ."

Intense worry raced across Rachel's chest; whoever it was who had attacked her uncle might still be lurking around! Nervously, she looked up and down the alleyway, but it was swathed so deeply in shadows that she couldn't be completely certain that they were alone. Still, her responsibility to see to her uncle's injury was her primary concern. She would not let him lie there.

"Are you hurt anywhere else?" she asked, pulling herself together.

"Just . . . just my damn arm . . ."

As her uncle spoke, Rachel checked the rest of his body. A knot was growing on the side of his head, but that could very well have come from his hitting the ground. The real danger would have been from a vicious cut or another broken bone.

There was no denying that the damage to Otis's arm was severe: just above the elbow, it appeared to crook a bit in the opposite direction. When she was a little girl, she'd seen a boy fall from a tree and break his arm, a wound that looked extremely similar to her uncle's malady. Once again she tried to touch the arm, and again Otis yelped.

"We have to get you inside," she muttered.

Otis could only groan in answer.

Rachel understood that moving her uncle would be a difficult task; given his enor-

mous bulk, she worried that she would
never be able to manage alone. Neverthe-
less, Mason's continued weakness from
his illness made it impossible for him to
help. Since the only other man in the
boardinghouse was Jonathan Moseley,
and she wasn't about to go anywhere near
him, she knew that she was on her own.

"Uncle Otis," she said, "I'm going to
need your help to do this."

"I'll give you all I got, darlin'."

Carefully, they rolled Otis slightly to his
right where he was able to use his good
arm to push himself into a sitting position.
Then, with Rachel making certain that she
didn't bump his wounded arm, they managed to get him forward onto his knees.
Finally, with every muscle in her body
straining with the effort, they succeeded in
getting him to his unsteady feet.

"Let's just get our bearings," she said,
resting for what was to come.

"I ain't got much of those to begin with."

With both of them breathing hard, Rachel
could plainly smell the alcohol on the man.
She was not surprised to learn that Otis
had been attacked as he returned from
the tavern. Still, she was a bit disheartened;

this would've been hard to do if he were sober.

Slowly, taking each step carefully, they made their way across the courtyard. Closer and closer they came toward the back door, but Rachel's fears only intensified. She worried that Otis would fall and hurt himself more, but somehow he managed to stay on his feet.

"The fella . . . who attacked me . . . said . . ." Otis said hesitantly.

"What? What did he say?" Rachel prodded.

"He . . . he said we . . . need to sell . . . the house . . ."

"Hush, Uncle Otis," she shushed him as the reason for the attack became obvious to her. "Let's just get you inside."

Without a shadow of a doubt, Rachel knew that Zachary Tucker was behind the attack upon her uncle. Before that moment, she'd thought the banker to be nothing more than a despicable snake only after profit, but now she knew she had underestimated his capacity for evil. Upset that his bid to purchase the boardinghouse had been declined, he'd undoubtedly sent some lackey to apply pressure, to make them all so fearful for their safety that they had no choice but to cave in to his demands.

That no-good bastard!

Not for the first time, Rachel marveled that Zachary Tucker and his brother were related. Mason, she knew, was honorable and decent, and she believed that, in the end, he would do what was right by Charlotte. That fate had been so cruel as to take Mason from all of their lives and leave Zachary in his place, working his wicked machinations, was nearly more than Rachel could accept.

Carefully the two of them made their way through the back door, across the small kitchen, and through a narrow doorway before settling Otis in his favorite chair in the sitting room. Lowering his ample girth into his seat, the wounded man grimaced in obvious pain.

"I need to go for the doctor," Rachel explained. "Can you stay here?"

"I'd be better . . . if I had my flask . . ."

"That'll just have to wait," she said with a weak smile. "Once I fetch Dr. Clark, I'll be right back."

"Me and my broken arm . . . ain't goin' nowhere."

With her heart full of equal measures of worry and anger, Rachel left the house.

By the time Dr. Clark had come and gone, Otis was sleeping fitfully. Thankfully, the freshly wakened physician had been able to reset the broken arm. Otis had shouted so loudly that he would have roused the whole town had it not been for the leather strap he had been given to bite down on.

"I'm sorry about all this, Otis," Dr. Clark said.

"Not . . . not as sorry . . . as I am . . . I bet . . ." Otis replied tearfully.

A makeshift sling had been improvised to keep the arm immobile. Come morning, Dr. Clark would return to set it in plaster. A pill he had been given and the contents of the flask Rachel had retrieved from the yard put Otis to sleep, but this was an injury he would be suffering from for some time to come.

With Otis repositioned in his own room, Rachel shut the door behind her as she left, closing off the sound of her uncle's snoring. The rest of the house still remained silent except for the usual creaking and groaning of the old building. Regardless, Rachel's heart thundered.

Her anger at Zachary Tucker had not subsided since she first had realized it was he who was behind the attack on her uncle. *How dare he do something so very cowardly as harm an innocent old man!* She had every intention to go down to the bank, march into his office, and give him a piece of her mind. If his goal was to make them frightened enough to sell the boardinghouse, he was going to be in for quite a surprise.

Thinking about one Tucker man made Rachel aware of the other. She made her way up the tall flight of stairs and carefully opened the door to Mason's room. From the sliver of light that followed her in from the hall, she could see that he was sleeping soundly, the wool blanket that covered his chest rising and falling rhythmically. Tomorrow, she would tell him of her many concerns about Zachary; maybe Mason would have a clearer idea of what they should do. Watching his peaceful sleep, Rachel found it so inviting that she decided to go and get some of her own.

Rachel had no more than pulled the door shut when strong hands grabbed her by the waist and yanked her backward. She scrambled wildly for something to grab hold of, but the strength of her attacker was too great for her to fight off. Before she knew what had happened, she had been dragged from the light of the hall to a place of darkness, a hand pressed down so tightly over her mouth that she found it hard to breathe.

There wasn't even time to scream.

Chapter Twenty

EVEN AS RACHEL WATKINS struggled futilely against him, Jonathan Moseley could not help but revel in the warmth of her body, the fragrant smell of her skin, and even the spirit of her fight. After all, there was much to love about this woman who eventually would become his wife.

Jonathan pushed the door shut with his foot and they were both instantly plunged into darkness. Although Rachel's heart was thundering as her breath frantically filled and emptied her lungs, he remained the essence of calm; there was no doubt in his mind that what he was doing was right. Regardless of how hard she fought to free herself from his grasp, Jonathan felt safe in the fact that his body was far stronger than the impression given by his tall, spindly frame; besides, he knew there would never come a day where he would be so weak as to let her go.

"You don't need to fight it any longer, my dear," he whispered in her ear.

For an instant, Rachel's struggle subsided, no doubt because she now knew who had placed hands upon her. When that realization completely sank in, her resistance grew even more intense.

"Hush, hush, darling. You're with me now."

And that is exactly as it should be . . .

Jonathan had been wakened by the sound of voices rising from the first floor of the boardinghouse. Opening his door slightly, he had strained to listen as the doctor and Rachel cared for Otis. Later, he had watched Rachel come up the stairs. For the briefest of instants, he thought that she would come to his door, to finally acknowledge her own passionate feelings for him and that he had been right about their being destined for each other. His heart began to pound loudly with anticipation of his fondest dreams coming true. As she had drawn nearer, Jonathan led himself to believe that they were about to begin the life he knew they were destined to lead.

But then she had gone to the stranger's door . . .

In that moment, Jonathan had known that Rachel was truly confused. That she was choosing to care for a man she knew nothing about, a man who could potentially pose a danger to them all, was more than he could continue to bear. He had waited angrily, ears straining to hear her come back out into the hall, and then he had struck.

"Everything will be all right, my dear," he soothed, knowing that if she could just listen to him for a moment, hear his loving voice, she would surely understand and would no longer fight. "Now that we are together, everything will be as it should, as it always was meant to be."

But even as Jonathan spoke to calm her, he could feel his own ardor stirring, his very loins afire with a burning passion. He had never before allowed himself to be so close to her, to touch her, close enough for his true feelings to be released. As if it had a mind all its own, his free hand began to roam beneath Rachel's skirt, up her quivering thighs, across her squirming stomach, and finally to squeeze her breasts.

"We belong together . . . as husband and wife . . ." he moaned.

Rachel struggled mightily, shouting something into the palm of his hand still clamped down over her mouth; Jonathan couldn't be certain, but he could hope that she was declaring her own pent-up feelings for him.

"I know just how you feel," he whispered in her ear.

Touching Rachel after so many long weeks of frustration now stoked his fires to fury. An aching spread across the front of his trousers; his manhood was fully erect. He had little doubt that his pain would end only upon its release.

"You should have just taken my offer and come with me to the woods," he panted as his free hand struggled to undo his trousers, and he used the weight of his body to prevent Rachel from breaking free of his grasp. "If you had, you would have

known me to be an honorable man, someone you could love and trust, and all of
this would've been unnecessary."

Just as Jonathan finally managed to
thread the clasp of his belt, Rachel drove
her elbow into his ribs, and in the immediate
mixture of stinging pain and startling confusion, he let go of her. In an instant, she shot
for the freedom beyond the door to his room,
but he managed to fall toward her and with
his long reach snatched her by the skirt and
pulled her to the floor directly in front of the
door. Both of them landed with a resounding thud, a sound Jonathan feared might
bring unwanted attention.

Clawing desperately for the door, Rachel
gave him more reason to worry. She
shouted, "Help! Somebody help me!"

Instantly, Jonathan was upon her. Strad-
dling her chest, he pinned her to the floor
as his previously tender feelings gave way
to a blinding anger. Savagely, he slapped
her across the face, first with the front of
his open hand and then with the back,
snapping her head from side to side. Rachel offered no more resistance, the fight
draining out of her as easily as if he had
smashed a grape under his foot.

"Why do you deny this?" he snarled. "Why must you make me do this to you? Don't you know what is for the best?"

Angrily, Jonathan tore open the front of Rachel's blouse, popping several of the buttons. In the scant moonlight that filtered in through his window, the rosy tint of her skin was revealed. Her hands never moved to stop him as his fingers sought the soft feel of her breasts, and the excitement coursing through him threatened to overwhelm his pounding heart and the continued pressure in his groin.

It's time for me to take what is mine!

Mason suddenly woke from a deep sleep, his chest filled with a feeling that something was wrong. It was a sensation to which he was well accustomed; for during his years traveling the iron rails that crossed the country, there had been many occasions when his intuition had saved his belongings, not to mention his life. In the darkness of his room, he waited, listening.

". . . help . . . somebody . . ."

In an instant, he was alert. Sliding from between his covers, Mason tentatively put one foot on the floor. In the last several days, with both Rachel and Charlotte's many words of encouragement, along with plenty of nourishment, he had managed to regain a fair amount of his former strength. He had done a little walking around the room, but always with Rachel at his side, ready to catch him if he began to fall. This would be the first time since he collapsed in the cabin that he had attempted to walk by himself.

Before Mason could so much as stand, the sound of a man's angry voice came to his ears. Rachel was in trouble.

Testing first one foot and then the other, Mason stood and began to move along the edge of the bed, one hand upon the mattress and then the footboard. Though his room was dark, he had no trouble seeing, another benefit of his years spent sleeping in rail cars. Finally, reaching the far end of the bed, he knew that he would be forced to let go and walk the few feet to the safety of the door.

I can do this . . .

Taking deep breaths, Mason finally convinced himself to let go, traversing his way across as sporadic tremors shot up the length of his weak legs. His knees quaked, but he didn't fall. The coolness of the November night touched upon the sweat standing on his brow, but he didn't shiver, his mind set firmly on the task before him. After a brief pause leaning against the doorframe, he opened the door to the hall.

Outside, faint light rose up from the bottom of the stairs. In the scant illumination afforded him, Mason could see that all the doors in the upper hallway were closed. Because this was the first time he had been out of his room, the memories of his many visits to the boardinghouse at Alice's side began to rush back at him, but he tamped down the flood, choosing instead to focus upon his worries for Rachel.

"Hello?" he called into the quiet house. "Who's down there?"

He received no answer. There was little doubt that the sounds he had heard had come from nearby, so he moved first to the door next to his own. Tentatively, his hand still on the doorframe, he leaned toward the door and listened. Faintly came the rustling of clothing. Though he couldn't be certain he wasn't making a rash mistake, his hand grabbed hold of the door-knob. Steeling himself, he threw it open, and what he saw inside made him gasp with disbelief.

Rachel lay unconscious on the floor, her blouse violently torn open and her naked flesh exposed. Her arms lay defenseless at her sides, her coal-black hair splayed out on the floor around her unmoving head. Kneeling before her, caught as he was lowering his trousers to the middle of his pasty thighs, was a man Mason didn't recognize. When he looked up, his wispy hair flung helter-skelter around his balding head, instead of the expected surprise at being caught, his bony face became a mask of anger and indignation.

"What the hell? Get out! Get out!" he demanded.

"You no-good son of a bitch!" Mason roared in answer.

Fueling Mason's arms and legs with a strength he hadn't known for many years was a burning, relentless drive to save Rachel. He leapt forward as if he were a wolf protecting its cub, passing over Rachel's unconscious body and barreling into the man. Even though the stranger raised his hands to defend himself, it was a useless gesture. Jamming the would-be rapist back onto the floor, Mason knelt upon his chest and drove his fist hard into the man's jaw, following up with another blow to his midsection. Over and over he swung, punch after punch connecting, his thoughts a whirling torrent of both pain and anger.

"How dare you touch her!" Mason thundered.

Desperately, Rachel's attacker tried to fight back, throwing feeble punches of his own, but even those that connected had little impact; to Mason they were nothing more than the gentlest of taps. His anger at what this man had done, let alone what he had intended to do, fueled him ever forward. *I will make him pay for what he has done to you, Rachel.*

But just as Mason was about to throw a punch laden with all of his remaining might, to try to end the whole horrific affair, the rapist managed to buck his hips and tip him on his side. Unable to balance himself, Mason fell on the floor, but before he could right himself, the bastard scuttled away from him. In a flash, the man jumped to his feet, desperately yanked his trousers up, and then barreled over Rachel and out the door. The clatter of footsteps rose from the staircase and was followed by the slamming of the front door.

We belong together . . . as husband and wife . . .

Rachel woke with the suddenness of a gunshot, her mind racing as fast as her heart. Gripped by panic, she felt the touch of a man's arms on her shoulders and was certain that she was in grave danger. In that split second, she remembered what had befallen her: she had just left Mason's room, tired from having cared for Otis's wounds, when a hand had clamped down on her mouth and she had been dragged away into darkness.

As she had struggled to get away, to get back to the safety of the light, she hadn't been able to think straight, hadn't been able to ascertain who it was that was attacking her. Not until her assailant had shut the door behind them and spoken had she learned his identity, and with that knowledge had come a hopelessness, an icy dread that had latched on to her heart and refused to let go no matter how much she fought.

Now that Rachel was once again alert, that dread returned. Her arms jerked outward, scratching and fighting to push him away. Though her vision was still clouded, which made it impossible for her to clearly see Jonathan Moseley's face, she knew that she needed to get away from him as quickly as she could. While her legs felt as weak as a newborn calf's, she implored them to move, to push with all that she had.

"Rachel, stop fighting!" a man's voice pleaded. "It's me!"

Instantly, she knew that the person who held her was not Jonathan; instead of his reedy, nasal voice, what she heard was much deeper, the sound of a man infinitely more sure of himself than the salesman. Blinking rapidly in the dim light from the hallway beyond, Rachel recognized her rescuer.

It was Mason.

He leaned down over her with the slightest wisp of a smile, a lightness that was betrayed by the grave seriousness of his eyes. Though some dizziness washed over her, Rachel couldn't help but notice the tiniest of details in his face; the dark stubble that graced his cheeks, the faint wrinkles that spread at the corners of his eyes, and even faint strands of his black hair. Still, these pleasant features couldn't calm the terror in her heart.

"He . . . he . . . he was going to rape . . . me," she whispered.

"I stopped him."

"Where . . . where   is . . . he . . . ?" Rachel panicked, looking about the room for some sign of Jonathan.

"He's gone from here," Mason answered reassuringly. "When I opened the door and found him with you, I tried all that I could to stop him from doing any more harm, but he managed to get away. I would have gone after him, but I'm not well enough to run down the stairs. Besides, I need to know if you've been hurt."

Even as Mason spoke, Rachel realized that she had been saved. With shaking hands, she touched the tattered front of her blouse, realizing just how much horror Jonathan had wished to visit upon her.

Seeing her naked flesh exposed made her flush crimson with embarrassment.

"I tried my best to cover you," Mason explained, his own modesty keeping his eyes from meeting hers. "Thank God that I was able to reach you before he could do real harm."

Suddenly, the enormity of what had nearly happened struck Rachel. Tears began to fall in a cascade that showed no sign of stopping. She knew that she had made a terrible mistake in not reporting to her mother Jonathan's improper advances toward her, beginning with the day at the laundry line. By not drawing attention to him, by not calling him out for the bastard he was, she had allowed him to gain confidence, to believe that nothing and no one would stop him. Only because of Mason had she been allowed to maintain her dignity.

But I've lost a lot more than pride . . .

While sobs racked Rachel's body, Mason took her into his arms. There, in the darkness of her attacker's room, he held her close, allowing her to shed her emotional burden. His touch comforted her. Nestled into the crook of Mason's muscular arms, she wasn't ashamed of her fear, but instead allowed it to be revealed and then cast out.

"Hush now," he soothed. "You're safe with me."

And at that moment, she knew it was true.

Chapter Twenty-one

MASON STOOD BEFORE the window of his room in the boardinghouse, staring at the raging storm beyond. Angry rain fell, needles of cold water lashing against the glass panes as gusts of intermittent wind pushed insistently upon the branches of the dappled trees. Occasional forks of lightning laced across the sky, followed moments later by the deep bass rumbling of thunder. The weather, dark and gloomy, was nearly as brooding as his own mood.

Three days had passed since Jonathan Moseley had attacked Rachel in the middle of the night. Mason had hoped that they would talk about what had happened, but Rachel had done little more than confirm that she had spoken to her mother about her assault and had rejected any suggestions that they call the police. She had told Eliza that she alone had fought Jonathan off and had omitted Mason's part in saving her. When he had pressed her, she had given him a weak smile and told him that she was over it all, water under the bridge, but he knew she was lying. Since he knew nothing more of the bastard than that he had assaulted her, he was frustrated that because of the darkness he didn't even have a face to hate.

Since that night, Mason's strength had steadily returned. Though he had been sore the morning after he chased away the salesman, he'd taken his mobility as a blessing and had begun to make his way around the confines of his room. Slowly, inch by inch, he had pushed himself, never settling for any amount less than he had done the time before. Now he knew that he was almost fully recovered.

While Mason had taken great pains to regain the use of his body, he had also paid attention to the needs of his mind and spirit. His return to Carlson had been difficult; hearing of Alice's death had nearly been a mortal blow to his heart, and learning that he had a daughter both delighted and disturbed him. He also often thought of the heated words Rachel had spoken to him when he first admitted his true identity.

But because you ran away, you've lost everything!

The harsh truth of the matter was that Rachel was right; by running away from everyone and everything he knew, Mason had forfeited all that he valued in life. Now, eight long years later, he had to pick himself up and begin again. While he could never be certain of his future path, he knew that he could no longer hide from his responsibilities as he once had.

To that end, I will resemble the man I once was . . .

Over the last three days, Mason had acquired everything he would need, with Charlotte as his enthusiastic accomplice. Turning from the window, he approached the bureau in the corner and looked upon his arrayed treasures that she had managed to procure for the task ahead: a pair of scissors, an ivory-handled straight razor, a dish containing a cake of shaving cream and a brush pilfered from Otis's room, and a towel. The final addition, just delivered, was a basin of hot water, the steam still rising from its surface and fogging up the mirror that hung above the bureau.

Using the palm of his hand, Mason wiped a clear swath across the mirror's clouded surface. In it, he found the reflected image of himself that he had been carrying with him ever since he was wounded on the battlefields of France, but nearly impossible for him to see was the man he had once been.

Can I ever be that man again?

"You can't turn back," he muttered to himself. "Never again."

Dipping two hands into the hot water, Mason splashed it onto his face, wetting his beard. Then, with the pair of sharp scissors, he began to cut the damp hair off in clumps. Slice by slice, cut by cut, the façade he had painfully constructed over the years was snipped away until only a residue of whiskers remained on his face. Then he lathered it, being careful not to take too long a look at himself in the partially fogged mirror. He had resolved before he began to let his eyes dwell only upon the final result.

As Mason was about to start shaving, his hand that held the razor began to shake. Tightening his grip upon the ivory handle, he closed his eyes and took a deep breath, summoning all the courage he could muster. He had resolved that he would not run from the problems that confronted him, but instead would meet his challenges head-on.

For Charlotte, for Alice, for Rachel and even for myself, I will not run . . .

Slowly he began to shave his face. Starting with his unscarred cheek, he scraped the sharp blade upward, cutting off his dark whiskers. He worked carefully, dipping the razor back into the scalding water after every pass. Over and over he repeated his work, working from cheek to lip to chin to neck. Finally, all that remained was what he had kept hidden.

Avoiding eye contact with the mirror, he shaved by touch, the fingers of his other hand guiding the blade where it needed to go. Within minutes, he was finished. With great trepidation, he opened his eyes.

Mason's first thought was that he was most certainly not the monster he had feared he had become. Though the scarring of his cheek was visible, it was not revolting: whitish-pink ridges rose and fell where the skin had been melted across his cheek and jawline. But the effect wasn't widespread, more splattered than spread; it was almost certainly this fact that had allowed him to grow a beard in the first place. Turning first one way and then the other, he closely examined the face he had allowed to become a stranger to his own eyes. Touching the scars caused him no pain. While it would have been impossible to completely ignore his obvious disfigurement, he realized that Alice would have recognized him.

Did I stay away all of these years for nothing?

Almost immediately, Mason knew the answer to his own unspoken question. The fact was that he was no longer the man who had left Carlson so many years before, but the realization struck him that he wouldn't have been that man even if he had never been wounded. Even if he had come home unscathed and been met at the depot by a band and a banner blaring his triumph, he would not have been the Mason Tucker who left. The horrors of war, the wanton blood and death and destruction he had witnessed, would have changed him every bit as much as an exploding shell.

Besides, he had shaved off his beard not because of a desire to return to the past, but because he had finally realized that what mattered was the man he would become.

Mason was lost in these thoughts when there was a soft knock on the door. It swung open and standing there, staring at him, was Rachel.

Rachel knocked softly on the door to Mason's room before entering, just as she had done many times before in the days since Charlotte found him. He had chosen to take all of his meals in his room, just as her mother did, but today Rachel intended to ask him if he felt like joining her for lunch at the dining room table.

"It's just about time for lunch and I wondered if—" she began before falling silent at the sight before her.

Gone was the disheveled, scruffy beard that had covered Mason's face. Before him was a still steaming bowl of water and his shaving instruments, a testament to what he had done.

At the sight of her, Mason quickly turned toward the wall, showing her only half of his face. His deep blue eyes darted toward her and then back to the safety of the wall in a look of embarrassment. It took only an instant for her to understand why.

The wounds to his face!

Suddenly, all of the words that Mason had spoken to her about his traumatic experiences on the war-torn battlefields of France came rushing back; the explosions that tore up the earth, the mud mixed with the blood of his fellow soldiers, but particularly the attack that led him from the relative safety of the trenches into a bombardment that sent him hurtling through the air and away from all he had known and loved. She recalled the tension in his voice as he spoke of waking in a hospital surrounded by the screams and moans of the wounded and dying. All that he had done since that day was aimed at hiding what had happened to his face.

"You don't have to hide from me," she said softly.

"It's still hard enough for me to look at," he answered, his deep voice resounding in the quiet room. "I don't want you to be afraid."

"Why would you say such a thing?"

"Because the last thing I would want is for you to be frightened of me."

Purposefully, Rachel crossed the small room to stand at Mason's side, her eyes never leaving his, never straying to catch the tiniest glimpse of what he'd chosen to keep hidden from her. Though she desperately wanted to see his face, to know how it had changed, she wanted him to be the one to let her in, to trust her enough to share that part of him.

"I would never be scared of you, Mason," she reassured him, gently placing her hand upon his arm. "Besides, if you were really that afraid of frightening people away, you never would have shaved your beard off in the first place."

Slowly, Mason nodded. "You're right," he agreed. "I chose to shave away my past because I'm tired of running away from who I am and from everything that I left behind. If I'm not willing to show myself to you, to let you see what that damned war turned me into, then how would I ever be able to walk out of this room and back into the world?"

Without expecting any answer to his question, Mason turned toward Rachel, allowing her to see all of his face: the scarring that ran angrily along the right side; the pink-and-white ridges that rose from his jawline and colored his cheek in splotches. To her eyes, it was as if someone had splashed candle wax onto Mason's face. Looking intently, she realized that she had expected it to be much worse.

But now that Mason had removed the dark beard from his face, Rachel felt a stirring of joy at having once again laid eyes upon the man she had known many years before. A sliver of memory at the way he had looked the day he married Alice rose in her thoughts; he had been dashingly handsome in his suit, his immaculately shined shoes gleaming in the sunlight, and she had been uncomfortable at finding her soon-to-be brother-in-law so attractive. Today, standing before her, unwanted scars and all, Mason still resembled the younger man who had sent butterflies racing through her stomach.

"I bet I'm a hell of a sight," Mason offered with a weak smile.

"All I see is the same Mason Tucker I knew eight years ago."

"I don't look like a monster?"

"Not to my eyes."

As if she had no control over her own body, Rachel's steady hand rose toward Mason's scarred face. Though surprise was clearly written across his features, he didn't flinch, did not make any move to avoid her touch, instead held her gaze steadily. When her fingertips touched the raised ridges of his scars, Rachel felt a chill race across her skin. Mason's flesh felt both warm and smooth, undoubtedly because of his recent shaving, but she swore that she could feel the rhythmic pulse of his heartbeat, a steady thrumming that seemed to hurry with every passing moment.

Though Rachel knew that it was inappropriate for her to be touching Mason in such a way, she found herself unable to remove her hand. Seconds passed as slowly as if they were hours, but still her fingers caressed his skin. Vivid memories of Mason's rescue of her flashed across her mind. Tremors of emotion cascaded in her breast and she had to fight back tears. A sudden desire to have Mason take her in his arms welled up in her heart, and she began to feel uncomfortable with her own thoughts. Quickly she removed her hand and turned away from him.

What . . . what am I feeling . . . ?

For a moment, the room was silent except for the continued lashing of rain against the windowpanes. Mason was the first to speak, asking, "Do you suppose that Charlotte will be frightened at how I look?"

"I don't think so," Rachel answered, thankful to have something beside her own confused emotions to consider. "If anything, Charlotte will find it a bit exciting, just another reason to spend all of her time at your side."

"I hope you're right. I'd hate for her to be scared of her own father."

"Are you going to tell her the truth?"

"I'm tired of running from my past, Rachel," he declared. "All these long years away have done nothing but spread pain across the lives of everyone I'd intended to protect. I can never make up for what happened to Alice, though I would give my own life in exchange, but I'll be damned if I'll allow anyone else to suffer because of my cowardice. It's past time that I began to make amends for what I have done. There are so many people I need to apologize to, and I intend to start doing that right away."

"*Where* do you intend to start?" she asked.

"With the most important person of all," he answered softly. "I need to talk to Alice."

Chapter Twenty-two

NEEDLES OF STINGING RAIN continued to plummet from the heavy, dark clouds above as Rachel hurried across the street beside the depot, intent upon keeping up with the pace that Mason set. Pulling her shawl tightly around her shoulders, she shivered and did her best to avoid stepping into the wide puddles still filling with water.

I'll be soaked to the bone in seconds!
Though the storm's ferocity had subsided somewhat, it remained unpleasant: periodic gusts of wind howled at her feet and threatened to sweep her to the

drenched ground; the chill that hung in the air grew heavier with every passing moment, carrying with it the promise of snow in the days and weeks ahead; and while no more tongues of lightning forked across the heavens, the deep bass rumble of thunder still occasionally rolled across the afternoon sky.

Ahead of Rachel, Mason plodded steadily forward. It surprised her that he was even able to walk, let alone move so quickly. But now he moved as if he were a man possessed, drawn to something or somewhere he could no more control than the raging of the storm.

"There's one good thing about this weather," he said over his shoulder.

"What's that?"

"No one else will be willing to come outside in it."

Mason was right; Carlson's streets were so empty that it could have been the middle of the night instead of the middle of the day. Nearly every window they passed was shuttered against the miserable weather, and even in those that were open, no faces were pressed to the glass. Only an occasional dog, too de-

spondent in the rain even to bark, witnessed their passing.

And that was just the way that Mason
wanted it.

Though he didn't have a hat to cover his
head, Mason had turned up the thick collar of his coat; Rachel knew that this was
not entirely for protection from the elements, but also to prevent him from being
recognized. His many long years away
had made him overly cautious and his
eyes constantly darted to some distant
place, searching for a face that might lin-
ger upon his own for a moment too long.
Still, he hurried on.

Lifting the hem of her skirt so that it
wouldn't drag in the mud, Rachel struggled to keep up. There was no need for
her to show Mason where to go and he
never faltered, though she still wondered
where he found the strength to move so
quickly. They crossed Main Street at its
northern end, made their way past a group
of houses, and then down a short lane
before the cemetery came into view.

Though she had just been to visit Alice's grave with Charlotte only weeks before, Rachel felt her breath being taken

away at the sight of the cemetery. Wisps of hazy clouds hung as if they were cobwebs above the tombstones. Shivering, she flinched as another rumble of thunder echoed from the distance.

Mason came to a halt at the base of the cemetery's hill. Running a hand through his wet hair, he stared solemnly at the dark iron gates and the tombstones that lay beyond. Rachel wondered if he had finally been struck by the enormity of it all. Though he had undeniably felt pain when he first learned of his wife's death, realizing that she lay in the cold earth, forever beyond his embrace, now seemed to have paralyzed him.

"Mason, I—" she began, unsure of just what to say.

"It's all right, Rachel," he reassured her. "I suppose I thought that I was ready to see this, to see Alice's grave, but the hurt is more than I thought it would be. Convincing myself appears to have been easier than doing the deed. It's just . . . hard to believe . . ."

"You don't have to do this now, not today, not if you're not ready for it," she said carefully. "We can come back later, sometime after you've regained more strength, after you've had more time to come to grips with all that has happened while you were away."

Slowly, Mason turned to face her, fixing her with a gaze that was heavy with sadness and pain. "I don't think there will ever come a day when I'll be able to accept what my actions have caused."

"Mason, I didn't mean that you—" she said quickly, fearful that she had offended him, but he silenced her by placing a hand upon her shoulder.

"If I were to walk away from here now, I would never be able to return," he explained. "There have already been far too many excuses. After what happened to you, and my needing to stop that bastard from hurting you, I made the decision to change my life, and that is just what I intend to do, no matter how much it might hurt. I won't do any more running . . . that's already cost us all far too much."

Together they made their way in silence up the gently sloping hill toward the cemetery. The going was difficult across the wet grass and muddy earth; occasionally, Mason offered his hand to steady her.

Even in the aftermath of the storm, the gate's hinges squeaked when opened.

To Rachel's eye, the cemetery seemed bigger than she remembered; it was as if the tombstones, glistening wet with rainwater, darker than they'd be under the glare of the sun, had multiplied. The wooden markers at the rear of the encircled graveyard, the oldest graves in the cemetery, seemed so frail in the aftermath of the storm, warped and swollen from so many previous downpours, that she wondered if they wouldn't collapse. A large raven took flight from atop a stone near them, its long wings flapping quickly, a scornful caw directed at their interruption.

Rachel gently led Mason to Alice's tombstone. Cut from a lighter stone, it hadn't grown as dark as those around it, but it still looked gloomy. Immediately after they stopped before the marker, a break appeared in the still swiftly moving storm clouds above and a shaft of sunlight fell upon the cemetery, sending dazzling reflections of light off the tombstones; the brilliance was so intense, so surprising, that Rachel had to shade her eyes. Mason didn't notice the change, his gaze never leaving the grave where his wife lay.

Tentatively, his shaking hand reached out to grasp the wet stone. Rachel watched silently, remembering how she had struggled with the same emotion that Mason surely felt. Though Alice's death had been painful for her to bear, and even though she still missed her sister, she'd been able to use the passage of time to dull her ache, comforting herself with her memories of their time together. For Alice's husband, only now discovering what terrible things had happened in his absence, the pain was much sharper.

As if he had been felled by a mighty blow, Mason dropped to one knee in the wet grass before Alice's tombstone. His hands gripped the top of the marker, his shoulders shaking violently as his sorrow finally overwhelmed him. Still, he didn't make a sound, his silence in the face of his wife's death louder than any words.

Rachel began to move away, to allow Mason the time and space to properly grieve for Alice, but she had not gone more than a couple of steps before he implored

her to stop, looking upon her with red-
dened, wet eyes and a tight face full of
pain. "Please don't leave, Rachel," he re-
quested. "There's nothing I could say that
you can't hear."

"I shouldn't hear the words that you
want to speak to her," she disagreed.
"Whatever you have to say should be for
her alone."

A hurt smile flitted across Mason's face.
"Long ago I might have agreed with you,
but I worry that I will lose my nerve. Please
stay with me until I've had my say."

Part of Rachel still wanted to disagree,
but she nodded her head.

For a long while, Mason was silent, his
fingertips tracing the indentations of the
carving of Alice's name into the tombstone.
When he finally spoke, his trembling voice
was little more than a whisper.

"When I left Carlson . . . I believed that
I would be . . . true to our words to each
other, my dearest Alice," he began, "but
then . . . then things changed. That godforsaken war, with all of the explosions and
screams and mud and blood, all things
that I naïvely hadn't expected, overwhelmed
me. They changed me into something that

I believed you wouldn't be able to understand, wouldn't accept.

"My decision not to return I misguidedly believed was for your benefit, when I should have seen that I was only being selfish," Mason kept on, the timbre of his voice growing with his inward anger. "And now that I've come back home, I find our daughter, Charlotte, waiting for me and I realize how many lives my failure has changed."

It was all that Rachel could do to hold her tongue, not to offer some defense regarding Mason's behavior, but she remained silent.

"It's," Mason continued, "unbearable for me to think of what you must have gone through in those days. I see you brokenhearted, pregnant with a child your husband never knew about, struggling to find some reason to keep going, and, in the end, not succeeding. I wish I could have taken away your fear, comforted you, but I failed you. For that, among many other things, I wish I was the one who had died."

"Mason—" Rachel blurted before clamping her hand upon her mouth.

"It's true," he said, turning to her.

All she could offer in answer was to shake her head as tears began to well in her eyes.

"But that is a wish that can't ever come true," Mason continued, turning back to his wife's grave marker. "And because of that, all I can do is to make the best effort I can to raise our daughter . . . and to ask for your forgiveness for what I have done."

Shakily, he rose to his feet and added, "I'll always love you, Alice."

Just as Mason was about to turn back to Rachel, his eyes caught sight of the tombstone lying next to Alice's and a startled expression crossed his face as he realized that his name was carved upon it.

"My own . . . tombstone," he muttered.

"Alice had it placed here several months after you were reported as having been killed," Rachel explained gently, wiping the tears from her eyes. "I think she waited so long in the hope you somehow might return, that there had been some mistake."

"I should have proven that thought true."

As another peal of thunder rolled across the countryside, Rachel remembered her own thoughts the last time she had stood at Mason's grave. Before she could stop herself, she began to speak of them. "For the longest time, I hated you for what happened to Alice," she said. "I believed that if she hadn't met you, if she hadn't loved you so deeply, then your death wouldn't have broken her heart."

Mason nodded, his eyes fixed upon her.

"Every year, my mother insists that I bring Charlotte to the cemetery on the date of Alice's death, Charlotte's own birthday," Rachel continued. "And every year I've stood here and cursed you and the day you came into my sister's life. I've held such terrible resentment."

"Do you still feel that way?" he asked.

Rachel regarded Mason closely. So much had happened since Charlotte had first found him racked by illness out in the woods. While she had felt some undeniable anger toward him when he finally revealed his identity, most of that had vanished. When he had rescued her from Jonathan Moseley, something else had come over her, an emotion that still proved elusive, but it was certainly not anger.

"No, I don't," she answered.

"You have every reason to hate me for what I've done."

"Like you, I'm ready to put the past behind me."

"Thank you, Rachel," Mason said humbly. "Let's hope the next person I have to see will be as forgiving."

"Who's that?" she asked.

"Your mother."

"Are you sure you want to do this?"

Mason stood beside Rachel in the hallway outside the door to Eliza's room, the scant light rising from the ground floor of the boardinghouse casting deep shadows across the walls. The sun had long since set and Rachel had collected all of the dishes from suppertime, a meal he had skipped as he had screwed up his courage to do what he knew needed to be done. The only sound to compete with his own ragged breathing was the rumbling of Otis's snores coming from somewhere below.

"I am," he answered.

Rachel knocked gently before opening the door and stepping inside. He followed her and shut the door behind them.

The entryway was gloomy, full of deep shadows that filled much of the rest of the room; only the faint, flickering light of a candle on a dresser gave any illumination. Mason's first reaction upon seeing the room was surprise; his memories of Eliza Watkins were of a woman who surrounded herself with the brighter things in life. Then he glimpsed her for the first time as she stood over by the window, peering through the curtains, a sad figure alone in the gloom.

Am I responsible for what she has become?

"Mother, I don't know how to tell you this, but—" Rachel began but faltered as she moved farther into the room.

Mason had stayed close behind her as she had advanced, and for the first time, Eliza's eyes went to him, peering intently for a better look at the man who accompanied her daughter. As, suddenly, a fork of lightning lit the room, his identity was revealed to her.

She recoiled. "No . . . no, it can't be . . ."

"Mother," Rachel said, stepping toward her mother, "please don't . . ."

But it was already too late. Eliza backed

away quickly, one hand flying to her throat and another wildly grasping about. She brushed against a small table, sending a teacup hurtling to the floor where it shattered into pieces.

"How . . . how is this possible?" Eliza exclaimed. "You're dead! It can't be you, it can't be . . ."

Stumbling backward, she bumped into a chair and fell to the floor. Before Rachel could react, Mason was already beside Eliza. Still, she did her best to stay away from him, cringing against the wall with nowhere else to go. Mason, dropping to one knee, gently extended his hand.

"This isn't real! I must be dreaming . . . a nightmare!"

"Maybe so, Mrs. Watkins, but it's me, Mason."

"It can't be!" Eliza cried in disbelief. "It just can't!"

"But it is."

"But your . . . your face . . ." she said, shaking her head, her eyes unwilling to look upon the mess that war had caused of Mason's handsome features. "It's . . . it's so scarred . . . it's . . ." she stammered. Tentatively, Eliza reached out her trembling hand to touch the ragged ridges on the side of Mason's face; the instant her fingers made contact, she recoiled as if she were the one being burned.

Rachel knew that her mother's reaction to Mason's burns must be causing him incredible dismay; but if he was upset, he didn't show it.

"Mrs. Watkins, please, take my hand," Mason implored. "I'll tell you everything you want to know."

"But, I—"

"Let him help you up, Mother," Rachel said.

With only a little more hesitation, Eliza allowed her hand to slip into Mason's, and he helped her to a soft chair near the window. Rachel fetched a pitcher of water and poured her mother a glass, which Eliza drank; all the while, her disbelieving eyes never left Mason's face.

Mason felt a stab of guilt as he looked upon Alice's mother. While he had imagined that her reaction would be one of surprise at seeing him again after so many emotional years apart, especially since she imagined him to be dead, but her horror upon recognizing him had been more intense than he had expected. He'd hoped that she would respond much like Rachel had, more with disbelief than outright shock.

"How can it be you?" Eliza asked after she had regained some measure of composure. "They told us that you were dead! Your own father came and told Alice that you had died in France! How can this be?"

Patiently, Mason began to explain what had happened to him since he had left Carlson eight years earlier. Much as he had with Rachel, he talked about the trenches of France, the explosion that had mistakenly led to his being pronounced dead, and his rehabilitation at a military hospital. He told Eliza of being unable to come to grips with the extent of his injuries, his fears of how everyone would react to his disfiguring scars, and how that had led him to avoid returning home.

Mason summed up the life he had been living, traveling the rails and hiding from trainyard authorities. He went so far as to detail some of the violent episodes that had led him to decide to return to Carlson. Through it all, Eliza's expression grew harder, less friendly, until she was frowning.

"But I don't understand why, once you had returned to America, you didn't tell anyone that you were alive."

"I just . . . just thought it was best—"

"The Mason Tucker that I knew would never have let those he had left behind believe he was dead," Eliza said emphatically. "To think that your own poor father has been led to believe a lie! Why, the shock of such deceit would probably be enough to kill him!"

"Mason felt so damaged . . ." Rachel began defensively.

"He's not the only one that I'm cross with," Eliza interrupted, turning her anger toward her daughter. "How long have you known that Mason was still alive? Why didn't you tell me?"

"Do you remember when you told me to follow Charlotte?"

Eliza nodded.

Rachel explained how she had done as her mother had told her and followed the little girl out into the woods to the north of the lake. She told of her discovery of Charlotte caring for a haggard man in a decrepit cabin and, truthfully, she admitted that she hadn't been certain of who he was until after she had brought him to the boardinghouse to recover.

"Why wasn't I told that there was a stranger living under my roof?" Eliza demanded.

"Mason isn't a stranger," Rachel disagreed.

"You didn't know that when you brought him here."

"Because I—"

"Rachel didn't say anything because I asked her to keep my identity a secret from everyone," Mason cut in. "There's no reason to be angry with her for failing to tell you I was here."

"I believe there's plenty of anger to go around for this," Eliza snapped.

For a moment, silence filled the room. Mason knew there was nothing he could do to make up for all hurt he had caused. Over the years, he had imagined Alice's suffering, but he hadn't given much thought to how her distress would affect those around her. Standing before Eliza Watkins, feeling her anger, made him realize how wrong he had been.

When Eliza finally spoke, her voice trembled with fury. "I've sat here and I've listened to everything you've had to say, Mason," she said, "about what happened in the war and why you chose not to come home, allowing everyone to believe you were dead. But what I hear are the words of a coward, excuses filled with more excuses. Am I wrong . . . am I to believe that you've stayed away because you were afraid?"

Slowly, Mason shook his head. "No, you're—"

With an alarming suddenness, Eliza rose from where she sat and slapped Mason across the face. In the close confines of the room, the sound seemed thunderous. Mason's head snapped to the side more out of surprise than pain, but the sheer violence of Alice's mother's reaction unsettled him.

"How dare you!" she bellowed as tears began to form in her eyes. "How dare you come back here after all of these years! Your fear, your cowardice, your vanity caused Alice's death just as sure as if you had stabbed her heart! Nothing will ever return her to us! Nothing!"

Throughout the barrage of words and accusations, Mason did nothing to argue with Eliza; the truth was that he knew he deserved everything being levied against him. Even as tears began to fall from the older woman's eyes, he refused to turn away.

"I want you to get out!" she finally shouted. "Get the hell out of here!"

"But Mother," Rachel began to protest, before Mason gently grabbed her by the arm and headed back toward the door.

"She's right," he admitted. "Everything your mother says about me is right."

While Eliza began to sob hysterically behind him, Mason couldn't help but wonder that if Alice were still alive to see his fateful return, she wouldn't have hated him just as much.

Chapter Twenty-three

THE NEXT DAY MASON awoke to sunlight pouring through the windows; the gentlest of breezes rustled what few leaves remained on the storm-shaken trees, and birds chirped hungrily at the dawning of the new day. He was marveling at it all and buttoning his shirt when the unmistakable sounds of Charlotte and Jasper racing down the hallway came to his ear.

"Charlotte!" he called. "Could you come in here for a moment?"

Instantly the tramping of feet came to a halt just outside his room and the door cracked open a couple of inches; Charlotte looked in hesitantly, clearly a bit fearful that she had done something wrong.

"Don't worry," Mason reassured her with a gentle laugh. "I'm not mad at you for running down the hall."

Her face brightened. "Good." She sighed. "'Cause Grandma doesn't like it."

"Then why do you do it so much?"

"It's fun!" she declared as if it were the most obvious thing in the world.

Playfully, Charlotte bounced into the room with Jasper, as always, at her heels and just as full of mischief. Dressed in a simple blue dress, her black boots still flecked with the mud of an earlier day's play, she looked amazingly like her mother. Charlotte regarded Mason curiously.

"Your face looks different," she commented.

"Yes, it does," he agreed. "I shaved off my beard yesterday."

Mason watched as Charlotte's eyes drifted across his face. Turning her head slightly to the side, she focused upon the scarring on the side of his face, her eyes narrowing to get a better look.

"Does what you see frighten you?" Mason asked.

"Nope," she answered immediately with a sideways shake of her blonde braids. "I like you better without that big old beard."

Mason couldn't stop a smile from forming at the corners of his mouth.

After Charlotte had taken the seat he had offered on the edge of his bed, her legs kicking out rhythmically, Mason said, "I asked you to come in here because I want to tell you a secret."

"Really?"

Mason took a deep breath. "Do you remember, in the days after you found me out in the cabin, when I was really sick, and I called you by another name . . . when I called you Alice?"

"That's my mother's name!"

"Yes, it is." He smiled. "Well, the reason that I called you by her name was that you reminded me of her. You see, besides your aunt Rachel and grandmother, I knew your mother better than anyone in Carlson, even in the whole world."

"You did?" Charlotte asked, wide-eyed.

"Yes," he answered carefully. "The secret I wanted to tell you is that your mother was my wife, which makes me your father."

"But . . . but my father . . . is dead," Charlotte said, puzzlement on her face. The kicking of her feet had stopped and her eyes looked up at him brimming with confusion; it was clear that she expected him to provide answers to her dilemma.

"Oh, Charlotte." He sighed. "I know that's what you believed to be true, but sometimes things aren't what they seem."

"But he's buried next to my mother in the cemetery!" she exclaimed, unwilling to believe the explanation Mason gave her. "Rachel and I were just there for my birthday and I saw it!"

"Sometimes people make mistakes," Mason patiently explained. "They don't mean to, but it happens all the same." He sat down beside Charlotte and tenderly took her hand in his own. "Many years ago, even before you were born, I went a long way away to war and I didn't come back when everyone expected me to. I was really sick, not like how I was when you found me, but sick in a different way. Do you understand?"

Charlotte nodded.

"When I didn't come back when I was supposed to," he continued, "your mother and grandmother and even Rachel thought that I had died, but I . . . just . . . couldn't make my way back home as fast as I should have."

For a long moment, both of them were silent. Mason looked down at their entwined hands. In that moment, he truly felt that *this girl was his daughter* and that nothing would ever change that. He vowed that even though he had failed Charlotte's mother, he wouldn't fail her child.

"I know this has to be hard for you to understand, Charlotte," Mason said, "but I want you to believe that if I had known you were here, or that your mother had been sick with worry, I would have done everything I could to come back to you. Nothing I say can make it right, but I hope you can believe me when I tell you that I'm sorry."

"But . . . but, I . . ." Charlotte began, then fell silent.

"Tell me," Mason encouraged.

"But . . . but does this mean that my mother might be alive, too?"

"No, Charlotte," he managed through the sorrow her question evoked. "I'm afraid she's gone from us now, no matter how much we wish otherwise."

Suddenly, the little girl sprang from where she sat on the bed and turned into Mason's arms, a move that startled him. As she sank into him, he tenderly embraced her, and from somewhere deep in his chest, he felt a growing sense of completeness, the filling of a void he hadn't even known existed. That she hadn't been repulsed by his scarring gave him a glimmer of hope that his life could be repaired. He felt a tear slide free from his eye and descend down his cheek, but he didn't mind, not in the slightest.

Their moment was broken by a sharp bark from Jasper.

"Hush, now," Charlotte scolded him. "You don't have to be jealous . . . He'll be your daddy, too!"

Mason laughed heartily at his daughter's words as he rose from the bed and walked over to where he had hung his worn coat. From the inside pocket he retrieved the photograph and letter he had treasured for so many years. "I have something for you," he said.

"You do?"

"These were the last things I received from your mother . . . before I got sick," he explained gently. "They've helped me through some very rough times, and whenever I look at them, I remember her as clearly as if she were standing right before me. Now I want you to have them."

"Really?" she exclaimed.

"Yes, really. They're yours."

Without having to be cautioned, Charlotte took the photograph and letter from Mason as delicately as if they were made of glass. As she examined the photograph, a bright smile spread across her face. Looking up at Mason, she said, "That's my mother!"

"Yes, it is," he agreed as he again marveled at how much of Alice lived on in Charlotte.

In that moment, he knew that Alice, wherever she was, was smiling.

Rachel knocked gently on the door to her mother's room before entering. Carefully balancing a tray with that afternoon's lunch, she found her mother once again standing in front of the window, brilliant sunlight streaming in through the crack in the curtains; the rest of the room was still dark with gloomy shadows. Eliza glanced at her daughter for only a moment, her face a mask of frustrated anger and spite, her jaw rigid and her mouth pulled into a tight line, before returning her gaze to the street below.

Setting down the tray, Rachel mumbled, "I'll be back for it later," and began to turn back toward the door.

"How could you have lied to me in such a way?" her mother asked suddenly.

Rachel sighed. As she had prepared her mother's tray, she had known that this was going to happen. Even the night before, well after she and Mason had left her mother's room, she had lain awake in bed, unable to sleep, thinking of how her mother had reacted to the surprising news that Mason was still alive. Over and over, she saw the horrified look in the woman's eyes as she gazed upon Mason's scars. While Mason had been the one slapped, she had known that Eliza Watkins's ire would eventually find a familiar target.

"It's just as Mason told you, Mother," Rachel explained, turning back to face the woman's accusing stare. "He asked me to keep his identity a secret. Besides, when we first brought him to the boardinghouse, we had no idea who he was."

"I just bet you didn't!" Eliza said sarcastically.

"What I'm telling you is the truth," Rachel answered defiantly. "If you had seen him lying in that cabin, if you had seen the disheveled mess he had become, you wouldn't have known who he was either. Even if Zachary Tucker himself had stumbled across him in the woods, he wouldn't have had any idea he'd found his brother."

The sudden realization that Zachary had no idea of his brother's return sent shivers racing down Rachel's arms. With everything that had happened lately, particularly the revelation of Mason's true identity and the vicious attack by Jonathan Moseley, it had been easy to forget Zachary's desire to own the boardinghouse and use it for the incoming lumber company. But the threat hadn't disappeared.

"I still don't understand why you didn't tell me once you had learned the truth," Eliza continued. "Regardless of what he asked you to do, there was no reason for you to keep it from me."

"Maybe I didn't say anything because I could see how genuinely hurt Mason was to learn about Alice."

"He didn't know?" Eliza asked incredulously.

"How would he? He's spent the last several years hiding in darkened rail cars, moving back and forth across the country. When he finally decided to return to Carlson, the first thing he did was to go to his and Alice's old house, but before he could find an answer to any of his questions, he became ill. He didn't know about Charlotte either."

"But Alice wrote to him," her mother said. "She told him!"

"He never received the letter."

"Does Charlotte know who he is?"

Rachel nodded. "He told me that he was going to tell her."

"You can't let him!" Eliza shouted, finally stepping away from the curtains and approaching her daughter, her face creased with worry. "Just imagine how much that would hurt her!"

"Why?" Rachel frowned. "The poor child has had to live with the burden of her

mother's death her whole life, every birthday being dragged out to see a tombstone
of a woman she never knew. She'll be
happy to have at least one parent! She
and Mason get along wonderfully."

"How can you allow them to be together? Have you forgotten that it is his
fault that Alice is gone?"

Rachel knew that her mother's angry
words were meant to upset her, but she
was beginning to see that there was another side, a different truth; what had happened to Alice was as much a result of her
sister's inability to deal with her grief as it
was about Mason not returning from the
war. For many years she had blamed Mason for what occurred. But now, even if
there was still lingering anger in her heart,
she knew that it was time to let it go and,
just as Mason had begun to do, try to re-
claim what was left of their lives.

**Clinging to the past won't help any
of us any longer . . .**

"Mother," she began as gently as she
could, "what's done is done. I can't keep
hating him for what happened, and neither
should you."

"Don't think you can tell me how I should feel! It's his fault!"

"That's not fair," Rachel disagreed, standing her ground in the face of her mother's ever-increasing fury. "Some of the blame has to rest with Alice. She was the one who chose not to live without Mason, even though she knew she was bringing his child into the world."

"Don't say such things about her!"

"But it's true, Mother. Deep down, you know that I'm right."

Surprise and indignation filled Eliza's face as she listened to Rachel's defiant words. Crossing her thin arms over her chest, she declared, "I can't believe you would say such things. For that matter, I don't know how you can stand to even be around him!"

"Because, just like Mason," Rachel explained, her own ire rising right alongside her mother's, "I want to put the past where it belongs! There's no need to carry all of this anger and pain around anymore. Blaming Mason will do nothing to bring Alice back and will only cause more hurt. What has it gotten any of us but needless suffering? Look at yourself, Mother. All it has given you is such fear that you never leave your room!"

"What is that supposed to mean?"

"It means that you've spent the last eight years carrying Alice's death around as if it were your own personal cross to bear," Rachel argued, allowing the thoughts she had held within herself for so many years finally to be let loose. "You lock yourself in this room as if you were in a prison! While life goes on as it always has just outside your windows, you remain here, acting as if we are still in the days when Alice and I slid down the banisters. You still act as if you expect her to come walking through your door!"

"You can't know the pain I've gone through!" Eliza shouted.

"I do, Mother!" Rachel answered truthfully. "I went through it too, remember? I'm the one who has cared for Charlotte as if she were my own daughter! I'm the one who has turned away each and every suitor who ventured to court me because of my responsibilities here in the boardinghouse! I'm the one who has had to bring meal after meal into this gloomy room!"

"I never asked you—" her mother began but was cut off.

"Every one of us has suffered and sacrificed, and for what?" Rachel vehemently argued. "We keep living in the past, feeling sorry about what happened, but never doing a damned thing about it! Well, I've had it and it's time for us to stop!"

Eliza could only stare at her daughter in disbelief.

"Mason is right," Rachel said, suddenly aware of just how much she had finally allowed herself to say, but not feeling the slightest bit sorry at having said it. "We have to go on living. Though we all miss Alice, Mason included, we have to go on if we truly want to live again. These days alongside him have reminded me of all that we have lost, and I know, in the bottom of my heart, that Alice wouldn't want that . . . for any of us."

Without waiting for an answer, Rachel turned and walked to the door. With her hand on the doorknob, she turned to find her mother still silently staring, emotion beginning to get the better of her.

"I hope that you can find it in your heart

to forgive, Mother," Rachel explained. "Because if you can't then you will have lost the part of you that Alice and I loved best."

With that, Rachel went out and shut the door behind her.

Chapter Twenty-four

ZACHARY TUCKER STOOD silently at the side of his father's bed, watching the old man as he slept. Outside the room's windows, the breaking November morning was brilliant; rays of golden sunlight streamed down from a nearly cloudless sky, warming away the stubborn frost that had settled upon the ground overnight. The weather, however, would go unnoticed by the room's sole occupant; in Sherman Tucker's narrow world, there was no longer much of a difference between day and night.

Though he was just sixty years of age, Sherman Tucker bore the outward appearance of a much older man. Deep, insistent wrinkles lined his worn skin; age spots dotted his scalp, swept over by wispy, thinning hair as white as snow. While he slept soundly, dark circles underlined his rheumy eyes. Once upon a time he had been a fit, robust man who had led his bank through tough times with a fiery, strong resolve that never wavered. Now he was a shell of that man. The reason for such a profound change was simple.

When his older son had first gone off to war, Sherman Tucker had been very proud to be his father. But after he received the fateful communication that Mason had been reported as missing, presumed killed in action, he had gradually lost interest in the world. All he had worked for was gone. The legacy he had sought to leave his son no longer mattered. In the beginning, his despair showed in a slumping of his broad shoulders, a watery look in his eyes as he tried to carry himself through another day at the bank. Soon it became a chronic pain in his back, a nagging cold that never seemed to go away, before finally depression overcame him, sending him to his bed, never to leave.

And that was the day when all that you had created became mine . . . Zachary gloated at the thought.

When Sherman's misery forced him to step away, Zachary had filled the void in his business that had been left behind, even if that had never been his father's intention. Within months, he had consolidated control, removing anyone stubborn or unwise enough to stand in his way. The power and authority he had always lustfully craved from a distance was finally his. Now, with his father's death more imminent, he felt no remorse, no impending sense of loss. In fact, he found himself filled with anticipation.

You'll finally be out of my way, Father . . . just like Mason . . .

Zachary had never been his father's favorite. Where Mason seemed to be able to do no wrong, every attempt that Zachary made to please his father met with unmitigated failure. He could still see the look of displeasure in the man's eyes when he made a mistake in the bank's ledgers, the first of many such disappointments. Mason had been the brother brought before important investors and visitors from out of town looking to bring business to Carlson. At Christmas parties and other celebrations, Mason was marched up before the throng and asked to say a few words about how much their work was appreciated.

Sherman Tucker had known that his younger son would never be able to emulate his sense of fairness and honesty in business, his strong ethic of doing what was right in preference to what was profitable. That was why Mason had been given every opportunity to be the one to replace him.

"But then he had the good sense to go and get killed," Zachary muttered to himself.

He walked over to the window and looked down upon Carlson. As pleasant as it was to be reminded of how he had managed to acquire all he desired, gaining control of his father's financial empire, his thoughts at such an early hour were more troublesome.

Inside his coat pocket, pressed against his chest, was yet another telegram from the Gaitskill Lumber Company pressuring him for an immediate update on the status of the boardinghouse property. He didn't need to look at it again to remember the impatient tone that had been used.

. . . for unless this matter is resolved to our satisfaction per the letter of our earlier agreement, we will have no choice but to . . .

Not an hour passed without Zachary cursing the stubborness of Eliza Watkins and her family. Even after the savage beating of that damned drunkard Otis, they still refused his demands. He had begun to realize how misguided his faith in Rachel was; in the end, she had proven no smarter than the rest of them, and all his entreaty to her had done was waste more of his valuable time, time he wouldn't be able to regain.

Below, Carlson was still awakening to a new day, but Zachary's mind was already working at a feverish pace. As his stomach tied itself into spastic knots, he was busy formulating his next plan of attack, something that would undoubtedly have to involve Travis Jefferson.

It's nearly time to let him do whatever is needed . . .

Zachary turned back to where his father

still slept soundly. In that moment, he knew that he and his father actually did have something in common: both precariously held on to what they deemed valuable, a hold that was slipping away, for both of them, by the hour. The difference was that Zachary wasn't willing to go without a struggle. He would do whatever was necessary, no matter how unseemly or violent, as long as in the end he was the victor.

His father and Mason's memory be damned.

"The way I hears it, a fella out travelin' them there rails can find himself with a whole mess of good drinkin', what with the 'shine and road whiskey and such," Otis offered in all seriousness. Wincing, he rubbed at his broken arm; he'd just returned from the doctor's office with a new plaster cast. When Rachel had pressed him about what had happened out behind the boardinghouse, his recollection of events was hazy at best; flashes of a face he couldn't recognize mixed with a great deal of pain.

"I can't say that I've ever been one to do much drinking," Mason answered.

"And that right there is a damned shame!" With that declaration, Otis fished out his flask from his shirt pocket and took a gulp. When he noticed Rachel glowering at him, his voice rose in mock indignation. "It's for the pain, darlin'! Honest it is!"

Mason sat opposite Otis at the rickety table in the back of the kitchen of the boardinghouse, the cramped quarters made tighter by the fact that the other man's enormous belly couldn't fit under the table's top. Rachel worked diligently on supper, and soon the scent of roast and boiled vegetables filled the room. She glanced at Mason, holding his eyes for a moment to share his amusement at Otis's bravado. Charlotte sat at the end of the table, Jasper contently curled on the floor beneath her.

When Rachel and Mason had first approached Otis with the obvious, startling fact that Mason hadn't died in France as had been claimed, the man had at first thought that he was in the clutches of a drunken hallucination. When he'd been convinced that he was indeed sober, he'd reacted with little more than a whistle and a shrug of his shoulders, although he eventually admitted that he could see little of the old Mason in the man with the ugly scars on his face and had been surprised to learn that Charlotte hadn't minded. Now, sitting in the kitchen, he seemed happy to have a captive audience for another of his drinking stories.

"Every man goin' about on his own, travelin' the rails or otherwise, should always count on doin' some drinkin'," Otis explained. "Hell, if it ain' the law it oughta be!"

Mason laughed in answer.

Rachel's heart leapt to hear Mason's laugh; it was low and gravelly, as if he hadn't used it in a long time. When he noticed her watching, he shot her a grin, his mouth crooked; but even with his scarred face, she saw a glimmer of the man she had once known. Conscious that she was staring, she turned back to her guffawing uncle. "Don't you ever get tired of talking about drinking?"

"Why on earth would I?" Otis said in mock indignation. "Why, the very best things that have ever happened to me have occurred while I've been drinkin' . . . although what they might be seem to be escapin' me at this here moment . . ."

"Surely you can't mean that," Mason said. "What about your arm?"

"What about it?"

"Maybe if you hadn't had so much to drink down at the tavern, you might have been able to fend off whoever it was who attacked you. If nothing else, you could've been clearheaded enough to be able to identify the man."

"What happened to my poor arm ain't got nothin' to do with my havin' too much to drink," Otis explained with the air of a schoolteacher stating the obvious truth. "I'd of beat the tar outta that ruffian if I hadn't slipped on a damn piece of ice, that's all."

"This sounds like another of your stories," Mason chided.

"Uncle Otis tells good stories," Charlotte added.

"Darn right, my dear!" Otis exclaimed.

"I just don't understand why, since this is the first time that you've seen Mason in over eight years, you feel the need to bore him with stories of your exploits," Rachel continued. "Especially considering what just happened to you."

"It's fine, Rachel." Mason smiled. "I don't mind."

"There, you see?" Otis bellowed triumphantly. "Besides, with Mason's bein' gone from Carlson for so many years, he ain't gonna know any of the true and bestest gossip. All I'm tryin' to do is educate the fella! Everyone in town knows I'm the one with the biggest mouth!"

Inwardly, Rachel cringed at her uncle's words. From the moment Mason had suggested letting Otis in on their secret, she'd been reluctant; all it would take would be one slip of the man's drunken tongue and all of Carlson would know that Mason had returned. In counterpoint, Mason had argued about the difficulty in continuing to keep it from the man, and besides, if Otis were to find himself on another bender and drunkenly talk of what he knew, no one was likely to believe him.

"Hopefully you can keep your mouth busy with other things," she teased Otis playfully, "because supper is ready."

Shooing Jasper out from underfoot, Rachel put one hand on Mason's shoulder as she placed the plate of roast on the table. In that instant, she could clearly feel the warmth of his skin beneath his shirt and her heart began to beat just a little bit faster than before. Quickly stepping away from the table and back toward the stove, she wiped at her brow in embarrasment.

Since Mason had come to her aid in the darkness of her room, chasing away the lecherous Jonathan Moseley, she had begun to feel differently in his presence. After so many years struggling to care for Charlotte, attending her many chores in the boardinghouse, and watching as life went by outside with little care whether she were a part of it or not, she had a sense of expectation. She found herself looking forward to seeing him each morning, to hearing him talk and laugh, to simply being with him. Even when they had been in the cemetery, standing before Alice's grave under miserable skies, it had meant a great deal to her that he had asked her to stay.

Just as Rachel was becoming lost in her confused thoughts, the door to the kitchen suddenly opened, and standing there, looking at the shocked and quite startled faces of everyone in the room, was her mother.

Eliza Watkins stood in the doorway dressed primly in a white blouse and dark skirt, her thin arms folded over her chest. A string of pearls circled her neck, its color only a touch whiter than the paleness of her skin. She smiled a bit weakly.

"Oh my!" Rachel gasped.

"Grandma!" Charlotte shouted happily.

"Well don't that there just about beat all," Otis declared as he and Mason got to their feet.

Unable to control herself, Rachel rushed to her mother's side as her own heart raced. She could scarcely believe what she was seeing with her own eyes. So many long years had passed since Eliza Watkins had ventured from her room that it was almost as if she were looking upon a dream, something that couldn't possibly be real.

Happiness flooded her face. In many ways, the person who had been most affected by Alice's death had been her mother. Unable to accept that Alice had not wanted to live, even when giving birth to her own child, Eliza had placed the greatest blame upon herself. That was why she'd refused to come out of her darkened room; life had seemed too perilous for her to control.

Until now.

"Mother," she said, "why . . . what are . . ."

"You were right, Rachel," Eliza said with a faint smile, embracing her daughter in a warm hug. "You were right. The time has come to stop living in the past."

Tears welled in Rachel's eyes.

Turning from her daughter, Eliza looked at Mason as he sat at the table, her gaze again lingering upon the scars that had disfigured his face, the markings responsible for her revulsion of the night before. "I want you to know that, while I can't let go of all of my feelings of anger, I do feel sorry that I slapped you," she explained. "I suppose that I've been every bit as unfair to you as I've been to myself over the years, so I finally decided, with a bit of encouragement from Rachel, that it's time to move on, well past time, as a matter of fact."

"There's nothing to apologize for, Mrs. Watkins," Mason answered.

"So are we gonna stand here jabberin' away and let this here roast grow cold or are we gonna eat?" Otis asked, licking his lips in anticipation.

"Yeah!" Charlotte echoed.

"Am I welcome to join?" Eliza asked.

"For today and forever more," Rachel answered, happier than she had been in a long time.

Shortly after she had finally managed to put Charlotte to bed, and only after agreeing to let Jasper sleep on the bed, Rachel stepped out onto the boardinghouse's small back porch, facing the alley and clothesline. The November night's air was crisp and she tightened her shawl around her shoulders. Above, thousands of stars twinkled in the black sky, as dazzling as jewels. Though happy to be outside, she looked about carefully; after Otis's assault, she was on guard against some despicable act to which Zachary Tucker might stoop.

"The night is beautiful, isn't it?" a voice asked from the shadows.

Rachel recoiled in fright, her eyes searching the depths of the inky darkness at the far end of the porch. There, shrouded in the night, she found Mason as he leaned up against the rickety railing.

"Oh! You startled me!" she explained in surprise.

"I didn't mean to," he apologized.

"It's all right," Rachel said. "I never thought you'd be out here. I thought I'd be alone."

"I occasionally like to sneak out here after everyone has settled down for the night," Mason explained. "With everything that's happened as of late, it's a welcome respite to be able to stare up at the sky and count a few stars. What brings you out?"

"I suppose for the same reason." She sighed, momentarily imaging how much *both* of their lives had changed with his return. "Things have been a bit . . . out of sorts, but now that you're back on your feet, and especially now that my mother has finally left her room, it seems as if life is returning to normal."

"Although I still believe she has every right to be mad at me for what happened. You all do," Mason said simply. "I have no expectations that my many transgressions will be forgiven overnight."

"They won't be, I can promise you that."

"Understandably so."

"But I believe that we all agree that what matters now is what you do from now on," she explained, speaking the feelings she had been unable, maybe even unwilling, to voice for days. "As I told my mother, we need to look toward the future instead of living only in the past. Alice is gone, and the truth is that none of us can change that."

For a moment, both of them were silent, each giving thought to what the future might mean for them. High above, Rachel watched as a shooting star streaked across the darkness, before vanishing without a trace.

"Charlotte said that you told her you were her father," she finally said.

"Yes, I did." Mason nodded, faintly visible in the darkness. "To tell you the truth, I was pretty damn nervous, but it felt wonderful that she did not seem opposed to the idea. The more thought I gave to what you said, I knew that I had to be there in Charlotte's life, if she'll have me."

Rachel's breath caught in her chest at the recognition of the man who she had

known so many years before; Mason Tucker
had always been a truly honorable, up-
standing man who accepted his responsibilities willingly, no matter how heavy his
burden might be to bear. With every passing day, he did more to rehabilitate himself
in her eyes.

"She will accept you, Mason," she said.
"It's my hope that we all will."

"I'd like to believe you could be right."

"You can start by watching her perform
in the school play," Rachel announced
warmly. "It's the day after tomorrow and
it's about the only thing half as exciting as
you coming back into her life."

"I don't know . . . I don't think that I'm
ready . . ." he replied haltingly.

Without Mason giving her a full explanation, Rachel knew well the dilemma he
faced. As difficult as it had been for him to
go to the cemetery and look upon Alice's
grave, as hard as it had been to face Eliza's wrath, the very idea of revealing himself to the good townspeople of Carlson
was almost certainly more than he was
ready to endure.

Rachel nodded. "I understand. I'll do

what I can to smooth it over with Charlotte, although it won't be easy."

"Any help you can give would be appreciated."

Rachel tugged at her shawl, then said, "What do you plan to do next, Mason?"

"I need to see my father," Mason answered simply. "He needs to know that I'm alive."

"You'll have to get past your brother in order to tell him."

"What do you mean?"

As carefully yet as thoroughly as she could, Rachel explained to Mason all of the things that had befallen Sherman Tucker in the years his elder son had been gone. Delicately, she described his father's decline in health, his eventual withdrawal from the Carlson Bank and Trust, and Zachary's rise to power over the community. In no uncertain terms, she told Mason of how Zachary's dealings had ruined people's lives and, with anger rising in her voice, of how he had made a play for ownership of the boardinghouse. She even went as far as to surmise that Zachary had been behind the attack upon Otis, and that if he knew his brother were still alive, there would be no telling to what ends he would be willing to go.

"He lives with your father in his home," Rachel added. "Though some people believe that he does so in order to care for Sherman, there are others who are of the mind that he's only protecting his own interests. With your father gone, ownership will be his."

"That sounds like Zachary. I'm sure he's plotted and schemed for years."

"I can believe that," Rachel said knowingly.

"I saw him when I first came to town," Mason said, giving thought to how Zachary had rushed down the street in such a hurry that he resembled more a fat chicken with its head cut off than a banker. "I suppose I should be thankful that I didn't get close enough for him to recognize me."

"Knowing all of this, how are you going to be able to see your father?"

"There's a way," he answered confidently.

Again, the silence returned between them. Rachel wondered silently if it was really proper for her to be enjoying Mason's

company as much as she did; after all, he
was once married to her sister. She was
lost in her complicated ruminations when
he spoke.

"If you're cold, you don't need to stand
out here on my account," he said.

"I'm fine," Rachel answered, even as
the hairs on her arms stood on end from
the chill. The truth was that there was nowhere she'd rather be than standing there
with him. That she had so much as thought
such a forward thing made her face flush
with embarrassment.

"Thank you, Rachel."

"For what?"

"For everything that you've done for
me," Mason said, his voice as soft as the
night breeze.

"You don't have to thank me." Rachel
smiled, relieved that his words had given
pause to her conflicted thoughts. "Nursing
you back to health really wasn't that
hard, other than the smell," she joked.

"That's not what I mean," he explained,
ignoring her attempt at humor. Confidently,
he took a couple of steps toward her, stopping only when he was at her side; though
he wasn't touching her, Rachel could feel

warmth coming from his very presence. "I'm talking about what you've done for Charlotte and the burden you've had to carry here at the boardinghouse. Such a weight shouldn't have been yours to bear."

"You don't have to say a word about Charlotte. I love her as if she were my own daughter."

"I thank you just the same."

Gently, Mason reached out and placed his hand upon Rachel's shoulder. In that instant when they touched, confusion reigned in her heart, filling her bewildered mind with as many questions as there were stars in the sky. On the one hand, she wanted to melt pleasurably into his arms, but she couldn't help but wonder at how she could feel such things about a man who was once married to her sister. So instead Rachel remained frozen, unsure of what to do. Though she wanted to ask Mason his thoughts, to try to find answers to her endless stream of questions, in the end there was nothing for her to do but escape.

"I . . . I should get some rest," she said, the words rushing from her mouth as she stepped back away from Mason and toward the door. "I . . . I just . . ." was all she could manage before hurrying back inside.

By the time she had reached the stair-case, her eyes were already filling with tears.

Chapter Twenty-five

RACHEL SAT QUIETLY in the stifling heat of the school's gymnasium, facing the impromptu stage that had been constructed for the night's performance. Brown and orange leaves had been made from paper and paint and then strung along the front of the stage like bunting. A hand-drawn sign declaring a "Celebration of Harvest" had been placed upon an easel fronting the crowd. A makeshift tree had been set out as a prop.

Folding chairs were arranged in neat rows for the audience, which was made up entirely of parents and other children who had been dragged along. With the performance soon to begin, most of the seats were full. Up near the stage, one of the teachers was tuning the piano, carefully plunking each key. Occasionally a head poked out from the shadows for a brief look at the crowd before its owner was shooed backstage.

Rachel had already been to a couple of these performances to watch Charlotte and her fellow classmates struggle through their show. The theme of the play changed little; with Carlson's lifeblood so closely connected to the land on which it had been settled, most plays were about one harvest or another. There would be plenty of polite applause, a laugh or two, often unintended, and finally a standing ovation as all of the children came back onstage for an encore.

The room was growing warm. All around her, men and women fanned themselves with the homemade programs the students had made. Though a couple of ceiling fans had been installed in the last year, they did little to alleviate the discomfort, only managing to stir the heat. Beads of sweat began to appear on Rachel's forehead and cheeks, but she ignored them.

Two days had passed since her encounter with Mason on the back porch of the boardinghouse, and since that time he had constantly been in her thoughts. Over and over she had replayed the events of that night: the way he had smiled, how he'd eased over to where she stood, but particularly the words he had spoken. Ever since, whenever she was around him, she'd been so conscious of what had happened that she'd been unable to simply be herself. She wondered if he had noticed.

Her life had been made more difficult as a result of Mason's unwillingness to come to the play. Though she recognized his reasons for not attending, Charlotte hadn't been as understanding as Rachel would have hoped. When informed of her father's decision, she had burst into tears and gone running up the stairs to her room. It had taken all of the coaxing and cajoling that Rachel could muster to persuade her to come out and go to the school. She had sulked the whole way, sniffling and pouting with every step.

Rachel had also hoped that her mother might attend, but she hadn't been the least bit surprised when Eliza declined the offer. Though she had already remained outside of her room more than Rachel had expected, going out to such a public event was still a step too far. So while Otis headed off to the tavern and Mason remained at home, Rachel had accompanied Charlotte alone.

Suddenly, a shout of "I don't want to!" echoed through the gymnasium. Instantly, Rachel knew just who had yelled; it had been Charlotte. The play hadn't even begun and already there was drama.

What more could possibly go wrong tonight?

With her small arms crossed defiantly over her heaving chest and her lips pursed into a fierce pout, Charlotte frowned up into the eyes of her distraught teacher, Mrs. Schumacher. Even though the woman's mouth was fixed in a permanent smile, her full cheeks pushed up in a sort of grimace, her tired eyes betrayed her mounting unease; she had the harried look of a rabbit that knew the fox was lurking nearby. All around, children dashed about wildly, most of them in various states of dress and all of them wound tighter than grandfather clocks. But even in the midst of such chaos, the teacher's eyes remained fixed upon Charlotte and the orange-leaf costume she was trying to coax her to put on.

"But I don't wanna wear that stupid thing!" the girl shouted.

"Now Charlotte, you—"

"I said I don't wanna do it!"

"We just need you to put this on, sweetheart," her teacher pleaded in a syrupy sweet voice, as sweat began to bead on her upper lip. "After all, your family has come to watch you perform and it would be a great disappointment to them if they didn't get to see you in your lovely costume."

"Not all of them, and I'm just a dumb old leaf!"

"Just wear it, dear," Mrs. Schumacher said, finally showing some of her mounting exasperation as she handed the costume to Charlotte. For a moment, it looked increasingly likely that she would have to force the girl to put it on, but just then a pair of children dashed by, a boy chasing a girl and grabbing menacingly at her pigtails, and the teacher's attention was drawn elsewhere. "Walter Wiggins!" she snapped. "Walter, you stop that this instant!"

Left by herself, her ridiculous costume dangling limply from her hands, Charlotte felt miserable about what her teacher had said; the truth was that everyone in her family *hadn't* come to watch her in the play—only Rachel was there.

Even though he and Rachel had tried to explain it to her, that it wasn't the right time for her father to be seen out in public, she was still resentful. All she wanted was for him to come watch her, to be proud of her, so that she could finally tell all of the other children that she too had a parent.

Why is that too much to ask?

Near the front of the stage, Catherine Nichols was getting ready to be the star of the show, dressed in a bright blouse and skirt for her role as the farmer's wife. Even Charlotte had to admit that she looked better than anyone else. With her long blonde hair and cheery smile, it wasn't hard for her to be the center of attention. Charlotte cringed when Catherine saw her looking her way, giving her a knowing, confident smirk.

Charlotte groaned and looked down at her costume. She supposed that her teacher *was* right about something: Rachel would probably be disappointed if she'd come to the gymnasium for nothing. Reluctantly, she slipped on her leaf outfit just as Mrs. Schumacher returned, as frantic as ever, and began rounding up all of her charges and getting them in their places.

"Now remember," she encouraged. "Big smiles, everyone!"

Charlotte stood offstage as the tall curtains were opened and the piano began to play robustly. As the lights were dimmed over the audience, a polite clapping echoed through the gymnasium.

While watching the first children run out in front of the audience dressed as squash and ears of corn, Charlotte wished that she could have been traipsing around the woods with Jasper instead of sweating heavily inside her ridiculous costume.

The play proceeded just as it had been practiced; after the first crops had made their appearance, Catherine and the boy playing the farmer sauntered onstage and recited their lines about the hard work being no burden in the face of such a plentiful harvest. Then other children went out and reaped the now abundant crops, just as the weather began to take a turn for the worse. Finally, it was Charlotte's turn to perform.

There were four other children playing leaves; a couple of them orange, one brown, and one a deep purple. The script called for them to run out onto the stage and act as if they were being blown haphazardly by the autumn wind, lingering at the front of the stage before making their way to the other side. Charlotte went out with the rest of the leaves and dashed about as she had been instructed, but just as she was about to make her exit, she took a moment to look out into the audience in the hopes that Rachel might be visible and instead saw something that stopped her in her tracks.

There, at the far back of the gymnasium, leaning against the wall and visible only in the light that poured through the door to his right, stood her father.

He had come to the play after all!

Rachel was furiously fanning herself with her program when the lights to the gymnasium went down and the makeshift curtain on the stage parted. The man at the piano began to play and the first of the children rushed out onto the stage, went to their positions, and began to recite their lines.

Watching the expressions of the parents seated around her, pleasant smiles broadening across their sweat-covered faces, Rachel felt her own sense of pride growing at Charlotte's accomplishments. Though she had been thrust into the role of mother by forces beyond her own control, it was a role she had assumed willingly. She had been there for every one of Charlotte's successes and failures, watching the girl grow into the image of Alice, and she didn't want anything to change.

But it already has changed . . .

Mason's return to Carlson meant, for better or worse, that nothing in Charlotte's life would ever be the same. For now, the girl was elated, thrilled to finally have what she had been denied her whole life. But what would the next day hold, or the day after that? When Rachel and Mason had spoken the night before, he had expressed a desire for things to remain as they were. "There's no reason for that to change," he'd said.

Rachel's attention was drawn to the stage. After the first group of children had performed an unintentionally funny song-and-dance routine that was met with enthusiastic applause from the audience, the scenery was changed and a new batch of performers came onstage. This group portrayed a family of farmers anxiously awaiting the harvest in the face of the rapidly approaching winter; Rachel was struck by how accurately this depicted what the good people of Carlson went through each fall.

Then there was a calamitous banging on the piano, clearly meant to announce the arrival of something dreadful—in this case the sudden rising of the fall winds. It was then that Charlotte and four other children, all of them dressed as differently colored leaves, ran out onto the stage and began darting first one direction and then another, blowing about as if the announced wind really was pushing them.

Just as those parents around her

had beamed with obvious pride at the appearance of their own children on the stage, Rachel felt her own heart swell at the first sight of Charlotte. Though she knew that the girl's part was small, only a quick sighting until the last song, which would be performed by everyone in the production, she reveled in every second. As Charlotte crazily rushed around in her costume, her blonde braids bouncing about, Rachel's eyes never left her, pleasantly regarding every step the girl took.

That's my daughter!

When Charlotte reached the front of the stage, she clearly began to look around in the audience, her eyes searching across the rows of chairs. Rachel thought to raise her hand, to make it easier for the girl to spot her if only for a quick moment, but just as she was about to do so, Charlotte came to a sudden and complete stop, her acting role forgotten, her eyes fixed upon something in the rear of the gymnasium.

Even as the other children continued to do as they had been instructed, never forgetting their role as leaves, blowing here and there but always moving to the opposite side of the stage, finally passing behind the curtain, Charlotte stood planted in place as surely as if she were the tree she was supposed to have fallen from. At first her arms hung limply at her sides, but as a spectacularly broad smile spread across her face, she lifted a hand and waved.

"Charlotte!" a voice whispered from backstage. "Charlotte! You're supposed to be off the stage!" Rachel caught a glimpse of a frantic woman, her eyes wide and pleading, waving one arm about in the hope of gaining the girl's wandering attention.

Instead, Charlotte continued to stare.

Intensely curious, Rachel turned in her seat and followed Charlotte's gaze. At first, she could see nothing but the faces of those seated around her, many regarding what was going on with bemused interest, but then she let her eyes travel farther, finally noticing what had caused all of the commotion.

Mason!

He leaned against the back wall of the gymnasium, standing mostly unseen in the deep shadows; if it hadn't been for the sparse light seeping in through the door at his side, Rachel was quite certain she would never have seen him. With a hat pulled down low over his brow and his arms folded across his broad chest, Mason would have been impossible to identify without closer scrutiny. She thought she could see him smile in answer to his daughter's broad grin and wave.

Though Mason had told Charlotte that he wouldn't be able to attend her performance, something had happened to make him think better of his decision. Whether it had been the copious amount of tears his daughter had shed that had swayed him or if it had been his intention to come all along, Rachel couldn't know, but her heart soared at the surprising sight of him. She knew it was impossible for him to sit beside her in the crowd, to allow his former friends and neighbors to look upon him and his scars, but that hadn't been enough to keep him from watching his daughter on her important day.

But what Rachel felt most was more than her happiness for Charlotte; seeing Mason raised feelings of her own. She turned away from him quickly, suddenly aware that questioning eyes were falling upon her. Her heart beat thunderously and she was thankful for the relative dimness of the makeshift auditorium, if for nothing more than it masked her blushing cheeks.

As Charlotte's teacher went out onto the stage to retrieve her wayward pupil, a sudden truth revealed itself to Rachel; she was beginning to have feelings for Mason Tucker, the man who had been married to her sister.

Just as soon as Charlotte was reluctantly pulled off the stage and behind the curtain by her teacher, Mason quietly turned and slipped out the door that led from the gymnasium. Even with his hat pulled down low, the glare of the lights felt blinding. Thankfully, the short hallway that led from the auditorium to the street was empty. Within seconds, he was stepping out into the chilly November night.

It might have been risky, but it was worth it!

Seeing Charlotte on the stage had warmed Mason's heart in a way that hadn't happened once in the eight years since he had set off for France. Though she was only a little girl, from a distance she so reminded him of Alice, particularly the color of her hair. From the moment she stepped onstage, he found himself holding his breath, his heart pounding full of pride, full of feelings he'd never imagined existed.

Mason's intention *had* been to stay away; he'd meant what he'd said to Charlotte and Rachel when he'd explained why he couldn't attend the performance. But somehow, watching out the window of his room in the boardinghouse as they set off for the school, he had known that if he didn't see his daughter at such an important moment of her life, even for an instant, he would regret it for the rest of his days.

"I'm through missing out on the events of her life," he'd muttered to himself.

Grabbing up his long coat and hat, Mason had practically leapt down the staircase and out the door, but he had still been cautious, finally deciding to approach the gymnasium only after he'd felt certain that everyone who was planning to attend was already inside. Entering the building carefully and standing beside the main door, he'd been ready to make a quick exit if it was called for. In the deep shadows, he believed it was impossible for Charlotte to see him, but when she had, he'd felt his heart nearly burst with pride.

Mason felt bad that Rachel had had to sit by herself, but he had no doubt that she would have realized who Charlotte was waving at; what finally necessitated his leaving was that nearly half the audience turned to see what the leaf found so fascinating. He hoped that Rachel understood what he was trying to do for his daughter.

Thinking about Rachel made him recall what he had said to her the other night on the back porch. His words had surprised even himself, falling out of his mouth as easily as rain from the sky. Declaring that he didn't want anything to change in Rachel's relationship with Charlotte undoubtedly was heartfelt, but complicated nonetheless. The simple truth was that he enjoyed her company in ways he had never anticipated; the thought of her leaving his life, as well as Charlotte's, unsettled him.

Still, so much else in his life was similarly unsettled.

Sooner or later, Mason knew that he was going to have to face the people of

Carlson without standing in the shadows. The list of those to whom he owed amends was long, but it began with his father. Sherman Tucker had always remained the largest figure in his life. From what Rachel had told him, Mason himself was the one responsible for the hard times that had befallen the man.

Mason was lost in these difficult thoughts, wondering how he might be able to speak with his father privately, when he rounded the corner of Main Street to see a man hurriedly approaching. Even lost in concentration, his head down, the man was instantly recognizable.

It was his brother, Zachary.

Fearful that he might have another collision, one from which he would be unable to escape unrecognized, Mason stepped back into the inky shadows between two buildings and watched as Zachary came closer. Well-dressed and groomed, considerably overweight, his brother was oblivious to whatever was going on around him. As he watched, Mason became aware of an insistent tugging at the back of his thoughts, one that told him that encountering his brother was a sign and that to ignore it would be every bit as regrettable as having missed Charlotte's performance.

With resolve, Mason turned and walked into the night.

Chapter Twenty-six

ZACHARY TUCKER WALKED quickly down the main thoroughfare of Carlson, his shoulders slumped as low as his mood. A brisk, chilly wind raced down from the north, and he turned up the collar of his wool coat for what warmth it provided. No one else was foolish enough to have ventured out on such a night; he had the streets all to himself.

Only minutes earlier, Zachary had finally left the bank for the night. He'd spent the entire day pouring over the piles of paperwork he had done in requisitioning property for the Gaitskill Lumber Company: promissory notes, ledgers full of figures, and even the telegrams that had been sent by both parties. Everything was in order.

Except . . .

Never in his wildest imagination would Zachary have believed that the success of his ingenious plan could hinge upon the whims of his brother's former family. He felt naïve for having believed that he could go to Rachel and receive a fair turn. She had proven every bit as stubborn as her mother. Even the attack on her uncle hadn't proved enough to sway them to his cause.

But what could I possibly have expected?

Still, Zachary knew that no amount of anger or frustration, no matter how justified, was going to change a single thing. After all, what could he even conceivably do; have Travis Jefferson burn the boardinghouse to the ground? At such a late date, the options remaining to him were few: maybe he could attempt to sway the company's board of directors to believe that there was another spur of railroad they could use; maybe he could persuade them to give him a bit more time; or maybe he could convince them to speak to that bitch Eliza Watkins and negotiate a better deal . . .

What in the hell am I going to do?

Loath as Zachary was to admit it, his grandiose schemes seemed to be blowing away like so much smoke. Months and months of planning, meticulous manipulation of funds and people, all would be ruined by the stubbornness of one woman, one family. He would still be wealthy, would still hold his position of authority in town, but it wouldn't be as much as he had wanted. There would be no choice but to settle.

Turning the corner that led to the home he shared with his bedridden father, Zachary came to a sudden halt. For an instant, out of the corner of his eye, he thought he had seen something dart between the houses on the other side of the street. Was it a deer or some other wild game? Hell, it was probably some drunken slob like Otis Simmons looking for a place to relieve his booze-laden bladder. The poor bastard would probably be lucky not to fall asleep outdoors and freeze to death because of his own stupidity.

Shaking his head and chiding himself for his nerves, Zachary plodded on, the weight of the moon and stars above pressing down on him.

Mason hurried along in the darkness, carefully picking his way behind the buildings that lined Main Street. He was careful not to trip over anything lying in the way as he wove past crates and grease-stained barrels, yet he was still able to keep Zachary in sight. Thankfully, his brother's pace was easy to maintain; one good thing about Zachary's new girth was that he wasn't going to be going anywhere in a hurry.

The moon looked down from above, just short of half full, surrounded by thousands of stars; the light that shone from the heavens was faint, hardly illuminating the ground at Mason's feet. Hastening along, he worried that he might encounter a barking dog that would alert Zachary, but he couldn't hear anything except for his own breathing.

So far, so good . . .

Even as he moved forward, Mason wasn't entirely sure of what he was doing;

he knew that he should be staying as far away from Zachary as possible. With all that Rachel had told him, combined with his own bad experiences with his younger brother, it was clear that Zachary had grown into an outright scoundrel.

Still, seeing Zachary on the same night that he'd felt such a strong urge to see his father was too much of a coincidence for Mason to ignore. While it would undoubtedly have been wiser to wait a day or two longer, until he was certain that Zachary was busy at the bank and his father was alone, he felt drawn to look upon Sherman Tucker with an insistence he was unable to ignore.

Moving ahead of his brother's pace, Mason slipped behind Carlson's Lutheran church, its tall white steeple standing out in stark contrast to the black sky above. Paralleling a row of well-groomed hedges, he hurried around the church in order to keep Zachary in his sight. Though the temperature continued to drop, driven downward by the breeze, Mason felt no cold, his chest burning with the desire to complete the task he had set for himself.

On and on they went, Mason shadowing

Zachary, who remained unaware of being followed. Suddenly, crouching in the shadows between two houses, Mason was startled to see his brother come to an abrupt halt, looking in his direction. Faster than a spooked rabbit, Mason darted behind a nearby evergreen, certain that he had been seen, his heart hammering. Seconds dragged on. A cold sweat beaded his forehead, but finally he forced himself to move. Between the next gap of houses, Zachary came back into view showing no sign of having noticed him. Mason kept on cautiously.

Finally they came to the home that Sherman Tucker had built in the years before his sons were born. On the far northern edge of Carlson, standing splendidly against a backdrop of grand evergreens and elms, Lake Carlson no more than a stone's throw away, the two-story home was one of the nicest in town. With an elegant wraparound porch, beveled glass windows, and gabled roof, it represented the success that its builder had accrued for himself and his family. As Mason warily approached, a careful eye kept upon the single light that shone through the downstairs windows, memories of all the years he had spent growing up inside the home's grand walls flooded his thoughts. Somewhere inside was his father.

Mason watched as Zachary made his way up the short walk and let himself in through the front door, leaving behind him the audible click of the lock being turned, the noise carrying out into the cold night.

Hurrying toward the rear of the house, Mason saw more lights being turned on as his brother proceeded deeper through the darkened rooms. Ever darker shadows enveloped him as he headed closer to the trees at the back of the property, their tall branches stretching into the night sky, blocking out the brilliant moon and stars above. Crunching sticks and pine needles, his approach startled a pair of rabbits, who scampered away.

As a child, Mason had spent hours playing on his father's property, learning each and every secret it might hold. In order to escape from Sherman's overly protective eye, he'd needed a way to get in and out of the house undetected; it was this avenue he would use to gain entry.

Mason jumped up and grabbed the

low-hanging branch of a maple tree that grew beside the big house, pulling himself up from the ground with little effort. Scaling a series of branches, he easily found the familiar handholds. Quickly rising in the leafless tree, he shimmied out onto a branch that overhung the roof. After listening for any signs of movement, he took a deep breath and dropped onto the house, fearful that the sound of his heavy landing would echo throughout the house.

Don't hear a thing, Zachary . . .

His breath caught in his chest, Mason waited for some sign that he had been detected, but the only answer was continued silence.

The pitch of the roof was steeper than Mason remembered, but he managed to pull himself upward by holding on to the outside edge. He maintained his precarious balance carefully. Close above him, two windows looked out onto the lake and the southern horizon; he knew that his father's room was the one on the right.

Inch by inch, Mason made his way, wary of losing his footing. Finally, he reached out and held fast to the pitched edge of the window's roofed overhang.

Mason's heart beat furiously in his chest, but he knew it wasn't from the exertion of climbing the roof; on the other side of the window, he was sure to find his father. While he had rushed to the house so that he could look upon Sherman Tucker, now he hesitated.

"C'mon now," he chided himself. "It's too late to turn back."

Peeking out in front of the glass, Mason tried to see inside the room, but only darkness was reflected back at him. As usual, the window wasn't latched; for as long as he could remember, his father enjoyed having a breeze while he slept, something that Zachary clearly hadn't paid much attention to, and thus the window remained unlocked. Mindful of any squeaks that might inadvertently announce him, Mason lifted the sash and stepped into his father's room.

For a long moment, Mason stood frozen, fearful even to breathe. The inside of the room seemed darker than outdoors, but his eyes slowly adjusted to the blackness. Eventually, he saw clearly enough to recognize that his father's bedroom had changed little in eight years; though the house was representative of the wealth Sherman Tucker had accumulated, the room in which his son stood was much simpler. Only sparse furnishings were visible: an ordinary dresser, a well-worn table, and a plain lamp complemented the bed.

Still crouched by the window, Mason followed a faint sliver of moonlight to where it illuminated a patch of the bed. There, with a wool blanket covering him, lay his father.

As he moved closer to the bed, Mason's breath was torn from his lungs when his eyes fell upon Sherman Tucker as he slept soundly, so great was the change that had fallen upon the man. Deep lines and wrinkles creased his forehead, his cheeks, and the corners of his eyes. Age spots haphazardly dotted his skin. His hair, once black with tinges of white, was now snowy wisps. But worst of all was the way his mouth sagged, turned down in a permanent frown, unwilling or unable to right itself. Tears welled in Mason's eyes as he saw what his father had become in his absence.

"Oh, Papa," he choked out. "I'm so sorry."

Regret clutched at Mason's heart. For all the long years he had been gone, he'd never once imagined that a man as vibrant, as full of life as Sherman Tucker would be struck so low.

Mason cursed the day he had decided to remain away from Carlson and those he loved. In all of those years, he'd never truly grasped the many consequences of his actions. With Zachary more than willing to snatch the reins of power at the bank, his father had been forced aside, not just from the institution he'd built from his own sweat and will, but from life itself.

Just as Mason was about to offer whatever futile apologies he could muster for all that he had caused, he was startled by the sight of his father sputtering to consciousness, his eyes fluttering as he began to stir.

"Who . . . who's there?" he asked feebly, his gaze searching.

Mason was stuck in place, uncertain as to what, if anything, he should do. Part of him wondered if he shouldn't make a break for it, rush back to the window and escape out into the night, fearful that looking upon his disfigured and scarred face would only cause his father more hurt. But he had no more than possessed the thought when he dismissed it; the time for running away from life's difficulties had ended. With unsteady fingers, he gently took his father's feeble hand into his own.

"It's Mason, Papa," he said softly. "I've come home."

Even in the meager light of the moon, Mason could see the outright shock and disbelief that raced across Sherman Tucker's disheveled features, his eyes growing wide and his lower lip trembling. When he had finally composed himself enough to speak, his voice, while frail, still carried with it the unmistakable sound of hope.

"How . . . how can it be . . . ?" he asked. "My son . . . is long gone from me . . ."

"I'm here with you now."

"No . . . no, I can't . . ." Sherman faltered.

"I know how hard this must be for you to hear, Papa, how impossible it must be for you to believe," Mason explained; with each and every word he spoke, he felt the older man's grip tighten. "I can't begin to tell you how sorry I am that I've been gone so long."

Sherman's eyes narrowed in the gloom, straining for a better look at the man who had entered his room, suddenly opening wide as he saw enough to dispel whatever suspicions he harbored. His breathing grew and tears soon streaked down his cheeks.

"My . . . my boy . . ." he sobbed.

"Please, Papa," Mason soothed, barely able to contain the emotion that rose in his own heart.

"Your face," Sherman said as he raised one gnarled hand up to press it against Mason's scars, his eyes brimming with both concern and surprise. "What . . . what happened . . . ?"

"There will be time for us to talk soon, Papa, but . . . but, I . . . I . . ."

Mason faltered, unable to say more. So much of him wanted to stay and make the amends that were needed, but he knew what was risked at Zachary's hands. If he were to do what was right, if he were to protect Rachel, her family, and the future of his own daughter, he had to be patient.

"But why . . . why must you go?" his father questioned.

Before Mason could answer, the sound

of footsteps, undoubtedly those of his brother as he made his way up the stairs, rose outside his father's door.

In that moment, Mason knew that he had a difficult choice to make; he could either stay and confront Zachary, bring the real story of his absence out into the open, or he could go quickly and choose another moment for the confrontation he knew was inevitable.

Releasing his hand from his father's grip, Mason said, "I have to go now, Papa, but I'll be back. I promise." He bent and kissed his father on the forehead, then swiftly crossed the room and threw open the window. He had just managed to get outside when the door behind him opened, framing Zachary in silhouette.

Panic gripped Zachary's chest at the sight of a stranger standing outside the window to his father's room. He recoiled in fright, but soon calmed whatever thundering remained in his chest and rushed over to engage the window's lock.

By the time Zachary reached the glass, whoever had been there had slid down the roof's incline and leapt into the limbs of the maple tree that overhung the house; all that remained to be seen of the intruder was the irregular swaying of several large branches.

Who in the hell was that?

"Come . . . come back, Mason . . ." his father croaked behind him.

Zachary turned quickly, unable to believe what he thought he had heard. He was at his father's side in an instant, his hands clenched tightly into fists. "What . . . what did you just say? Who was that?" he demanded.

"Mason . . . it was Mason . . ." Sherman smiled, showing the first real emotion that his younger son could remember seeing in his face in years. Joyful tears rushed freely down his wrinkled cheeks. "Mason . . . was here . . ."

Stunned, Zachary turned back to the window half expecting the shadowy figure to have returned. His first instinct was to believe that his father was delusional, that his illness had progressed to the point where he was imaging his long dead son coming to visit. But that ignored the fact that he had seen someone as well.

Questions   exploded   in   Zachary's

thoughts. He wanted to press his father to tell him *exactly* what had happened in the room, to shake the cobwebs from the old fool's head and learn who the visitor had been, but looking down, he saw that his father had returned to his slumber, his eyes closed and his face somehow pleasant.

"It's not possible," he said to himself. "It cannot be."

But somewhere in Zachary Tucker's stomach, concern gnawed at him. There had been a man, a man who looked vaguely as Mason once had, but such a resemblance was no great stretch. The very idea that he was Mason was ridiculous even to entertain! But why had his father believed the man was Mason, why had he seemed so full of life when he otherwise looked close to death?

A sudden rush of wind rattled the glass panes of the window, and Zachary shivered.

Someone has been here! Who?

Chapter Twenty-seven

WITH CHARLOTTE FINALLY put to bed and the dishes from dinner washed and set out to dry, Rachel looked curiously out the window of the boardinghouse's kitchen, watching Mason stand solemnly on the back porch. The old hat he had worn to the performance at the school the night before was pulled down low over his face, but she could see enough of what remained visible to notice his wistful expression.

Around him, the night hung heavily. Earlier in the day, the first flakes of snow had begun to cascade lazily from the steel-gray clouds above, covering Carlson in a

soft blanket of ivory. Teasing winds pushed
it about in billowing sheets. Though it was
only a precursor to what would eventually
come, the snow had been accompanied
by a deep chill; Rachel could see Mason's
breath being exhaled in puffy clouds.

Throughout the day, Mason had remained largely silent and distant, respond-
ing only when spoken to and giving only a
weak smile when Charlotte tried to joke
with him at the dinner table. Even now, his
arms were folded across his broad chest,
more a sign that he wanted to be left alone
than to ward off the cold. Clearly, the decisions he must make were weighing on
him.

The absence of Mason's attention bothered Rachel more than she would have
ever thought possible. Though he had
been missing from her life for years, she
now had come to truly enjoy his company,
the deep sound of his voice, and surprisingly to her, the way he looked at her. Even
his scars, the reason he had remained
away for so many years, did not repulse
her. She still remembered the night, much
like this one, only days before, when he
had spoken words that had both thrilled

and unsettled her, feelings she still felt. To have him so clearly upset bothered her.

Watching Mason brood, Rachel knew that she could no longer ignore what remained unspoken between them. Hanging her apron on a hook beside the stove, she grabbed her shawl, wrapped it tightly around her shoulders, opened the door, and stepped outside.

"A penny for your thoughts," she offered.

"That's about all that they're worth these days," he answered, smiling easily as he turned toward her.

"You've been awfully quiet today, not that any of us would have been capable of getting a word in edgewise at supper with the way Charlotte carried on."

For almost the whole meal, Charlotte had chattered away, recounting her surprise and excitement at seeing her father watching from the rear of the gymnasium. Though her teacher had been irate at having to go out on the stage and drag her kicking and fussing back behind the curtain, the young girl cared little, and recounted her story as if it were another of her and Jasper's exploits in the woods.

She was so intent on talking that Rachel had to remind her to finish her supper.

"It meant a lot to her that you went to the play," Rachel added.

"Almost as much as it meant to me, I reckon."

"What changed your mind? You said you wouldn't go."

Mason shrugged his shoulders. "I realized that missing her performance and having to see the disappointment in her eyes was more than I could bear," he explained. "I already have hundreds of regrets for what I've done, regardless of my intentions, but now I want to make it up, if I can. Charlotte is the one person I'll not let down again."

His promise warmed Rachel's heart. Gone was the man who had purposefully stayed absent from Carlson, never willing to let those who loved him know that he hadn't perished on some foreign battlefield. In his place stood a man who understood the priority of family and was willing to make whatever sacrifices were necessary in order to uphold that bond.

"I'm glad you're home," Rachel told him.

"I didn't know what I had waiting for me here."

"I cannot imagine how it must have felt to learn you had a daughter."

"But she's not the only reason that—" Mason started to answer, turning to face Rachel for only an instant before falling silent and returning his gaze to the star-filled sky.

Rachel desperately wanted him to speak to her, to say the words she knew he was choosing to leave unspoken, but understood that she couldn't force him. Regardless of how badly she wished it were otherwise, Mason would only tell her when he was ready. For that matter, she found it nearly impossible to speak of the feelings buffeting her own heart.

Don't let things remain unsaid, Rachel chided herself.

"What is . . . what's bothering you, Mason?" she finally asked.

Rachel watched as Mason took a deep breath, wondering if her wish that he would confide in her was about to come true, but when he eventually spoke, his words surprised her. "Yesterday, I . . . I went to see my father."

"But . . . but when?"

"Last night," he explained. "After I left the school, I'd meant to come back here to the boardinghouse, but then I nearly ran into Zachary on his way home from the bank."

Rachel gasped. "Did he see you?" she asked nervously.

"No," he answered. "At least not right then."

Mason explained that ever since the day he had gone to the cemetery and had made his peace with Eliza, he'd been doing a lot of thinking about his father. Undeniably, Sherman Tucker had played an essential role in Mason's life, as a mentor as well as a parent. That he hadn't told his father he was still alive, especially considering Sherman's failing health, was something he needed to rectify. When he had encountered his brother, the desire to see his father simply became too great to ignore.

"So you followed Zachary?" Rachel asked.

Mason nodded. "You had mentioned that Zachary still lived with my father, so I kept pace with him until he arrived. Once we came in sight of the house, absolutely nothing was going to stop me from seeing Papa."

"But with Zachary there, how did you manage?"

With his face touched by a hint of mischief, Mason told her of how he had accomplished his goal; Rachel listened breathlessly as he recounted climbing the tree, scaling the roof, and making his way into his father's darkened room.

"When I looked down at him, when I saw how much he had changed, maybe because he thought I'd died in the war, I felt devastated. I couldn't believe my absence had caused that much pain. Even after learning that Alice had died in childbirth and seeing the burden that was placed upon you and the void that it made in Charlotte's life, it wasn't until that moment, seeing my father in that state, that I truly realized how much anger and suffering I caused for everyone."

Though there had undeniably been a time when Rachel would have been a willing voice in the raging chorus of hatred for Mason Tucker, blaming him for the misfortune that had befallen Alice and her family, her feelings had unquestionably changed. Listening to him speak with such heartfelt anguish filled her with compassion.

"When my father spoke to me, my heart nearly broke," Mason added.

"Did . . . did he know that it was you?"

"He looked at me and said my name, reached out and put his hand on my scars and appeared to have recognized that it was me, but with his health so clearly deteriorating, I wonder if he'll even remember I was there the next time he wakes. Hell, even if he does recall my visit, he'll probably think it was nothing but an unwelcome dream."

"But you fulfilled your wish," Rachel argued. "You got to see him."

"I did," Mason acknowledged with a frown. "Unfortunately, that's not the worst of it."

"What happened?" she asked, her voice panicked.

"I think that Zachary might have seen me as I was leaving."

"Oh, dear!" Dread filled Rachel's chest at the thought of Zachary once again becoming involved in their lives. Having already stated his intense and seemingly insatiable desire to own the boarding-house, demonstrating it through his will-ingness to have Otis attacked as Rachel believed, she knew that there was no tell-ing what Mason's brother was capable of. "Are you sure?"

"Not entirely," Mason admitted truthfully. "The room was almost as dark as mid-night, and by the time he opened the door, I'd already made my way back outside. By the time he made it to the window, I would have been shooting down the tree. The problem is that I *don't* know for sure. There's no way of knowing whether he got a good enough look to identify me or not, but know-ing what Zachary is like, the lengths to which he will go, taking such a risk doesn't strike me as very smart."

"We need to be extremely careful now, Mason," Rachel fretted. "If he even sus-pects that you've returned, we're all in for a peck of trouble! You can't even risk going outside! If he were to know for certain—"

"No, Rachel," he answered firmly.

"But—"

"I will not spend the rest of my life hid-ing," Mason said calmly. "What am I sup-posed to do? Stay locked up here in the

boardinghouse, never so much as showing my face in public again? We both know
that such a way of living isn't for any of us.
No, the time has come for me to reenter
the life that I left behind. I've already done
too much hiding."

"What if he—"

"Trust me. I won't allow anything to
happen to you or yours, I promise."

Listening to Mason speak, Rachel allowed herself to be soothed by his assur-
ances. She knew that her initial reaction
had been wrong, even a bit cowardly, but
with all that had happened since the day
she followed Charlotte out into the woods,
she found her concern difficult to ignore.
Though she was still frightened of what
Zachary Tucker was capable of, she trusted
Mason to do what was right.

"I didn't mean that you should run," she
said regretfully. "I truly didn't."

"I know," he quieted her, "but if I intend to
resume some semblance of the life I once
had here in Carlson, I am eventually going
to have to let people know that I'm alive."

"That's what you want? To resume your
life?"

"What I want is to go forward, to stop

running and be the parent that Charlotte needs me to be," Mason said, taking a step toward where Rachel stood. "But I don't want to do that alone. I want . . ."

"Mason?" she said. Her heart was pounding. "Tell me what you want . . . please tell me . . ."

Mason drew nearer, taking her hands in his own. The heat of his touch surprised her. For a long moment, neither spoke, content simply to stare into each other's eyes. Rachel felt as if she were swimming in the blue depths of Mason's gaze.

"The other night I told you that I didn't want your role in Charlotte's life to change," he said, speaking of the memories that had roiled about in Rachel's anxious heart only minutes earlier. "But that's not all I want."

"Tell me," Rachel said softly.

Mason's eyes held her every bit as solidly as if she were in his arms. When he spoke, his words drove the very breath from her chest. "While I can never completely know what my future will hold, I do know what I desire for it, and that is for you to be part of it. I'm asking for you to share in my life as well as Charlotte's."

"But Mason, how can that be?" she protested, voicing the very fear that had been nestled deep in her heart from the first moment she had acknowledged that her love for him was not sisterly. "I'm not Alice, and she was the love of your life."

"And she was my wife," he answered swiftly.

"But doesn't that mean that—"

"The truth is that Alice is gone, Rachel," Mason said. "Gone from both of our lives. Spending the rest of our days needlessly wishing it to be otherwise will only make us miserable. But just as I can't allow myself to live in the past, to stop jumping from one train car to the next, I refuse to deny what I've been feeling for you."

He loves me!

To hear Mason speak such heartfelt words, to learn that the man she yearned for wanted her too, sent shivers of joy racing through Rachel. Desperately, she searched for words to answer, to finally reveal her own feelings for him, but found herself speechless, silent in the face of the glory of the moment, helpless to fight any longer against the emotions she had been feeling.

Mason was right; Alice was gone. Making peace with that fact had been hard, but she had done so. Being in love with her sister's former husband was complicated and confusing, but it wasn't wrong. It was possible, wonderful—and right! There might be those who found their love inappropriate, but there was no denying that it existed and could warm them the rest of their lives.

Impulsively, Rachel rose up on the tips of her toes and brushed a caressing hand against his scarred cheek. There was no going back. Tenderly, he lowered his face toward hers, his fingers delicately lifting her chin.

Just before their lips touched, he asked, "Is this what you want, Rachel?"

"Yes," she answered. "Oh, yes, Mason."

Straining upward toward him, she melted into him. His arms enveloped her, pulling her to him. Closing her eyes, Rachel allowed herself to surrender to the emotions that coursed between them, to answer his demanding kiss with passion of her own, to succumb to the overwhelming desire that pulsed through their entwined bodies.

One of Mason's hands found the small of her back and the desire that cascaded through Rachel made her weak in the knees. With a feeling that was almost desperation, she kissed him even more passionately, her mouth exploring his, hungry for something she had longed for, when Mason met her intensity with more of his own.

In that moment, nothing mattered: not that Mason had once been Alice's husband, not that he had been gone for eight long years, not that he had been scarred by the ravages of war, not that everyone in Carlson still believed him to be dead, and not even that Zachary posed a danger to all of them. The only thing of consequence was that they were together, that they had declared their feelings for each other, and that they would go forward together.

When their kiss finally ended, Rachel opened her eyes to find that heavy snowflakes covered their shoulders. Even as flakes melted against her hair, catching on her lashes, her eyes probed Mason's face.

"Where do we go from here?" she asked.

"Anywhere we want to," Mason answered simply.

Without any doubt, Rachel knew that he was right; now that they had admitted what lay in their hearts, and with Charlotte in the circle of their love, there was nothing they couldn't accomplish together.

Rachel set her oil lamp down on the floor and checked the lock on the front door of the boardinghouse. The old grandfather clock that had sat at the foot of the steps since she was a child chimed midnight, twelve uneven bongs that reverberated across the room. The only other sounds were the creaks and groans of the old building settling in the cold, snowy November night.

Glancing out the frost-dappled window, she saw that the snow continued to fall heavily; the hard ground was already covered with two inches of fluffy white powder. Smiling, she returned to her task; every night since Otis had been attacked on his way home from the tavern, Rachel had made it a habit to check all the doors and windows. With Zachary possibly having seen Mason, there was every reason to be careful. Even now, her emotions running unchecked, she knew that she had to remain diligent for the safety of the family.

And their futures . . . including mine and Mason's . . .

Parting with Mason on the porch had been one of the most difficult things she had ever done, so great was her desire to remain in his arms. Even bidding him a good night's sleep with another passionate kiss had done little to quench the fire that filled her. Though they had only been apart for just moments, she couldn't wait to see him again.

Picking up the oil lamp, she walked the short hallway to the kitchen, intent upon making certain that the latch on the window was secure; with that done, she could finally get some rest. With her every step, shadows danced on the walls in the flickering flame of the lamplight; though she was used to such illusions, the memory of being attacked by Jonathan Moseley suddenly rose up in her thoughts, unsettling her.

She pushed open the door to the kitchen and set the lamp down on the table. The flame jumped for a moment before settling into a steady burn. She checked the window, and found that the lock was still engaged, but as she turned back toward the lamp, she felt a draft of cold air race across her skin. Looking around the room, she noticed the door that led to the porch was ajar, a sliver of the night visible past the jamb. She was certain that she had locked it only minutes before . . .

Before she could turn around, a rough hand clamped down on her mouth, silencing the scream that rose in her throat. Though she tried to struggle, she was held in place effortlessly.

"Keep still, or you're gonna get hurt," a man's voice threatened in her ear. "Badly."

Chapter Twenty-eight

TRAVIS JEFFERSON ANGRILY clamped one hand down on the woman's mouth while his other arm firmly grabbed her about the waist. She struggled for a moment, unsure and frightened of what was happening to her, but she quieted a bit after he warned her of the consequences she would face in fighting him. He had no qualms whatsoever about hurting a woman; if this bitch must be roughed up a bit, he wouldn't lose one damn second of sleep over it.

He cursed himself for having been caught unawares in the kitchen; he took pride in doing his job properly, but this time it had all gone to hell.

Patiently, he had waited outdoors in the falling snow, watching through the frosted glass as Rachel Watkins left the kitchen for the deeper recesses of the boarding-house. Jimmying the lock had been so simple that he wondered why it had been installed in the first place. He'd just entered the kitchen when the flickering light once again began to move toward him.

Travis still might have gotten away without being seen, managing to hide in the inky shadows, but he had little doubt his goose was cooked when the woman had noticed the door still ajar. At that point, he had no choice but to act.

When Zachary Tucker had come to him earlier in the day with the proposition of returning to the boardinghouse, to see if the inhabitants had any sort of information about the banker's long-dead brother, Travis had jumped at the chance, smiling all the way out the door. It didn't matter to him that his odds of success were slim at best; after all, his employer was obviously feeling the stress of his negotiations with the railroad company. What *did* matter was that he had another opportunity to redeem himself.

The truth was that he was frustrated that his attack on that fat drunkard of an uncle had not worked, that his clear message to sell the property had fallen upon deaf ears. He thought that a broken arm would convey his message far better than any words ever could. Failure was something he refused to tolerate in his profession. This time, he would be successful, no matter what means he had to employ. To that end, he'd come with a knife safely tucked into the cuff of his boot. If someone ended up cut, then so be it. He was ready for whatever might come his way.

"Now, I'm gonna ask you some questions," he growled into the woman's ear, "so you just nod that pretty little head of yours in answer, unless you got some desire to lose it. You follow what I'm sayin' to you?"

Rachel Watkins nodded her head emphatically.

"Good girl," Travis praised her. "If you lie to me, I'll know."

She nodded again.

Maybe this ain't gonna be so damn difficult after all . . .

"Do you know of a fella goes by the name of Mason Tucker?" he asked, turning the woman to where he could see in her eyes; even in the dim light afforded to the kitchen, he felt confident that he would be able to see the truth, no matter what it might be.

Rachel Watkins's eyes grew wide as she slowly began to nod her head; Travis had known that she would recognize the name, what with the man having been married to her sister.

"Supposed to have died, didn't he?"

Another cautious nod.

"You don't suppose that he ain't as dead as people think?" the hired man snarled, adding as much threatening menace to his voice as he could. "Maybe even livin' here in this house?"

This time, Rachel's eyes grew even wider, and though she shook her head in response, it was clear to Travis that she was lying to him. A shivering sense of excitement wormed its way down the length of his spine; just the thought of discovering deception excited him, for now he would have no choice but to make things physical.

With his hand still pressed against her mouth, he violently shook her. "Don't think for one second I can't tell when I'm bein' lied to! That son of a bitch is here, ain't he? Answer me, goddammit!"

Letting go of his grip upon her, Travis struck Rachel with the back of his hand, slapping her so hard that she tumbled to the floor. Before she could stir, he was again upon her, roughly yanking her back to her feet, so that her head lolled from side to side.

"I'm gonna do a hell of a lot worse if you don't tell me what I want to know!"

"Let her go!" a man's voice commanded from behind him.

Swiftly, Travis turned the woman around, grabbing her by the waist and pulling her against him, the other hand around her throat. Together, spinning on his heel, he twisted to face the new arrival with Rachel as a shield.

Standing in the darkness of the hallway that led from the kitchen was a man, his hands balled tightly into menacing fists, his broad shoulders promising a potentially worthy adversary. With the scant, flickering light thrown from the oil lamp, the man's eyes shone like those of a wild beast whose brood was being threatened.

"I reckon you're Mason Tucker," Travis said.

Stars swam dizzily in front of Rachel's eyes as a result of the stranger's blow, but through the haze of confusion and tears, she was overjoyed to see Mason.

When she had first been grabbed, Rachel was overcome with fear that Jonathan Moseley had returned. She had screamed, but the sound had died in the cup of the stranger's hand. Not until her attacker spoke did she realize he was someone else.

Though Rachel had been frightened half out of her wits, she had done her best to remain calm, looking for any avenue of escape. At the mere mention of Mason's name, she had known that Zachary Tucker was behind this latest intrusion into the boardinghouse. To ask about Mason, to wonder if he weren't dead and even in the house, made it as clear to her as if Zachary himself had come. Mason's hope that his brother hadn't caught a good look at him in his father's bedroom hadn't held true. The man gripping her was probably Zachary's thug, the one who had brutalized Otis.

"I told you to let her go," Mason warned. "And I sure as hell meant it."

"Or what?" the man chuckled. "Way I see it, there ain't no way in hell you're gonna do shit, long as I got a hold of this here gal. That means that you and I is in a standoff."

Listening to the two men, there was nothing Rachel could do, no warning she could give; the man's hand was still clamped down tightly over her mouth. Stunned after being slapped, she still quivered slightly, and she didn't believe that she had the strength to fight her way free.

"You can't hold on to her forever," Mason snarled.

"Ain't gonna have to," the stranger argued. "Soon as I can get on out of here, there ain't gonna be a single person in Carlson who ain't gonna know you're alive, startin' with one in particular. With a face the likes of yours, ain't gonna be no easy task to keep on hidin'."

As the man spoke, Rachel felt his hand move ever so slightly. It had been pressed tightly over the whole of her mouth, but now it had begun to slide toward her chin, allowing her a bit more movement with her upper lip. While she still assumed that the man wanted to keep her silent, to prevent her from shouting and awakening the rest of the boardinghouse's inhabitants, what was most important was that she remained his hostage. He was sure that Mason would be reluctant to engage him if there were any chance of her being hurt in the process, a fact that was most certainly true.

Suddenly, Rachel knew what it was that she should do. If Mason were to have any chance to stop this man, as well as to prove once and for all that his brother was up to no good, she had to act.

"You best just stay away," the man began, "'cause there ain't—aaarrrhhh!"

Before the stranger could complete his thought, Rachel bit down on his finger as hard as she could, and in the instant when the man reacted, she jammed her elbow into his midsection, driving him away and escaping from his grasp. She had no more than broken free than Mason was across the room, hurtling into her attacker with all of his might; his first blow landed just as Rachel fell to the floor and relative safety.

"You bitch!" the man barked.

"Now it's just you and me," Mason snarled in answer.

Staring wide-eyed, Rachel watched as Mason landed a heavy punch that connected with the stranger's jaw, momentarily staggering him, but just as it seemed he might fall down, the man managed to right himself, slamming back into Mason. The two of them careened across the kitchen, smashing into the table on which she had placed the oil lamp.

The force of the collision immediately set the lamp wavering, and just before Rachel could rush over and rebalance it, it tipped over the edge and fell to the floor, where it shattered into pieces. The oil poured free from its container and instantly burst into flames, racing across the floor like water poured from a cup, burning a brilliant yellow and orange.

"Mason!" she shouted. "Fire!"

Rachel hurried to where the oil burned ever hotter and ever higher, desperately trying to stamp it out with her booted feet, but nothing she did seemed to make the slightest bit of difference. She was helpless to prevent tongues of flame from licking at the legs of the table and chairs and setting them ablaze. Within a matter of moments, the fire already appeared to be out of control.

Oh, no! Oh, please, Lord, no!

Mason moved quickly to his left, dodging a short right hand thrown by the stranger, crouched, and blasted a punch of his own to the man's ribcage. Rachel's attacker yelped in pain. Though Mason had thrown all the strength he could muster into the blow, the unknown assailant continued to show surprising resiliency, refusing to fall or yield.

Within the close confines of the kitchen, the two men did battle, each refusing to surrender even an inch to the other. After a terrific punch to the chin, Mason found himself momentarily dazed, but he kept fighting, connecting with one, two, and then three blows in succession. This time, the stranger snarled in response, pouncing like an animal on Mason, his hands clawing and digging into his flesh. Though his body ached from the fight, Mason's fury at the man continued to urge him forward.

"Fall, you son of a bitch!" Mason barked.

"Never!"

While he fought, Mason kept an eye on the fire that was rapidly spreading out of control. When the oil lamp fell, he'd been so preoccupied with confronting the other man that he hadn't given it any thought; not until the unmistakable sounds and smells of the fire assailed him did he realize there was a much greater danger than just this one man.

"Mason, the fire!" Rachel cried, panicked.

Faced with protecting the woman he loved, Mason would do absolutely anything to keep her safe. He had stumbled upon the assault by accident; he'd come back downstairs just to hold her in his arms once more before the night was out.

I will not lose my family again!

Shoving the man away from him, Mason

lashed out with a straight left that pounded his nose, causing an audible crack to explode into the room. The stranger fell back toward the stove, blood pouring out of the wound.

Sensing he had little time to waste, Mason turned and shouted at Rachel. "Get everyone out of here!" he ordered, his voice already struggling to be heard over the growing fire.

"But what about you?"

Before Mason could answer, the man was again upon him, driving an elbow into the meat of his chest and another heavy punch into his gut. Pounding the stranger in the back, Mason shouted, "Do it, Rachel! Do it now!"

For a moment longer, Rachel paused, but finally she ran from the kitchen to waken the family.

With fire all around him, Mason turned back to his violent task.

Rachel raced up the steps of the tall staircase two at a time. Holding her skirt in one hand and the railing in the other, she screamed, "Mother! Otis! Charlotte!"

At the top of the stairs, she dashed to her mother's door and whipped it open.

Eliza, who had been sleeping peacefully, startled at the sound of intrusion.

"What . . . what's happening?"

"Mother, get up," Rachel answered, lowering her face until it was inches from Eliza's. "The house is on fire. We need to get out."

"A fire?" her mother gasped. "But how did—"

"There's no time!" Rachel cut her off. "You get Otis. I'll get Charlotte. We have to hurry!"

Bursting into Charlotte's room, Rachel ran to where the girl continued to sleep soundly in her bed and urgently tried to shake her awake, while Jasper immediately came to his feet.

"Charlotte, wake up!" Rachel shouted. "Wake up!"

The girl's eyelids fluttered.

"Come on, sweetheart!"

Frustrated and fearful, Rachel picked the young girl up from the bed and cradled her against her chest; it had become apparent that no amount of encouragement was going to make the groggy child aware of the danger they were all facing.

"Wha . . . what's goin' on?" Charlotte asked, a sleepy pout on her lips.

"Let's go, Jasper!" Rachel shouted, and the dog followed her command and ran for the door.

When Rachel ran back out into the hallway, her arms straining to hold Charlotte's slumped weight, her mother and Otis were coming toward them.

"How in the hell did a fire start, anyhow?" he asked, wiping the sleep from his eyes.

"Everyone outside, quickly!" Rachel ordered, wanting to make sure that everyone was safe before answering any questions.

Descending the stairs more carefully than she had mounted them, Rachel waded into the dense and choking smoke that had filled the foyer. She made sure to keep Charlotte's face close to her chest, and held her blouse's sleeve over her own mouth. With every step, she strained to hear some sound from Mason, but none came.

At the bottom of the stairs, unable to

see Otis and her mother, though they were only a few feet away, Rachel was gripped by panic.

"Where . . . where in the . . . name of tarnation . . . is the damn door?" Otis managed between coughs.

Only minutes since the fire had been ignited in the kitchen, great waves of heat filled the boardinghouse.

"Rachel?" her mother called from somewhere in the smoke behind her. "Where are you?"

Just as Rachel was about to give in to her ever-mounting panic and just head straight ahead in the hope that she might chance upon a way out, the insistent sounds of Jasper's barking split through the crackling sounds of the fire. Over and over he barked, as if he were calling to them.

"Follow Jasper!" she cried. "Hurry!"

In the smoky entryway, they stumbled toward the incessant barking until they found themselves up against the front door. It was just as Rachel had thought; Jasper was leading them to safety.

With a grunt, Otis turned the knob, flung open the door, and they all ran outside as smoke poured into the night, rising skyward to mix with the still falling snow.

Breathing in huge gulps of the frigid, fresh air, Rachel handed Charlotte to her mother and she turned to look back at the boardinghouse; at the part of the building where the fire had begun, tremendous pillars of flame licked out of broken windows.

Someone was shouting, "Fire! Fire!"

Rachel knew the boardinghouse was lost.

But where is Mason?

Chapter Twenty-nine

As BLOOD POURED FREELY from the stranger's nose, Mason could see that the other man was finally weakening. His shoulders were slumped, his fists drifted down toward his waist, and he breathed heavily through his mouth, the clear result of both exhaustion and Mason's debilitating punch. He knew that it was time to finish things.

In the course of their battle, they had careened around the kitchen, down the smoke-choked hall, ending up in the seldom-used dining room. Behind them, catastrophe continued to rage as the boardinghouse burned uncontrollably. It had begun as a small spill of oil on the floor, but now it was an inferno. The sudden sound of the ceiling being rent asunder punctuated the sizzle and crack of leaping flames as the building itself was consumed.

Though the smoke was thick, pouring around every corner in the search for a new space to fill, Mason refused to back down. With his lungs burning and watery eyes, his determination never wavered.

"Just go down," he grunted.

"The only way . . . you're gonna beat me . . . is to kill me," the stranger huffed, his cut lips spitting blood.

"That can be arranged," Mason growled.

For a moment, neither man moved, but suddenly Rachel's attacker pounced, lunging with a punch that connected but, with his much-weakened state, wasn't powerful enough to do any real damage. With a grunt, Mason retaliated, delivering a crushing blow to the man's chin, sending him hurtling backward; his knees quivered, and he finally crashed to the floor. He tried to rise, but his senses had escaped him, and his head hit the wooden floor with a thud.

End this now! Mason told himself.

Striding over to the man, Mason meant to do just that, his fists still bunched to administer the crucial final blow. But just as he was about to reach down and snatch a handful of his opponent's shirt, his foe pulled the knife he had hidden in his boot, and swung it in a dangerous arc. Its long blade reflected the light emanating from the raging fire and caught Mason in his forearm.

Mason winced in pain. "Damn it!"

Before the man could even rise to his elbows, Mason angrily kicked the blade out of his hand, sending it skittering across the floor and into the depths of the burning kitchen beyond, safely out of reach. He followed this with another kick to the stranger's temple, rendering him incapable of further struggle. A red gash trickled blood down Mason's underarm, to his fingers, where it fell to the floor.

His anger peaking, Mason bent down and grabbed the beaten man by the collar. His head lolled unsteadily as Mason yanked him up until their faces were only inches apart.

"Who sent you here?" he demanded. "Why did you want to hurt Rachel?"

"You . . . you got it . . . all wrong . . ." the man answered through bloody teeth.

"Tell me, damn you!"

"Weren't her . . . that I was comin' for . . . was you . . ."

Shock rose in Mason's face so quickly that he couldn't mask it; when the stranger saw his reaction, he began to laugh, a wheezing, wet sound that struggled to fight its way out of his chest.

"Who sent you?" Mason demanded, regaining his wayward thoughts, refusing to relent until he got an answer.

"Shouldn't . . . be . . . too   damn . . . hard . . ."

"Who?"

"Your br . . . brother . . . Za . . . Zach . . ." And then the man was unable to answer any further, slipping off into the darkness of unconsciousness, his body surrendering to the pain of his beating. Mason let him fall to the floor. His fears had been realized; Zachary knew he was still alive.

Reaching down, Mason grabbed the unmoving man and, with some effort, lifted him up over his shoulder. As he made his way to the rear of the house, he did all that he could to shield his weary, beaten body against the heat emanating from the kitchen and the hallway beyond. He staggered to the door the assailant had entered by, yanked it open, and stepped out into the cold November night. One thought consumed him.

You will pay for what you have done. Brother, this I swear . . .

Rachel paced back and forth in front of the blazing boardinghouse, nervously wringing her hands. The building had begun to fall apart before her very eyes; waves of flame roiled across the outside walls, windows shattered spectacularly on both floors, and the occasional crash of a collapsing beam echoed into the night. Jasper began to bark, as if he wanted their attention, but Rachel knew that there was nothing that anyone could do; their home was being destroyed.

A small crowd of anxious neighbors had gathered in the November chill, offering their condolences and keeping a close eye that the fire would not spread any farther. The idea of forming a bucket chain had been suggested, but everyone present knew that it was far too little, far too late.

"Isn't there anything we can do?" Eliza fretted.

"Too late for that." Otis frowned. "All we're gonna be left with is a bunch of hot embers for our trouble."

"At least you all made it out alive," someone in the crowd added.

Not everyone . . .

All Rachel could think of was that Mason was still trapped inside the burning building. What a horrible choice he had forced her to make to leave him, but she knew that he had been right. Without warning, all of her family would have perished. But with every passing moment, her fear grew. Was he still fighting amid the flames?

Just as she was about to throw caution to the wind and try to find a way back into the raging inferno, Mason suddenly came around the corner, the man who had accosted her slung over his shoulder, arms hanging limply in defeat. As Mason reached her, an audible gasp went up from somewhere in the crowd, from someone who clearly recognized the man who stood before them. As if he were dropping a sack of potatoes onto the ground, Mason tossed down the unconscious man.

"Thank heaven you're safe," he whispered.

Without a word, Rachel hurled herself into his arms. She couldn't have cared less what anyone watching thought, content instead to bury her head into the crook of his neck as tears came to her eyes. Releasing her fear, sobs racked her body. All around them, whispered voices spoke.

"How . . . how can it be?"

"What happened to his face? How did he get scarred?"

"But Mason Tucker is dead, isn't he?"

"He looks like a . . . a monster!"

"There now," Mason soothed Rachel, paying no heed to the chatter. "Everything's all right."

"I . . . I did . . . did as you said . . ."

"That you did."

From over Mason's shoulder, Rachel could see her mother watching them, but though she had expected Eliza to have a disapproving look on her face, surprisingly, it was more one of curiosity. Hers was the only face that didn't reflect shock at their embrace.

"He told me that Zachary had sent him to look for me," Mason explained when they had finally separated, nodding at the unconscious man. "You were right."

Rachel took no satisfaction from Mason's words. "He'll pay for what he's done."

She began looking for Charlotte, wanting the young girl to join in their celebration, but glancing first from her mother, then to Otis, to Jasper, and eventually to the small crowd, she was surprised to find no sign of her. Shivers of dread raced down her spine. Suddenly, an earsplitting shriek managed to cut through the sounds of the raging fire.

It was Charlotte's voice . . . coming from inside the house.

Mason raced up to the front door and, kicked at the blazing knob, driving it inward with a crack to reveal a raging inferno beyond. Towering flames reached across every surface, leaving nothing but destruction in their wake. Waves of incredible heat rolled over his skin.

"How in the hell're you gonna get in there?" Otis marveled.

"She'll be so scared, Mason!" Rachel pleaded. "You've got to get her!"

"I won't let her be hurt," he vowed.

Mason took a deep breath and, with his sleeve held tightly against his face, just as quickly as he could raced into the foyer and past the hungry flames, only stopping when he had reached the bottom of the staircase. For an instant, the ever-present heat brought back the horrors he had experienced on the battlefield, of the explosion that had scarred him and taken him away from those he loved, but he refused to let himself be distracted.

"Charlotte!" he shouted. "Where are you? Answer me, child!"

There was no answer save for the sounds of destruction.

Suddenly, from somewhere behind him came the distinctive sound of a beam cracking, followed by the collapse of the dining room's ceiling. Debris, mostly plaster and wood, rained down on the floor, victim to the fire's relentless consumption of the boardinghouse. Still, in the din of noise, Mason heard the faintest of sounds, a voice, calling from the top of the stairs.

"Daddy! Help me, Daddy!"

It was Charlotte!

Mason had no idea how his daughter had climbed back up to the second floor, especially after Rachel had succeeded in bringing her to safety, but he was far more concerned about reaching her again, saving his child from the flames.

Before Mason, parts of the staircase burned in orange-and-yellow flame. Steeling himself, he raced quickly up the steps, leaping over a particularly nasty spot, but just as he tried righting himself by reaching out to the oaken banister, the railing gave way and he found himself balancing precariously, high above the burning floor below. Flailing his arms, he finally managed to regain his momentum before falling back on his rear.

Damn it, Mason! You won't be any good to Charlotte if you're dead!

Covering the short distance to the head of the stairs, Mason rushed to the open door to Charlotte's room, flame pursuing him at nearly every turn. What he witnessed inside made his heart stop: Charlotte cowered in the far corner of the room, her hands clutched to her chest as everything around her collapsed into ruin. Part of the ceiling just inside the doorway had fallen in, leaving a twisted, burning heap of wood blocking any entry or exit; it had clearly been what had caused her to scream.

"Charlotte?" Mason called. "Are you hurt?"

"No . . . no . . . Daddy," she whimpered.

"Don't move, honey," he reassured her, fearful to frighten her further. "I'm coming to get you."

Taking two short steps back, his feet precariously close to the railing, Mason girded himself and then raced back to the door, leaping into the mess of wreckage and flame. Searing heat singed his arms, tugged at his hair, and sucked the very air from his lungs. For a short, painful moment, he wondered if he would manage to clear the pile of debris, or if he would become trapped, dying a horrible death before his daughter's eyes, but somehow he continued on, landing in the relative safety beyond.

Rushing to Charlotte, Mason took the frightened girl in his arms as tears streamed down her face.

"What are you doing here, sweetheart?" he asked. "Why didn't you stay with Rachel?"

"I had to! I had to come back inside! I couldn't let Mama's treasure be lost!" Charlotte cried.

"What are you talking about?"

It was then that Charlotte revealed what she had been protectively clutching to her chest; Mason immediately recognized the well-read letter and worn photograph of Alice that Mason had given her.

Uncontrollably, a smile came to Mason's lips. While he wasn't happy that Charlotte had placed herself in such danger, he couldn't help but feel that she had done so out of love for her mother, even if her emotions had no memories to accompany them.

"Let's get out of here," he said.

It was impossible for them to go back the way that he had come; even if he managed to get past the rubble at the door, he had no doubt that the flames had nearly finished their work on the stairs. The only option that remained to them was the window.

The intense heat had already managed to crack the window's pane, splitting it nearly in two; Mason merely finished what the fire had started, kicking out the damaged shards, clearing an exit with his boot. Pulling Charlotte tight to his chest, he said, "Hold on to me as tightly as you can and don't look down. We'll be back with Rachel before you know it."

Mason winced painfully as a fragment of glass sliced into his back as they climbed out of the window and onto the short roof of the second floor. Aware of the layout of the house, he knew their best bet was to go to the rear of the building and use the gentle slope that covered the rear porch to get to the ground.

Moving carefully, watchful not to slip or break through a weakened portion of the boardinghouse roof, Mason picked his way toward the back of the building. He soon found that his plan wasn't perfect; at the boardinghouse's rear, the fire raged completely out of control. The kitchen, where the fire had first begun, was almost entirely consumed; only the barest framework remained, visible through the destroyed roof. Thankfully, some of the porch roof had survived, allowing Mason to inch his way out onto it. The ground, no farther than ten feet down, seemed miles away.

"We have to jump, Charlotte," he explained. "Can you hold on to me?"

Charlotte nodded fearfully, her blonde hair covering her face.

"That's a good girl."

Without hesitation, Mason leapt out into the November night. They landed on the hard ground with a thud, Mason rolling to protect the little girl, taking the brunt of the fall on himself. Gasping, he held Charlotte close to his chest, thankful that, somehow, he had saved them both.

"Are you all right?" he asked, wiping a strand of hair from her face.

Charlotte nodded weakly.

"That wasn't so bad, was it?"

"I don't want to do it again, not unless Jasper gets to come."

As Rachel ran toward them, Mason couldn't help but laugh.

Zachary Tucker paced nervously past the windows of his office, moving back and forth without ever coming to a complete stop. Outside, heavy snow continued to fall, signaling the certain arrival of winter, but he paid it little heed. The Carlson Bank and Trust was empty, all of the employees having left hours earlier, but Zachary was far too restless to retire for the night. With a half-full glass of whiskey and smoldering cigar for company, he knew he couldn't rest, *wouldn't* rest until he knew the truth.

Sending Travis Jefferson to discover the facts was risky. The man had a fondness for violence that could end up with someone being badly hurt, but it was a course Zachary was willing to take, no matter the consequences.

The thought that somehow his father hadn't been delirious, that he hadn't imagined his elder son had returned from the grave, unsettled Zachary. Though he felt it was impossible for Mason to be alive, he knew the mysterious stranger was not someone he could simply ignore. With his anticipated deal with the lumber company hanging precariously in the balance, there truly hadn't been a choice.

I need to know who was in my father's room!

Suddenly, the sound of the downstairs door being opened rose to his ears. Zachary relaxed, slipping behind his desk; the only person besides himself who had a key was Travis. He must have finally finished his work, returning to give up the information his employer desired.

But then more than one silhouette appeared in the frosted glass of his office door, and before Zachary could regain his feet, it swung open, revealing his unexpected visitors: Carlson's potbellied sheriff, Walter Kirby; one of his many deputies, a man he had once been introduced to but whose name he had long since forgotten; a battered and bruised Travis Jefferson, his eyes never wavering from the floor; and . . .

No! No, it cannot be! It simply can't!

Mason, his older brother, his *long-dead* brother, stood in the doorway. He was much as Zachary remembered him, except the hideous scarring that covered one side of his face. The very sight of it repulsed Zachary. If he had had such an affliction, he wouldn't be able to show his own face in public ever again. But what unsettled him the most were Mason's eyes, still a smoldering blue, staring straight through him, seeing him for what he was.

"How . . . how are you . . . here?" Zachary questioned in confusion.

No one said a word in answer.

"This isn't possible," he went on, giving a nervous laugh, his breathing ragged and his heart pounding. "I must be dreaming. You just cannot be here! You're dead! Do you hear me? You're dead!"

"Do what you need to do, Sheriff Kirby," Mason said simply.

"You heard the man, Clifford."

At the sheriff's words, the deputy walked over and grabbed Zachary by the shoulder, his grip as tight as a vise, and began hauling the overweight banker toward the door.

"What's the meaning of this?" Zachary thundered. "I haven't done anything wrong!"

"That ain't what your man here's been sayin'," Sheriff Kirby explained.

Travis Jefferson had spilled his guts to the law! In that instant, Zachary realized that all his plans were for naught; his contract with the Gaitskill Lumber Company would go up like so much smoke, all of his antici-pated riches lost in a sea of scandal; but, more important, he would lose his grip upon the Carlson Bank and Trust, forfeit-ing the wealth and power he had spent the last eight years painstakingly acquiring.

"Mason!" he shouted at the door, fight-ing feebly against the relentless march of the deputy, desperately hoping that his brother, who he still couldn't bring himself to believe was somehow miraculously alive, might still have some shred of compas-sion for his younger sibling. "Mason, you know me! You have to know that what you were told is nothing but lies! Please, dear God, you have to believe I wouldn't be a party to this!"

For a moment, Zachary believed he might have reached Mason, for he halted the deputy before he could reach the door. Stepping before his brother, Mason smiled wanly.

"I knew you would listen to reason!" Zachary rejoiced, even as he winced at just how disgusting the scars on Mason's face truly were. "You always were—"

Before he could manage another word, Mason drove a ferocious punch directly into the middle of his enormous paunch. The blow knocked all the wind out of his lungs, sent him crashing hard onto his knees, and eventually to his side, wheezing for his next breath. Pain the likes of which he couldn't remember crowded his senses, making his eyes water, before a steady darkness marched in from the edges.

The instant before Zachary slipped into unconsciousness, Mason bent down to where he could see his face. "You are going to pay for what you've done, you no-good worthless shit," he snarled. "If it's the last thing I ever do, there will be a reckoning."

And then he was gone.

Rachel was waiting, Charlotte at her side, when Mason came down the steps that led to his brother's office. Even as the sheriff and his deputy hustled the two accomplices past them to an uncomfortable cell in Carlson's tiny jail, she could see the toll the night had taken on Mason; fatigue was etched upon his face. His skin was streaked with soot as he favored the gash in his forearm. Still, she felt intense relief that their ordeal was at an end.

"Is it over?" she asked hopefully.

Mason nodded and gave a weak smile, walking over to tousle Charlotte's hair. "There's nothing more that Zachary can do to any of us. Where he's headed, he'll have a lot more concerns than trying to figure out how his brother managed to return from the dead."

"Then where do we go from here?"

This question had been rolling around in Rachel's mind from the moment that Mason had rescued Charlotte from the burning boardinghouse. With his surprise reappearance among the people of Carlson, there would be no end to the questions that would inevitably surface about his whereabouts for the last eight years. Witnesses had watched as she had leapt into his arms, and since Alice was her beloved sister, tongues would undoubtedly be wagging. All that she wanted was some guidance, some idea that Mason knew what to do.

"We go wherever we want to," he answered simply. "A good place to start would be to my father's house. He'll need to be reassured that he didn't imagine my late-night visit. Besides, with my brother's impending imprisonment, someone will need to look after the bank."

"And that will be you?"

"I hope so. I hope that I can regain everyone's trust."

"If my daddy says he can do it," Charlotte piped up, "then that's what he's gonna do."

Mason smiled. "I'm glad someone believes in me."

"She's not the only one." Rachel moved closer to the man who had returned from the dead, rose up on the tips of her toes, and gently placed a tender kiss upon his cheek. Mason put his arm around her and pulled her tightly against him. His kiss was all-consuming. It went on and on, stopping only when Charlotte insistently tugged on his arm.

Though the night had been filled with surprise and devastation, Rachel believed that Mason was right, that they could go wherever they wanted, rebuilding all that had been lost, reacquainting themselves with old friends and family members and making new ones. They wouldn't run from the past but embrace it, not stopping for any hardship, but overcoming all obstacles.

Their love for one another would see them through.

Epilogue

Carlson, Minnesota—June 1928

RACHEL crossed the bedroom and stood before the open windows as a gentle breeze pushed the curtains in a soft dance, kissing her bare arms with a comforting coolness. The late afternoon sun was just about to disappear over the far horizon and the sky was already dotted with the first twinkling of stars. Crickets and cicadas had begun to call out.

Leaning down into the cradle Mason had built, Rachel adjusted the blanket over their sleeping infant daughter. Christina Tucker, who had come into their lives only five months earlier, bubbled only slightly at her mother's touch before settling back into her peaceful slumber. Born with a full head of jet black hair, she bore a strong resemblance to Rachel, save for the piercing blue eyes that undoubtedly came from her father.

"Our little angel," Rachel whispered.

Thinking back on the strange events that had returned Mason to her life, Rachel could only marvel at all that had happened.

In the aftermath of the boardinghouse's destruction and Zachary Tucker's being revealed as the person responsible, much in Carlson had changed as the scandal reverberated through the community. Both Mason's brother and Travis Jefferson had been found guilty by a jury of their peers and had been sentenced to many long years behind bars. While their departure had meant the failure of the negotiated financial deal with the Gaitskill Lumber Company, a new compromise had been found, one that brought a new spur to the rail line and money to fill Carlson's coffers.

With Zachary removed from his position at the Carlson Bank and Trust, there had been some initial worry that his departure would signal the end of the once proud institution. But into that void stepped Mason. After he had returned to his father's home, proving to Sherman Tucker that his son's appearance before him wasn't a dream, he had resumed his previous duties at the bank, inspiring confidence and pursuing an honest, scrupulous way of doing business. Though there was the occasional stare at the scars on his face, most everyone came to see him as the man he was on the inside, paying no heed to how he might look on the outside. While Sherman had made a brief recovery after Mason's return, showing a happiness in his eyes that had been thought long gone, it was unfortunately short-lived; less than a year later, he died peacefully in his sleep.

One of the first things Mason did upon resuming his duties at the bank was to help finance the rebuilding of the boarding-house. Besides his own connection to the family, he believed that since Zachary had played an active role in its destruction, the bank held some responsibility.

With nearly the whole community chipping in, the building Eliza's father had long ago constructed was rebuilt. With Eliza's self-imposed exile in her room ended, she had introduced herself back into the society life of Carlson with a vengeance. The parlor of the new boardinghouse was opened to gatherings and socials, with coffees and teas, and all the gossip anyone could ever hope to listen to.

Since his sister had resumed such an active role in the running of the boardinghouse, Otis quietly and happily returned to his old habits, neglecting his work and drinking. Most nights he could be found sitting on a stool at the local tavern, regaling anyone who would listen of how he had managed to save everyone from the burning building.

Downstairs, Rachel smiled as she heard Mason, Charlotte, and Jasper burst into the house in a storm of laughter. Though she worried that they might wake Christina, she knew that the poor baby would have no choice but to get used to the noise.

From the moment Rachel and Mason had declared their feelings for each other, their love had grown each day. At first there had been some criticism about their relationship, mostly from those who found it unseemly for a woman to become involved with her dead sister's husband. Undeterred,

Rachel and Mason found sweetness and joy in their romance. By the time they were married in a simple ceremony at the shore of Lake Carlson, everyone in town had come to realize that their love was real and true.

After they moved into Mason's father's home, the place where he had been born and raised, Rachel was soon pregnant. After what Alice had endured, there was nervousness in the family. But Rachel hadn't been one of those worried; for her, carrying her first child was serene, pleasant, and full of moments she would undoubtedly cherish until the end of her days. When the day came for her to give birth to Christina, Dr. Clark had attended; her mother had been present, but her vow never to deliver another infant into the world remained steadfast.

Charlotte had benefited the most from her new family; where once she had been an irascible child, often seeking her own devices, she had embraced Mason as her father. She had become more sociable with the other children at school, improving her marks in every subject. Though she and Jasper were still apt to dash about the woods, poking their noses where they shouldn't, Rachel no longer worried as much about her. Now that she was someone's big sister, Charlotte had some new responsibilities, ones she was proud to bear.

Still, Alice had never really left their lives. But instead of taking flowers to her grave on the anniversary of her death, on Charlotte's birthday, they would visit when it felt right: on Christmas, Rachel's birthday, or an autumn afternoon resplendent with a spectacular sunset. In that way, Alice's absence no longer hung heavily over their heads; they included her in their lives. Though Rachel knew Mason still harbored feelings of guilt for what had befallen Alice, she saw that he no longer lived solely in the past, but embraced the present and the future.

Alice is watching us from heaven above . . .

"I hope we didn't make too much noise," Mason said from the doorway.

Rachel turned to him and smiled. "It sounded like a bunch of wild horses had been let loose."

"That would have been Jasper." He chuckled. "He gets so darn excited."

"As if he were the only one."

Mason walked over and put his arm around his wife, looking down into the crib as Christina slept on, unaware of how much her parents adored her. Something wonderful had happened to bring her into the world, something that would sustain them all.

"I love you, Rachel," Mason said softly, kissing her forehead.

Rachel smiled in answer . . . she knew no words were needed.